John Wesley, Charles Wesley

The Poetical Works of John and Charles Wesley

Reprinted from the originals, with the last corrections of the authors; together with

the poems of Charles Wesley not before published. Vol. 2

John Wesley, Charles Wesley

The Poetical Works of John and Charles Wesley
Reprinted from the originals, with the last corrections of the authors; together with the poems of Charles Wesley not before published. Vol. 2

ISBN/EAN: 9783337115494

Printed in Europe, USA, Canada, Australia, Japan

Cover: Foto ©Andreas Hilbeck / pixelio.de

More available books at **www.hansebooks.com**

ADVERTISEMENT.

In this Volume three publications of the Wesleys are substantially reproduced: the two first being the work of John Wesley, the third of John and Charles conjointly. This last is reprinted entire, with the exception of such pieces as are reserved to form part of subsequent volumes: while, in regard to the first and second the principle laid down in the Advertisement prefixed to Volume I. of this edition has been carried out. These two Collections of Psalms and Hymns, viz., those of 1738 and 1741, are not, strictly speaking, reprinted; but both are virtually preserved, and ample means of ascertaining what they contained are afforded, by the additions made in this volume to the original Tables of Contents. Such a method of perpetuating the knowledge of these two very scarce volumes has commended itself to the Editor's judgment, on the ground that most of the books from which the extracted psalms and hymns are taken are easily accessible; and also that the space obtained by this method will be available, when required, for compositions which are undoubtedly original.

One of Wesley's latest poetical publications was "A Collection of Psalms and Hymns for the Lord's Day." It was not published separately, but along with his Abridged Liturgy; nor was it original, but

composed altogether of extracts from the larger
" Collection of Psalms and Hymns " which was then
in stated use where public worship (strictly so called)
was conducted on the Lord's Day.   It was an object
of just solicitude with him to provide hymns suitable
for mixed assemblies, or as he has judiciously defined
them, (Minutes of Conference, vol. i., p. 562,) hymns
of praise and prayer, rather than such as describe
particular states of mind; and for this purpose both
the former and the later publications were well
adapted.   Wesley's great and early admiration for Dr.
Watts has been put on record in one of his sermons.
(Works, vol. vii., p. 292.)   The extent to which he
availed himself of the poetical labours of " that great
and good man " will not therefore excite surprise ;
and least of all when the admirable suitableness of
many of his psalms and hymns for public worship is
considered.   In this respect it may be freely admitted,
even by ardent admirers of the Wesley poetry, that
Watts has the pre-eminence, and has rendered in-
valuable service to the church of God.

Watts and the Wesleys, whatever their differences
in judgment or in taste, were one in spirit, and
are believed to have long since united " in nobler
worship" above.   There may the Editor, and all who
read these volumes, join them in due season !

Richmond, Surrey,
     January 20, 1869.

THE
POETICAL WORKS
OF
JOHN AND CHARLES WESLEY.

VOL. II.

THE

POETICAL WORKS

OF

JOHN AND CHARLES WESLEY:

REPRINTED FROM THE ORIGINALS,

WITH THE LAST CORRECTIONS OF THE AUTHORS;

TOGETHER WITH

THE POEMS OF CHARLES WESLEY

NOT BEFORE PUBLISHED.

COLLECTED AND ARRANGED BY

G. OSBORN, D.D.

VOLUME II.

LONDON:
WESLEYAN-METHODIST CONFERENCE OFFICE,
2, CASTLE-STREET, CITY-ROAD
SOLD AT 66, PATERNOSTER-ROW.

1869.

CONTENTS.

————

HYMNS AND SACRED POEMS, 1742.

PART I.

PAGE.

PART II.

Contents. xi

A

COLLECTION

OF

PSALMS

AND

HYMNS.

Published by JOHN WESLEY, M. A.,

Fellow of *Lincoln* College, Oxford.

LONDON:

Printed by W. STRAHAN. And Sold at the *Foundery*, near *Upper Moorfields;* at JAMES HUTTON'S, Bookseller, at the *Bible* and *Sun*, without *Temple-Bar;* and at JOHN LEWIS's in *Bartholomew-Close.* 1741.

[Price Bound One Shilling.]

VOL. II.   B

CONTENTS.

PART THE FIRST.

PART THE SECOND.

PAGE.

NOTE.

THE reader will observe that of the 160 hymns contained in
this volume as originally published, more than 130 may be traced
(by the references given above in brackets) to previous publications by other authors; and were merely selected, arranged,
and more or less altered by Wesley. Only three of those which
have been so traced are reprinted here; viz., "Resignation,"
"Submission," and the first "Hymn to Christ." The second
with that title, together with "A Thought in Affliction," "A
Prayer for the Light of Life," "A Prayer for Faith," and "God's
Love and Power," are also reprinted, because they have not
been identified in other Collections, and may possibly be Wesley's. The remainder are more probably his; though the two in
half-rhymed verse are subject to some suspicion on that account.
Two versions of Psalm cxxx., and the other Psalms which appeared in the second and following editions of this volume, are
reserved for publication hereafter.

A

COLLECTION

OF

PSALMS AND HYMNS.

A THOUGHT IN AFFLICTION.

1 WILT Thou, O Lord, regard my tears,
    The fruit of guilt and fear?
Me, who Thy justice have provoked,
    O, will Thy mercy spare?

2 Yes; for the broken contrite heart,
    Saviour, Thy sufferings plead:
O, quench not then the smoking flax,
    Nor break the bruised reed!

3 Thy poor unworthy servant view,
    Resign'd to Thy decree;
Ordain me or to live or die,
    But live or die in Thee!

4 Upon Thy gracious promise, Lord,
    My humbled soul is cast!
O, bear me safe through life, through death,
    And raise me up at last!

5 Low as this mortal frame must lie,
    This mortal frame shall sing,
"Where is thy victory, O grave!
    And where, O death, thy sting!"

GOD'S LOVE AND POWER.

1   I FELT my heart, and found a chillness cool
    Its purple channels in my frozen side ;
The spring was now become a standing pool,
    Deprived of motion and its active tide.
           O, stay ! O, stay !
I ever freeze if banish'd from Thy ray :
A lasting warmth Thy secret beams beget ;
Thou art a Sun which cannot rise or set.

2   Then thaw this ice, and make my frost retreat,
    But let with temperate rays Thy lustre shine :
Thy judgments lightning, but Thy love is heat ;
    Those would consume my heart, but this refine.
           Inspire ! inspire !
And melt my soul with Thy more equal fire ;
So shall a pensive deluge drown my fears,
My ice turn water, and dissolve in tears.

3   After Thy love, if I continue hard,
    If sin again knit and confirm'd be grown,
If guilt rebel, and stand upon his guard,
    And what was ice before freeze into stone ;
           Reprove ! reprove !
Thy power assist Thee to revenge Thy love.
Lo, Thou hast still Thy threats and thunder left ;
The heart that can't be melted may be cleft !

THE RESIGNATION.*

1   LONG have I view'd, long have I thought,
    And trembling held this bitter draught ;

* Altered from Norris's "Miscellanies," p. 83.

'Twas now just to my lips applied,
Nature shrank in, my courage died:
But now resolved and firm I'll be,
Since, Lord, 'tis mixt and given by Thee.

2 I 'll trust my Great Physician's skill,
What He prescribes can ne'er be ill:
For each disease He knows what's fit,
He's wise and good, and I'll submit:
No longer will I grieve or pine;
Thy pleasure 'tis, it shall be mine.

3 Thy med'cine puts me to great smart,
Thou wound'st me in the tenderest part;
But 'tis with a design to cure;
I must and will Thy touch endure:
All that I prized below is gone;
Yet still, Father, Thy will be done.

4 Since 'tis Thy sentence I should part
With what was nearest to my heart,
I freely that and more resign;
Behold, my heart itself is Thine:
My little all I give to Thee;
Thou hast bestow'd Thy Son on me.

5 He left true bliss and joy above,
Emptied Himself of all but love;
For me He freely did forsake
More than from me He e'er can take:
A mortal life for a divine
He took, and did even that resign.

6 Take all, Great God, I will not grieve,
But still wish I had still to give.
I hear Thy voice, Thou bidd'st me quit
My paradise, and I submit;

I will not murmur at Thy word,
Nor beg Thee yet to sheathe Thy sword.

A PRAYER FOR THE LIGHT OF LIFE.

1 O Sun of Righteousness, arise,
 With healing in Thy wing!
To my diseased, my fainting soul
 Life and salvation bring.

2 These clouds of pride and sin dispel
 By Thy all-piercing beam;
Lighten mine eyes with faith, my heart
 With holy hope inflame.

3 My mind by Thy all-quickening power
 From low desires set free;
Unite my scatter'd thoughts, and fix
 My love entire on Thee.

4 Father, Thy long-lost son receive;
 Saviour, thy purchase own;
Blest Comforter, with peace and joy
 Thy new-made creature crown!

5 Eternal, undivided Lord,
 Co-equal One and Three!
On Thee all faith, all hope be placed,
 All love be paid to Thee!

SUBMISSION.

[Altered from Herbert.]

1 But that Thou art my wisdom, Lord,
 And both my eyes are Thine,
My soul would be extremely stirr'd
 At missing my design.

2 Were it not better to bestow
    Some place or power on me?
  Then should Thy praises with me grow,
    And share in my degree.

3 But while I thus dispute and grieve,
    I do resume my sight ;
  And pilfering what I once did give,
    Disseize Thee of Thy right.

4 How know I, if Thou shouldst me raise,
  · That I should then raise Thee?
  Perhaps my wishes and Thy praise
    Do not so well agree.

5 Therefore unto my gift I stand,
    I will no more advise :
  Only do Thou lend me a hand,
    Since Thou hast both mine eyes.

———

A PRAYER FOR FAITH.

1 FATHER, I stretch my hands to Thee,
    No other help I know :
  If Thou withdraw Thyself from me,
    Ah! whither shall I go?

2 What did Thy only Son endure
    Before I drew my breath !
  What pain, what labour to secure
    My soul from endless death !

3 O Jesu, could I this believe,
    I now should feel Thy power;
  Now my poor soul Thou wouldst retrieve,
    Nor let me wait one hour.

4 Author of faith, to Thee I lift
  My weary, longing eyes;
  O, let me now receive that gift!
  My soul without it dies.

5 Surely Thou canst not let me die!
  O, speak, and I shall live!
  And here I will unwearied lie,
  Till Thou Thy Spirit give.

6 The worst of sinners would rejoice,
  Could they but see Thy face:
  O, let me hear Thy quickening voice.
  And taste Thy pardoning grace.

A HYMN TO CHRIST.*

1 MEEK, patient Lamb of God, to Thee
  I fly; Thy meekness give to me:
  I choose Thee for my life, my crown,
  I pant to have Thee all my own:
  Thou seest my heart, Thou know'st my love.
  From Thee I never will remove;
  No shame I fear, no pain, or loss,
  But gladly follow to the cross.

2 Make clean as wool my filthy heart,
  Wash white as snow my every part:
  Give me in stillness to sustain
  Whate'er Thy wisdom shall ordain.
  Carve for Thyself in me, and make
  My heart Thy lamb-like image take:

* Probably altered from an older translation of *O Stilles Gottes Lamm*, Hernhuth Collection, No. 412, ascribed by some to Gottfried Arnold. (1666—1714.) The next hymn is most likely a translation also, but has not been traced to its original.

Yea, slay me, Lord, and offer me
A pure burnt sacrifice to Thee.

3 Bind, Father, hand and foot Thy son,
  Nor leave the work till all be done;
  O, never let me, Lord, go free,
  Till all my heart's resign'd to Thee :
  Then quickly to the altar lead,
  And suffer me no more to plead :
  No longer with the' old *Adam* bear ;
  Lead on, dear Lord, consume him there.

ANOTHER.

1 JESU, Thy soul renew my own,
  Thy sufferings for my sins atone :
  Thy sacred body slain for me,
  From sin and misery set me free.

2 The water issuing from Thy side
  The soldier's spear had open'd wide,
  That bathe my heart, and all Thy blood
  Refresh and bring me near to God.

3 The blood-sweat trickling from Thy face
  Prevent my coming in disgrace :
  Thy holy passion, death, and tomb
  Shall screen me from the wrath to come.

4 O Jesu, grant this my request !
  Take, hide me quite in Thy dear breast.
  And make me in Thy wounds to dwell
  Secure from all the fiends of hell.

5 Call me in my last agony,
  And bring me, O my God, to Thee ;
  That I, with all Thy saints above,
  May never cease to praise Thy love.

AN HYMN FOR THE GEORGIA ORPHANS.

1 COME, let us join our God to bless,
   And praise Him evermore;
That Father of the fatherless,
   That Helper of the poor.

2 Our dying parents us forsake;
   His mercy takes us up,
Kindly vouchsafes His own to make,
   And God becomes our hope.

3 For us He in the wilderness
   A table hath prepared ;
Us whom His love delights to bless,
   His providence to guard.

4 Known unto Him are all our needs;
   And, when we seek His face,
His open hand our bodies feeds,
   Our souls He feeds with grace.

5 Then let us in His service spend
   What we from Him receive;
And back to Him what He shall send
   In thanks and praises give.

FOR THEIR BENEFACTORS.

1 FATHER of Mercies, hear our prayers
   For those that do us good ;
Whose love for us a place prepares,
   And gives the orphans food

2 Their alms in blessings on their head
       A thousand-fold restore;
    O, feed their souls with living bread.
       And let their cup run o'er.

3 For ever in thy Christ built up,
       Thy bounty let them prove,
    Steadfast in faith, joyful through hope,
       And rooted deep in love.

4 For those who kindly founded this,
       A better house prepare;
    Remove them to thy heavenly bliss,
       And let us meet them there.

BEFORE THEIR GOING TO WORK.

1 LET us go forth, 'tis God commands:
       Let us make haste away:
    Offer to Christ our hearts and hands:
       We work for Christ to-day.

2 When He vouchsafes our hands to use.
       It makes the labour sweet;
    If any now to work refuse.
       Let not the sluggard eat.

3 Who would not do what God ordains.
       And promises to bless?
    Who would not 'scape the toil and pains
       Of sinful idleness?

4 In vain to Christ the slothful pray:
       We have not learn'd Him so:
    No; for He calls Himself the Way
       And work'd Himself below.

5 Then let us in His footsteps tread,
   And gladly act our part;
 On earth employ our hands and head,
   But give Him all our heart.

A HYMN FOR CHARITY CHILDREN.

1 How happy they, O King of kings!
   How safe, how truly blest,
 Who under Thy protecting wings
   Both shelter find and rest !

2 Them wilt Thou lead, them wilt Thou keep.
   And with Thine arm uphold;
 O blessed Shepherd! blessed sheep
   Of *Israel's* sacred fold!

3 Nor does the tender wandering lambs
   His kindly care disdain;
 He knows them better than their dams,
   And better does sustain.

4 Behold, His flock from every side
   He is assembling still;
 And may He all in safety guide
   To *Sion's* sacred hill.

5 If thither He will us convey.
   Nor our mean vows despise,
 Our hearts we'll on His altars lay
   A grateful sacrifice.

6 To God the Father, and the Son.
   And Spirit, One in Three,
 As is, and was e're time begun,
   Eternal glory be.

ANOTHER.

1 To Thee, O Father of mankind,
    Shall our glad hymns ascend:
To anger slow, to love inclined;
    Thy goodness knows no end.

2 The poor and needy from the dust
    'Tis Thy delight to raise,
Who in the' assemblies of the just
    Will still record Thy praise.

3 Each hand and heart that lend us aid,
    Thou didst inspire and guide;
Nor shall their love be unrepaid,
    Who for the poor provide.

4 The choicest of Thy blessings shower
    On those who us have blest!
Unfailing streams of bounty pour
    On every bounteous breast.

5 Gather those outcasts who remain
    Exposed as we before;
So shall our still increasing train
    With louder songs adore.

ANOTHER.

1 When to the temple we repair,
    A numerous joyful throng,
Our praise shall fill the house of prayer:
    The Lord's our strength and song.

2 Should we be wanting to rejoice,
    Through deadness or delays,
The stones themselves would find a voice
    To celebrate His praise.

3 He found us in the desert wide,
  And did from thence remove:
Still may He us vouchsafe to guide,
  And lead with bands of love.

4 He is our Comforter and Light,
  We on His manna feed;
His cloud by day, His fire by night
  To heavenly *Canaan* lead.

5 To those calm happy seats may He
  In safety us convey,
With all whose love and piety
  Have placed us in the way.

6 To the blest co-eternal Three
  Whom earth and heaven adore,
As was, and is, all glory be,
  Till time shall be no more.

ANOTHER.

1 O THOU, whose wisdom, power, and love,
  For all Thy works provide;
Which those vast orbs that roll above,
  And our low centre guide.

2 The rich, the poor, the mean, the great,
  Are link'd by Thy strong hands;
Poised on its base, the work's complete,
  The firm composure stands.

3 The meanest worm that creeps on earth
  Is not below Thy care;
And we, although of humble birth,
  Thy Godlike bounty share.

4 Whoe'er Thy Being dare dispute,
　　Are silenced here with ease;
The stones themselves would them confute.
　　If we should hold our peace.

5 The' Almighty be their strong defence.
　　And multiply their store,
Who still concur with Providence
　　To aid and bless the poor.

ANOTHER.

1 FATHER of Mercy, hear our prayer.
　　In Thee we move and live:
How slow to wrath, how prone to spare,
　　And ready to forgive!

2 Thou chiefly dost Thy boundless power
　　In acts of goodness show;
Thy mercy all Thy works adore,
　　Thence all our blessings flow.

3 This still shall be our grateful theme.
　　Thy praise we'll ever sing;
Our friends the kind refreshing stream.
　　But Thou the' unfailing Spring.

4 Our joy would soon o'erflow the banks.
　　And inundations raise.
Did we not thus look down with thanks,
　　And look to heaven with praise.

5 To God the Father, God the Son.
　　And God the Holy Ghost,
Who yet are not three Gods, but One,
　　Revered by all His host;

6 The blest, eternal Trinity,
    Whom heaven and earth adore.
All honour, praise, and glory be
    Both now and evermore.

A YEARLY HYMN FOR CHARITY CHILDREN.

1 AGAIN the kind revolving year
    Has brought this happy day,
And we in God's blest house appear.
    Again our vows to pay.

2 Our watchful guardians, robed in light,
    Adore the heavenly King;
Ten thousand thousand seraphs bright
    Incessant praises sing.

3 They know no want, they feel no care,
    Nor ever sigh as we;
Sorrow and sin are strangers there,
    And all is harmony.

4 If aught can there enhance their bliss,
    Or raise their raptures higher,
New joys in heaven, at sights like this,
    New anthems fill the choir.

5 With what resembling care and love
    Both worlds for us appear!
Our friendly guardians, those above;
    Our benefactors here.

ANOTHER.

1 TRIUMPHAL notes, and hymns of joy,
  To Thee our God we'll sing;
Thy praises shall our lips employ,
  O *Salem's* peaceful King!

2 Thou mak'st the world obey Thy will,
  Whose will is always best;
Thy word bids winds and waves be still,
  And chides them into rest.

3 Thy sacred Spirit on *Jordan's* stream
  Decended like a dove;
Thou didst from wrath and sin redeem:
  Thy law is peace and love.

4 That law, by our kind patrons' care,
  We now are daily taught;
Though once far off, we now are near,
  As those to Jesus brought.

5 May He to every bounteous friend
  His favour still increase,
Till they and we with Him ascend
  To everlasting peace.

A HYMN AT THE OPENING OF A CHARITY SCHOOL.

1 LIFT up your heads, ye lofty gates;
  Unfold, each spacious door;
For here the King of Glory waits
  With blessings for the poor.

2 'Twas love Divine, 'twas sovereign grace,
  True bounty's endless spring,
Did us so near God's altars place,
  Where we may pray and sing.

3 To psalms and hymns we may aspire,
     If anthems are too high;
And follow the celestial choir
     In decent harmony.

4 With holy souls we here may meet,
     And learn their songs Divine;
Their Hallelujahs loud and sweet
     With our Hosannas join.

5 How blest, if always thus we might
     The coming hours employ,
And singing pass to realms of light,
     And endless worlds of joy!

A HYMN FOR ANY SCHOOL.

1 On this auspicious happy day
     What incense shall we bring?
What grateful humble homage pay
     To an Almighty King?

2 Be His dread name on earth confest,
     As 'tis by those above!
What is the' employment of the blest,
     But songs of praise and love?

3 The breath from heaven we did receive,
     We thus in hymns restore;
And while we on His bounty live,
     We'll wonder and adore.

4 Rescued from want, and vice, and shame
     We'll all our future days
Our great Creator's love proclaim,
     And live but to His praise.

5 May heart, and voice, and life combine,
    His goodness to express;
May all that hear us with us join,
    And our Redeemer bless.

ANOTHER.

1 FATHER of Lights, to Thee, from whom
    Each perfect gift descends;
To Thee with humble prayers we come,
    For all our bounteous friends.

2 Blessings, the payment of the poor,
    Our lips and hearts return:
May Heaven, which gave, augment their store,
    And comfort those that mourn !

3 O that we better could improve
    What's in such plenty sown !
But dews of grace are from above,
    Our wants and sins our own.

4 Only the lowly and the meek
    Shall rest of mind obtain:
Such followers does our Saviour seek,
    Such shall His kingdom gain.

5 Thither may we be safe convey'd,
    When life's rough storms are o'er,
And all who give their friendly aid
    To help us to the shore.

6 To God the Father, and the Son,
    And Spirit, One and Three,
As is, and was, for time to come,
    Eternal glory be !

ANOTHER.

1 To Thee, O Lord, our God and King,
    Whose mercies ne'er decay,
We thus in artless numbers sing,
    And thus our praise we pay.

2 Whate'er is human ebbs and flows,
    As wasting time prevails;
But grace Divine no changes knows,
    Charity never fails.

3 From thence flow plenteous streams and clea.
    And may they never cease:
'Tis you who plant and water here.
    'Tis God that gives the' increase.

4 May He your pious alms regard,
    Your warmth of zeal approve;
With ample blessings still reward
    The labour of your love.

5 May all the pleasing pains you share
    Be crown'd with wish'd success;
The present age applaud your care,
    And future ages bless!

A MORNING HYMN.

1   We lift our hearts to Thee,
    O Day-star from on high!
The sun itself is but Thy shade.
    Yet cheers both earth and sky.

An Evening Hymn.

2   O, let Thy orient beams
        The night of sin disperse ;
  The mists of error and of vice
        Which shade the universe !

3   How beauteous nature now !
        How dark and sad before !
  With joy we view the pleasing change,
        And nature's God adore.

4   O, may no gloomy crime
        Pollute the rising day !
  Or Jesu's blood, like evening dew,
        Wash all the stains away.

5   May we this life improve,
        To mourn for errors past,
  And live this short-revolving day
        As if it were our last.

6   To God the Father, Son,
        And Spirit, One and Three,
  Be glory, as it was, is now,
        And shall for ever be.

AN EVENING HYMN.

1 ALL praise to Him who dwells in bliss,
    Who made both day and night;
  Whose throne is darkness, in the' abyss
    Of uncreated light.

2 Each thought and deed His piercing eyes
    With strictest search survey;
  The deepest shades no more disguise
    Than the full blaze of day.

3 Whom Thou dost guard, O King of kings,
    No evil shall molest:
  Under the shadow of Thy wings
    Shall they securely rest.

4 Thy angels shall around their beds
    Their constant stations keep:
  Thy faith and truth shall shield their heads,
    For Thou dost never sleep.

5 May we with calm and sweet repose,
    And heavenly thoughts refresh'd,
  Our eyelids with the morn's unclose,
    And bless the Ever-bless'd.

A FUNERAL HYMN, FOR A SCHOLAR, OR OTHER YOUNG PERSON.*

1 VAIN man, of mortal parents born,
    Know thou art born to die!
  How frail our state, how short our life,
    How full of misery!

2 As flowers from mother-earth we rise,
    A fading bloom we spread;
  As soon we waste and pass away
    Among the' unnumber'd dead.

3 As shadows glide o'er hills and dales,
    And yet no tracks appear;
  So swift we vanish hence; our souls
    Have no abiding here.

* Omitted in the second and all following editions.

4 The mourners go about the streets
    With solemn steps and slow;
Thus must it be for you and me,
    To the same home we go.

5 So teach us, Lord, to number out
    Our life's uncertain days,
We sweetly may our heart apply
    To heavenly wisdom's ways.

6 O holy Lord! O mighty God!
    When we resign our breath,
Then save us from the bitter pains
    Of everlasting death.

A PRAYER FOR ONE THAT IS LUNATIC AND SORE VEXED.

1 Jesu, God of our salvation,
    Hear our call; Save us all
By Thy death and passion.

2 Jesu, see Thine helpless creature;
    Bow the skies; God, arise,
All Thy foes to scatter.

3 Jesu, manifest Thy glory
    In this hour, Show Thy power,
Drive Thy foes before Thee.

4 Jesu, help, Thou serpent-bruiser;
    Bruise his head, Woman's Seed,
Cast down the accuser.

5 Jesu, wound the dragon, wound him;
    Make him roar, Break his power,
Let Thine arm confound him.

6 Jesu, come, and bind him, bind him;
　　Let him feel His own hell,
　Let Thy fury find him.

7 Jesu, than the strong man stronger,
　　Enter Thou; Let Thy foe
　Keep Thee out no longer.

8 Suffer him no more to harm her:
　　Make her clean, Purge her sin,
　Take away his armour.

9 Jesu, mighty to deliver,
　　Satan foil, Take the spoil,
　Make her Thine for ever.

10 Jesu, all to Thee is given:
　　All obey, Own Thy sway,
　Hell, and earth, and heaven.

11 Jesu, let this soul find favour
　　In Thy sight; Claim Thy right,
　Come, O come and save her.

12 From the hand of hell retrieve her:
　　Jesu, Lord, Speak the word,
　Bid the tempter leave her.

13 Hide her till the storm be over:
　　King of kings, Spread Thy wings,
　Christ, her weakness cover.

14 Jesu, wherefore dost Thou tarry?
　　Hear Thine own, Cast him down,
　Quell the adversary.

15 Jesu, shall he still devour?
　　Is Thine ear Slow to hear?
　Hast Thou lost Thy power?

16 Shorten'd is Thy hand, O Saviour ?
   Save her now, Show that Thou
Art the same for ever.

17 O omnipotent Redeemer,
   Hell rebuke With Thy look,
Silence the blasphemer.

18 Jesu, all his depths discover ;
   All unfold, Loose his hold,
Let the charm be over.

19 Jesu, is it past Thy finding ?
   Find and show, Break the vow,
And let it not be binding.

20 Break the dire confederacy:
   Shall it stand ? No: command,
Say, " 'Tis I release thee."

21 *Satan*, hear the name of JESUS,
   Hear and quake: Give her back
To the Name that frees us.

22 Jesu, claim Thy ransom'd creature,
   Let the foe Feel and know
Thou in us art greater.

23 Strengthen'd by Thy great example
   Let us tread On his head,
On his kingdom trample.

24 Drive him to the' infernal region :
   Chace, O chace, To his place,
Though his name be legion.

25 Is not faith the same for ever ?
   Let us see Signs from Thee,
Following the believer.

THANKSGIVING FOR HER DELIVERANCE.

1 PRAISE by all to Christ be given;
    Let us sing, Christ the King,
King of earth and heaven.

2 Glory to the name of JESUS;
    Jesu's name Still the same,
From all evil frees us.

3 Jesu's name the conquest won us;
    Let us rise, Fill the skies,
With our loud Hosannas.

4 Christ, Thou in our eyes art glorious:
    We proclaim Christ the Lamb,
Over all victorious.

5 Lion of the tribe of *Judah*,
    Joyfully, Lo! to Thee
Sing we Hallelujah.

6 Hell was ready to devour;
    Thou the prey Bear'st away
Out of *Satan's* power.

7 See the lawful captive taken
    From the foe! Now we know
Satan's realm is shaken.

8 Thou hast shown Thyself the stronger:
    Still go on, Put it down,
Let it stand no longer.

9 Overturn it, overturn it,
    Down with it, Let the feet
Of Thy servants spurn it.

10 Surely now the charm is broken:
   Thou hast shown To Thine own.
Thou hast given a token.

11 Is there any divination
   Against those Thou hast chose
Heirs of Thy salvation?

12 Thou hast bought, and Thou wilt have us
   Who shall harm, When Thine arm
Is stretch'd out to save us?

13 Hell in vain against us rages;
   Can it shock Christ the Rock
Of eternal ages!

14 *Satan*, wilt thou now defy us?
   Is not aid For us laid
On our great Messias?

15 Past is thine oppressive hour:
   Where's thy boast? Baffled, lost:
Where is now thy power?

16 Serpent, see in us thy Bruiser;
   Feel His power, Fly before
Us, thou foul accuser.

17 Thou no longer shalt oppress us:
   Triumph we Over thee
In the name of Jesus.

APPENDIX.

To the "Collection of Psalms and Hymns" published by Wesley in 1741, as far as they are here reprinted. there is subjoined an exact account of the contents of a volume with the same title, which he published without the name of author, printer, or publisher, in 1738. The strong resemblance between the two publications thus is made apparent to all who may think fit to compare the two Tables of Contents; and also the reason why the book of 1738 was never republished by Wesley, and need not be included in this reprint. The lovers of the Wesley poetry. too. will, it is hoped, be gratified in having the opportunity of making themselves acquainted with a volume which has become so excessively rare. For their sakes there is added to the Table of Contents a copy of the only hymn in this volume which has not been traced in the Table of Contents ; which, like one or two others inserted in the foregoing " Collection," may not have been written by Wesley ; but, like them. will be read with interest, as having had his sanction at that early period. There are also added readings of the poem entitled " Home" in this Collection, which differ so much from those in Vol. I., as to make it desirable to give students the opportunity of comparing them.

A COLLECTION OF PSALMS AND HYMNS.

CONTENTS.

PART I.

PSALMS AND HYMNS FOR SUNDAY.

PART II.

PSALMS AND HYMNS FOR WEDNESDAY OR FRIDAY.

PART III.

PSALMS AND HYMNS FOR SATURDAY.

A SINNER'S SIGHS.

1 O, LOOK not, Lord, on my desert,
   But on Thy glory; for Thou art
   The mighty God, I a weak worm!
   Destroy me not; but, O, reform!

2 Put me not to eternal shame,
   Unfaithful steward as I am:
   I have consumed Thy goods; yet, O.
   Thy mercy, not Thy vengeance, show!

3 Suffer not an Egyptian night
   To cover me, though long Thy light
   I have despised; yet 'gainst vile clay
   Do not Almighty power display.

4 God of compassion, Lord of love.
   The vials of Thy wrath remove;
   Look where the' atoning blood doth stand.
   And quench Thy wrath, and stay Thy hand.

5 Thou art both Judge and Saviour. Lord,
   Both life and death attend Thy word:
   O, hear; O, spare me; O, forgive
   Once more, and yet my soul shall live.

"HOME;" AS PRINTED IN 1738.

Ver. 1. line 1. LORD, my head burns. my heart is sick,
      line 3. Thy slowness wounds me to the quick.

   2 How canst Thou stay? Think on the pace
      The blood did make which Thou didst waste
      When I beheld it down Thy face
      Trickling; I never saw such haste.
      Come. Lord. &c.

6 Yet if Thou stay'st, why must I stay?
  What is this weary world to me?
  This world of woe?—Ye clouds, away;
  Away, I must get up and see.
  Come, Lord, &c.

7 What is this world, this meat and drink,
  That chains us by the teeth so fast?
  This woman kind which I can wink
  Into a blackness of distaste?
  Come, Lord, &c.

9 Nothing but drought and thorn and brake,
  Which way soe'er I look, I see.
  Some dream of joy; but when they wake
  Hungry and faint, they fly to Thee.
  Come, Lord, &c.

10 We talk of harvests; no such things
  There are, while in this world we stay:
  No fruitful year, but that which brings
  The last and loved, though dreadful, day.
  Come, Lord, &c.

13 Come, dearest Lord, no longer stay,
  My heart and flesh and bones do say.
  Come, Lord, and show Thyself to me,
  Or take my longing soul to Thee.

HYMNS

AND

Sacred Poems.

Published by

JOHN WESLEY, M.A.,
Fellow of *Lincoln* College, *Oxford;*

AND

CHARLES WESLEY, M.A.,
Student of *Christ-Church, Oxford.*

For the Grace of GOD *that bringeth Salvation unto* ALL MEN *hath appeared;* ['Επιφάνη γὰρ ἡ χάρις τῶ Θεῶ ἡ σωτήριΘ- πᾶσιν ἀνθρώποις.] *Teaching us, that denying Ungodliness and worldly Lusts, we should live soberly, righteously and godly in this present World; looking for that blessed Hope, and the glorious Appearing of the great* GOD, *and our Saviour* JESUS CHRIST; *who gave Himself for us, that He might redeem us from* ALL INIQUITY, *and purify unto Himself a peculiar People, zealous of good Works.* Tit. ii. 11, 12, 13, 14.

BRISTOL: Printed and sold by *Felix Farley,* in *Castle-Green; J. Wilson,* in *Wine-street;* and at the *School-Room* in the *Horse-Fair:* In *Bath,* by *W. Frederick,* Bookseller: And in *London,* by *T. Harris,* on the Bridge; also, at the *Foundery* in *Upper-Moor-Fields.* MDCCXLII.

THE PREFACE.

1. PERHAPS the general prejudice against Christian Perfection (the subject of many of the following verses) may chiefly arise from a misapprehension of the nature of it.   We willingly allow, and continually declare, there is no such perfection, in this life, as implies either a dispensation from doing good, and attending all the ordinances of God ; or a freedom from ignorance, mistake, temptation, and a thousand infirmities necessarily connected with flesh and blood.

2. First, we not only allow, but *earnestly contend*, (as *for the faith once delivered to the saints,*) that there is no perfection in this life which implies any dispensation from attending all the ordinances of God, or from *doing good unto all men, while we have time*, though *especially unto the household of faith*.   And whosoever they are who have taught otherwise, we are convinced are not *taught of God*.   We dare not *receive* them, *neither bid them God speed*, lest we be *partakers of their evil deeds*.   We believe that not only the babes in Christ who have newly found Redemption in His blood, but those also who are *grown up unto perfect men, unto the measure of the stature of the fulness of Christ*, are indispensably obliged, (and

that they are obliged thereto, is their *glory and crown of rejoicing.*) as oft as they have opportunity, to eat bread and drink wine *in remembrance of Him;* to *search the Scriptures;* by fasting (as well as temperance) to *keep their bodies under, and bring them into subjection;* and, above all, to pour out their souls in prayer, both *secretly,* and *in the great congregation.*

3. We, secondly, believe, and therefore speak, and that unto all men, and *with much assurance,* that there is no SUCH perfection in this life as implies an entire deliverance, either from ignorance or mistake, in things not essential to salvation, or from manifold temptations, or from numberless infirmities, wherewith the corruptible body, more or less, presses down the soul. This is the same thing which we have spoken from the beginning: if any teach otherwise, *they are not of us.* We cannot find any ground in Scripture to suppose that any inhabitant of an house of clay is wholly exempt, either from bodily infirmities, or from ignorance of many things ; or to imagine any is incapable of mistake, or of falling into divers temptations. No ; *the disciple is not above his Master, nor the servant above his* LORD. *It is enough that every one who is perfect shall be as his Master.*

4. But what then, it may be asked, do you mean by *one that is perfect,* or, *one that is as his Master?* We mean, one in whom is *the mind which was in Christ,* and who *so walketh as He walked;* a man that *hath clean hands and a pure heart;* or that is *cleansed from all filthiness of flesh and spirit;* one *in whom there is no occasion of stumbling,* and who, accordingly, *doth not commit sin.* To declare this a little more parti-

cularly : we understand by that scriptural expression, *a perfect man*, one in whom God hath fulfilled His faithful word, *From all your filthiness, and from all your idols, will I cleanse you. I will also save you from all your uncleannesses.* We understand hereby, one whom God hath sanctified throughout, even *in body, soul, and spirit;* one who *walketh in the light, as He is in the light*, in whom *is no darkness at all;* the blood of Jesus Christ His Son having *cleansed him from all sin.*

5. This man can now testify to all mankind, *I am crucified with Christ; nevertheless I live; yet I live not, but Christ liveth in me.* He is *holy, as God who called him is holy*, both in life and *in all manner of conversation.* He *loveth the Lord his God with all his heart*, and *serveth Him with all his strength.* He *loveth his neighbour* (every man) *as himself;* yea, as *Christ loved us;* them in particular that *despitefully use him and persecute him*, because *they know not the Son, neither the Father.* Indeed his soul is all love, filled with *bowels of mercies, kindness, meekness, gentleness, longsuffering.* And his life agreeth thereto: full of *the work of faith, the patience of hope, the labour of love.* And *whatsoever he doth, either in word or deed*, he doth it *all in the name*, in the love and power, *of the Lord Jesus.* In a word, he doth the will of God *on earth, as it is* done *in heaven.*

6. This it is to be *a perfect man*, to be *sanctified throughout, created anew in Jesus Christ.* Even " to have a heart so all-flaming with the love of God," (to use Archbishop Usher's words) " as continually to offer up every thought, word, and work, as a spiritual sacri-

fice, acceptable unto God through Christ." In every
thought of our hearts, in every word of our tongues,
in every work of our hands, *to show forth His praise
who hath called us out of darkness into His marvellous
light!* O that both we, and all who seek the Lord
Jesus in sincerity, may thus be *made perfect in
One!*

HYMNS

AND

SACRED POEMS.

PART I.

THE FORTIETH CHAPTER OF ISAIAH.

PART I.

1 COMFORT, ye ministers of grace,
    Comfort the people of your Lord;
 O! lift ye up the fallen race,
    And cheer them by the gospel-word!

2 Go, into every nation, go!
    Speak to their trembling hearts, and cry,
 Glad tidings unto all we show;
    Jerusalem, thy God is nigh.

3 Accomplish'd is thy legal war,
    The mantle o'er thy sins is spread:
 Thy God the punishment hath bore,
    Thy God the debt hath more than paid.

4 Punish'd thou art, for He hath died,
    (The merit of His death is thine,)
 Absolved, and freely justified,
    And clothed in righteousness Divine.

5 Hark ! in the wilderness a cry,
    A voice that loudly calls, Prepare !
Prepare your hearts, for God is nigh,
    And means to make His entrance there.

6 The Lord your God shall quickly come :
    Sinners, repent, the call obey ;
Open your hearts to make Him room ;
    Ye desert souls, prepare His way.

7 The Lord shall clear His way through all ;
    Whate'er obstructs, obstructs in vain :
The vale shall rise, the mountain fall,
    Crooked be straight, and rugged plain.

8 Nature, perverse and rough, shall yield,
    The' aspiring droop, the abject dare ;
Alike by sovereign grace compell'd,
    Despair shall hope, and pride despair.

9 When all, into subjection brought,
    Level shall lie, and humbly low,
Who captivated every thought,
    His glory then the Lord shall show.

10 The glory of the Lord display'd
    Together all mankind shall view ;
And what His mouth in truth hath said,
    His own almighty hand shall do.

PART II.

1 WITHERING as grass is humankind,
    And fleeting as the short-lived flower,
The goodliness to-day we find
    To-morrow fades, and is no more.

2 Man, foolish man, his virtue shows,
    Which for a moment charms our eyes :
The sin-convincing Spirit blows,
    Withers the flower, and fades, and dies.

3 Die the gay flower of human pride :
    The word of God shall stand secure :
The word of God shall still abide,
    And firm from age to age endure.

4 *Sion*, ascend the mountain-top :
    Jerusalem, the grace proclaim ;
Herald of God, thy voice lift up,
    And strongly shout the SAVIOUR'S name.

5 Good tidings show to *Judah's* race :
    Publish throughout the earth abroad
Good tidings of redeeming grace,
    And cry to all, Behold your God !

6 Behold, the Lord your God shall come,
    And bow the world to His command :
His outstretch'd arm shall make Him room
    Who can His outstretch'd arm withstand ?

7 Lo ! an exceeding great reward,
    Himself, to humbled souls He gives :
He fills whom first He hath prepared,
    And All in All for ever lives.

8 Shepherd of Souls, His tender care
    Shall kindly for His flock provide ;
The lambs He in His arms shall bear,
    And sweetly in His bosom hide.

9 His sheep He shall protect, and feed,
   Bind up the maim'd, support the weak ;
The great with young shall gently lead,
   And seek the lost, and heal the sick.

PART III.

1 Nor doth His love eclipse His might.
   Or lessen His majestic powers,
Though stooping from His glory's height ;
   Who is so great a God as ours?

2 He in the hollow of His hand
   Measured the vast unbounded main ;
The wide-extended heavens He spann'd ;
   Infinity His arms contain.

3 He meted out the earth, and poised
   The mountains, hung on empty space,
When all the morning stars rejoiced,
   And shouted their Creator's praise.

4 Creation's line His wisdom laid,
   He grasp'd the chaos with His fist ;
Sea, air, and earth, and heaven He weigh'd,
   And bad the' exact machine consist.

5 Who with the great Omniscient God,
   Angel or man, in council join'd ;
To Him the way of judgment show'd,
   Or taught that all-informing Mind?

6 He, high enthroned above all height,
   A partner in His work disdains ;
In power and knowledge infinite
   The self-directed Spirit reigns.

7 See the vast tribes that crowd the face
    Of earth, the islands scatter'd wide ;
Survey the whole of human race,
    Their wealth, their number, and their pride :

8 Light as the balance-dust, and small
    To Him as the minutest grain,
Their millions into nothing fall,
    Or "swell to be discern'd in vain."*

9 The nations with their God compare,
    (A drop with the unfathom'd sea,)
They vanish all, dissolved in air,
    And lost in His immensity.

10 Lighter than vanity, and less
    Than nothing, He on all looks down ;
Nor can their services appease
    His wrath, or mitigate His frown.

11 *Lebanon* brings her stores in vain :
    Nor all her cedars can afford,
Not all her beasts for sinners slain,
    An offering worthy of their Lord.

12 Nothing the creature adds to Him
    From whom their borrow'd being flow'd ;
Who self-sufficient and supreme
    Exists, the One Eternal God.

PART IV.

1 Say, then, ye worms of earth, to whom
    Will ye your glorious God compare ?
Vainly through all His works ye roam,
    To find Jehovah's likeness there.

* Young's "Last Day," book ii., 195.

2 The vile idolater belies
        His image with a golden shrine;
    To counterfeit the Godhead tries;
        And stocks and stones become Divine.

3 Man his own deity reveres
        By self-delight, and self-esteem;
    Whate'er the sinner hopes, or fears,
        Desires, or loves, is God to him.

4 But have ye not His being known,
        And clearly seen by nature's light;
    Have not the ancient fathers shown,
        And you confess'd the Infinite?

5 The heavens His glorious power proclaim.
        The' Invisible on earth is show'd,
    Nature is written with His name,
        And all things speak their builder God.

6 Creation to His law submits,
        His rule He over all maintains;
    High on the globe of heaven He sits,
        And undisturb'd for ever reigns.

7 The' inhabitants of earth from thence,
        As grasshoppers, His eye beholds:
    His hand, and power, and providence
        The curtain of the heavens unfolds.

8 'Tis He who stretch'd them out, 'tis He
        Who still the wide pavilion spreads.
    That blue ethereal canopy.
        And draws it o'er His creatures' heads.

9 Princes, and kings, that dare withstand
    Their uncontroll'd Creator's sway,
Shall sink beneath His mighty hand,
    And fall, and fade, and die away.

10 Planted awhile, or sown below,
    Their stock accurst shall ne'er take root.
The Lord upon their pride shall blow.
    Wither the flower, and blast the fruit.

11 Say, then, ye abject worms, to whom
    Will ye your glorious God compare ?
Who shall His holiness presume
    To match. or who His power shall dare.

12 Lift up your eyes to things on high,
    Nor fix on earth your groveling thought :
Who built yon azure vaulted sky ?
    Who spoke those beauteous orbs from nought?

13 God only wise, and great, and strong,
    Made them to run their heavenly race.
(Knowledge and might to God belong.
    Honour. and majesty, and praise.)

14 Their radiant hosts He marshals right.
    Their nature, names, and number knows
He bids them in their courses fight.
    And blast their great Creator's foes.

15 They hear; and each His will performs :
    And. lo ! to man they ever call,
" Lift up your eyes, ye abject worms :
    Adore the glorious Cause of all !"

PART V.

1 THE world He made He still sustains.
　　Why then dost thou, O *Israel*, say,
" My God forgets His people's pains,
　　His *Jacob* is a castaway? "

2 Repent thee of thy peevish haste;
　　Recall the rash desponding word;
No more complain, " The hour is past,
　　And I have wearied out my Lord."

3 Hast thou not heard, hast thou not known
　　The everlasting God, that laid
The earth's foundations, rules alone,
　　Nor faints to bear the world He made?

4 JEHOVAH is unchangeable,
　　His ways, and thoughts, are not as ours;
He cheers the languid souls that fail,
　　And quickens all their drooping powers.

5 Gently He lifts the fallen up,
　　He gives them faith, and faith's increase.
Revives their feeble, dying hope,
　　And fills with love, and joy, and peace.

6 Blasted, the vigour of the young
　　Shall fade, and suddenly decay;
The bold, and confident, and strong
　　Shall fear, despair, and die away.

7 But they who wait upon the Lord
　　Shall surely find His promise true,
Receive the quickening powerful word.
　　And, born of God, their strength renew.

8 Their willing souls, from sin set free,
　　Shall swiftly in His statutes move,
　Shall walk in glorious liberty,
　　Shall fly upon the wings of love.

9 With eagle's wings their souls shall rise,
　　Steady and strong to heaven soar,
　Regain on earth their native skies,
　　And faint, and fall, and sin no more.

THE SIXTY-THIRD CHAPTER OF ISAIAH.*

PART II.

1 I too will magnify the Lord,
　　And emulate the angels' lays,
　His loving-kindnesses record,
　　In sounds of everlasting praise.

2 For all He hath on us bestow'd
　　This only tribute can I bring.
　Extol the mercies of my God,
　　His multitude of mercies sing.

3 How good to *Israel's* chosen race !
　　Who, who can all His goodness tell?
　So rich in unexhausted grace;
　　His riches are unsearchable.

4 Surely, He said, Mine own they are;
　　My people will not faithless prove ;
　My children will not slight My care,
　　Or disappoint a Father's love.

* The first part, altered from Mr. Norris, will be found in
Vol. I., p. 118.

5 Sweetly He strove their hearts to gain,
    He woo'd them to embrace His will.
They never ask'd His help in vain,
    But found a present Saviour still.

6 Dear as the apple of His eye
    In all their griefs He kindly grieved;
The angel of His presence nigh
    From all the favourite nation saved.

7 He rescued when to evil sold,
    He snatch'd them from impending harms,
Carried them all the days of old
    Safe in His everlasting arms.

8 He magnified His saving power,
    Call'd them His utmost grace to prove ;
With infinite compassion bore
    The objects of His tenderest love.

9 But O ! they soon forsook their God;
    The faithless and rebellious race
In devious paths of evil trod,
    And grieved the Spirit of His grace.

10 They vex'd; and forced His wrath to rise:
    His vengeance fell, so long delay'd:
Constrain'd the rebels to chastise,
    He pour'd His judgments on their head.

11 His mercy then He call'd to mind ;
    He call'd to mind the ancient days
When, only merciful and kind,
    He smiled on the peculiar race.

12 Where is He now—their God, their Guide!
    (He taught their hearts the powerful plea:)
Where is He now, their hearts replied,
    Who brought His people from the sea?

13 Who placed a shepherd o'er the rest,
    And gave him wisdom from above.
And breathed into his peaceful breast
    The meek, mild spirit of His love.

14 Them by the hand of *Moses* led,
    His power and goodness to proclaim,
Beyond the bounds of time to spread
    JEHOVAH's everlasting name.

15 The Lord of Hosts in all appear'd,
    He smote the sea with *Moses'* rod,
His glorious arm aloft He rear'd:
    The parting sea confess'd its God.

16 He brought them through the wondrous way;
    The deep was dry at His command;
Secure they march'd in firm array.
    Nor stumbled, till they reach'd the land.

17 Smooth as the generous-nurtured beast
    Into the verdant vale goes down,
To bring them to that promised rest,
    His Spirit gently led them on.

18 Thus didst Thou guide Thy chosen race,
    That every tongue might speak Thy fame,
And earth and heaven conspire to praise
    The God of *Israel's* glorious Name.

PART III.

1 GOD of eternal Majesty,
    High as Thou art, from heaven look down ;
 Holy and Just, we cry to Thee ;
    Behold us from Thy glorious throne !

2 Where is Thy strength to conquer sin ?
    Thy zeal to save a fallen race ?
 Thy bowels sounding from within ?
    Thy mercies, and Thy pardoning grace ?

3 Thy pity, and paternal care,
    The tender yearnings of Thy heart.
 Are they restrain'd ?   Is fury there ?
    Ah, no ! Thou still our Father art.

4 Doubtless Thou art our Father still,
    Though *Abraham* his seed disowns
 Debased by sin, though *Israel*
    Renounces his degenerate sons.

5 Our Lord, and our Redeemer now
    Thou art, and wilt be still the same :
 Our everlasting Father Thou ;
    JEHOVAH is Thy glorious name.

6 Why, then, O Lord, if ours Thou art.
    Why hast Thou suffer'd us to rove ?
 Withdrawn Thy Spirit from our heart.
    And left us to our want of love ?

7 Why hast Thou hid Thy lovely face,
    And caused us from Thy paths to err ?
 Abandon'd by restraining grace,
    Our hearts were harden'd from Thy fear.

8 Yet, Lord, for Thee again we mourn:
    Now let our prayers Thine aid engage,
Now for Thy servant's sake return,
    And cheer Thy drooping heritage.

9 The land we fondly deem'd our own
    (Alas ! how short a time enjoy'd !)
Our adversaries have o'erthrown,
    And trampled on the house of God.

10 Yet we are Thine, though dispossest,
    And outcasts from the promised land :
They never have Thy sway confess'd,
    Or yielded to Thy just command.

11 We, we are call'd by Thy great name ;
    Accept our plea, Thine ear incline ;
Thine, Lord, we are; renew Thy claim:
    Receive, and seal us ever Thine.

GOD'S HUSBANDRY.

*From the German.**

1 High on His everlasting throne,
    The King of saints His works surveys,
Marks the dear souls He calls His own,
    And smiles on the peculiar race.
He rests well-pleased their toil to see :
    Beneath His easy yoke they move,
With all their heart and strength agree
    In the sweet labour of His love.

* Compare the hymn No. 1004 in the Herrnhuth Collection (abridged by one-half in Knapp's *Ev. L.*, p. 501,) by Bishop A. G. Spangenberg, (1704—1792.) beginning "*Der König ruht und schauet doch.*"

2 His eye the world at once looks through,
   A vast uncultivated field !
Mountains and vales, in ghastly show,
   A barren uncouth prospect yield.
Clear'd of the thorns by human care,
   A few less hideous wastes are seen ;
Yet still they all continue bare,
   And not one spot of earth is green.

3 See where the servants of their God,
   A busy multitude, appear ;
For Jesus day and night employ'd,
   His heritage they toil to clear.
The love of Christ their hearts constrains,
   And strengthens their unwearied hands :
They spend their sweat, and blood, and pains,
   To cultivate *Immanuel's* land.

4 Alarm'd at their successful toil,
   Satan and his wild spirits rage ;
They labour to tear up and spoil,
   And blast the rising heritage.
In every wilderness they sow
   The seed of death, the carnal mind :
They would not let one virtue grow,
   Or leave one seed of good behind.

5 Yet still the servants of their Lord
   Look up, and calmly persevere ;
Supported by the Master's word,
   The adverse powers they scorn to fear,
Gladly their happy work pursue :
   The labour of their hands is seen,
Their hands the face of earth renew,
   Diversified with cheerful green.

6 Where'er the faithful workers turn.
    The steps of industry appear;
They labour the dry wood to burn,
    They labour with unwearied care
The fruits of Sodom to tread down.
    To root up each accursed seed.
By Satan and his servants sown,
    And plant the Gospel in its stead.

7 To dig the ground, they all bestow
    Their lives; from every soften'd clod
They gather out the stones, and sow
    The' immortal seed, the Word of God.
They water it with tears and prayers,
    They long for the returning word :
Happy, if all their pains and cares
    Can bring forth fruit to please their Lord.

8 Jesus their toil delighted sees,
    Their industry vouchsafes to crown :
He kindly gives the wish'd increase,
    And sends the promised blessing down :
The sap of life. the Spirit's powers
    He rains incessant from above.
He all His gracious fulness showers,
    To perfect their great work of love.

9 He prospers all His servants' toils :
    But of peculiar grace has chose
A flock, on whom His kindest smiles
    And choicest blessings He bestows :
Devoted to their common Lord,
    True followers of the bleeding Lamb.
By God beloved, by men abhorr'd ;
    And HERNHUTH is the favourite name :

10 Here many a faithful soul is found,
     With mystic powers of love endued,
   Full of the light of life, and crown'd
     A king and priest to serve his God.
   With flaming zeal for Christ they shine,
     Their body, soul, and spirit give,
   To Christ their goods and blood resign,
     For Christ they freely die and live.

11 What can we offer our good Lord
     (Poor nothings !) for His boundless grace
   Fain would we His great name record,
     And worthily set forth His praise.
   Dear Object of our growing love,
     To whom our more than all we owe,
   Open the Fountain from above,
     And let it our full soul o'erflow.

12 So shall our lives Thy power proclaim,
     Thy grace for every sinner free,
   'Till all mankind shall learn Thy name,
     Shall all stretch out their hands to Thee.
   Open a door which earth and hell
     May strive to shut, but strive in vain :
   Let Thy word richly in us dwell,
     And let our gracious fruit remain.

13 O, multiply Thy sower's seed !
     And fruit we every hour shall bear,
   Throughout the world Thy Gospel spread,
     Thine everlasting truth declare :
   We all, in perfect love renew'd,
     Shall know the greatness of Thy power ;
   Stand in the temple of our God
     As pillars, and go out no more.

IT IS MINE OWN INFIRMITY.

Psalm lxxvii. 10.   [P. B. V.]

1 HAVE mercy, Lord, Thy wrath remove,
   Nor let Thy judgments weigh me down :
I cannot live without Thy love,
   I cannot stand beneath Thy frown.

2 Wilt Thou not once Thy face display,
   And dart a ray of heavenly light?
Still must I urge my cheerless way,
   And mourn throughout my long-lived night?

3 Lo! in my prayer I ever mourn,
   Vext with the sad remains of sin,
Broken, and bruised, and rack'd and torn.
   How shall I bear this hell within?

4 This unbelief, these cruel fears,
   Distracting doubts, and torturing pain?
While Thou art silent at my tears ;
   Thou seest them ever flow in vain.

5 And must I yield to black despair?
   In vain on Thee for mercy call.
Tempted above what I can bear?
   And wilt Thou suffer me to fall?

6 Never again disclose Thy face.
   Or show me the atoning blood?
Have I exhausted all Thy grace?
   Hath God forgotten to be good?

7 For ever is Thy mercy gone,
   Thy truth. and faithfulness, and love?
Doth angry Justice rule alone?
   Have I no Advocate above?

8 Then pour Thy vengeance on my head,
　　And quench the smoking flax in me :
Break (if Thou canst) a bruised reed,
　　And cast me out who come to Thee.

9 Jesu, I come my doom to meet,
　　A sinner whom Thou wilt not spare :
But I will perish at Thy feet,
　　The first that ever perish'd there.

GENESIS III. 15.

*" I will put enmity between thee and the woman,
and between thy seed and her seed," &c.** *

1 God of Truth, and Power and Love,
　　Father, Friend of all mankind,
Let on me Thy Spirit move,
　　Influence my feeble mind ;
'Twixt the serpent's seed and me
　　Prevalently interpose,
Break the fatal amity,
　　Make us everlasting foes.

2 Sin hath poison'd all my soul,
　　Sin, the serpent's cursed seed :
No one part in me is whole ;
　　Yet will I the promise plead,—
Promise of all-saving grace,
　　Promise of an inward power,
Able to redeem the race,
　　Me, and all men, to restore.

Most of the thoughts in this poem are borrowed from a
sermon in Dr. Gell's " Essay toward the Amendment of the last
English Translation of the Bible."　1659, pp. 9—25.

3 Breathe the breath of simple life,
   O! be *Abel* born in me,
(Previous to the legal strife,)
   Innocent simplicity:
Give me childishness to' oppose
   To the subtle serpent's art;
Childishness no evil knows,
   Give me, Lord, a simple heart!
4 Or, if pride hath this destroy'd,
   Turn'd into self-righteousness,
Let the law supply the void,
   Seth * succeed in *Abel's* place.
Deeply root Thy law within,
   Parent of the *wretched man:* †
Check my forwardness to sin,
   Forcibly by fear restrain.
5 Bind in me the strong man, bind
   With the fetters of the law;
Curb and thwart the carnal mind.
   Keep the Man of Sin in awe:
Enemy to all that 's good,
   Never will he quite give place:
He can only be subdued
   By the sense of pardoning grace.
6 Tell me, Jesus died for me;
   Show some token of His love:
Love and sin can ne'er agree,
   Love shall still the stronger prove.
Love in the first measure give,
   Sin shall then no longer sway:
Flesh may for a season strive,
   I the Spirit shall obey.

* שֵׁת A positive law.   † אֱנוֹשׁ Enos. i.e. miserable

7 Patiently I then shall wait
    For the woman's noblest Seed,
JESUS CHRIST the MIGHTY HATE,
    Bruiser of the serpent's head :
O, reveal Thy Son in me,
    Bring the perfect nature in,
Now destroy the enmity,
    Now consume the Man of Sin.

8 *Adam*, flesh, and self, and pride,
    Antichrist. Perdition's son,
Let him not in me abide,
    Cast him out, and reign alone ;
Slay the dragon in the sea ;
    Make my soul Thy pure abode,
Fill'd with all the Deity,
    Swallow'd up and lost in God.

MORIAR UT TE VIDEAM !

Let me die that I may see Thee !

1 O THOU, who know'st what is in man,
    Who searchest out the reins and heart,
Me, Jesu, to myself explain,
    A ray of heavenly light impart ;
Impart Thyself, Thou real Light,
And manifest my nature's night.

2 Cause me, O God, myself to know,
    The depth of wickedness within ;
Show me, my inmost substance show,
    The' exceeding sinfulness of sin :

Such power belongs to Thee alone :
Show me, that sin and I are one.

3 Senseless alike of sin and Thee
   My unawaken'd soul remains ;
Fast bound in sin and misery,
   I slumber on, nor feel my chains,
Nor taste nor see how good Thou art,
For still the veil is on my heart.

4 O, might my heart at least relent,
   And feel the guilty mountain-load '
O, that Thy powerful word might rent
   The veil, and let me into God ;
The glories of Thy face display,
The brightness of eternal day !

5 I know the terms : I cannot see
   Thy blissful face, and live——in sin :
A flaming sword preserves the tree
   Of life, lest self should enter in :
It keeps out self, and every way
It turns, the Man of Sin to slay.

6 Be it according to Thy word,
   Ready to meet my doom I am.
O, let me rush upon that sword,
   And feel the sin-consuming flame !
Live only Christ in me, not I ;
O, let me see Thy face and die !

7 Die all of self to live no more,
   Die the old man no more to rise ;
Me to Thine image here restore,
   Receive me to Thy paradise,
(Whence I may never more remove,)
The paradise of perfect love.

A PASSION HYMN.

1 Ye that pass by, behold the Man !
    The Man of Griefs, condemn'd for you !
The Lamb of God, for sinners slain,
    Weeping to Calvary pursue.

2 See how His back the scourges tear,
    While to the bloody pillar bound !
The ploughers make long furrows there,
    Till all His body is one wound.

3 The abjects spit upon that face
    Which prophets wish'd in vain to see,*
On which the angels loved to gaze,
    Pleased with His milder majesty.

4 Adored by angels, mock'd by men,
    Speechless the form of guilt He wears :
Reviled, He answers not again,
    But meekly all their insults bears.

5 Nor can He thus their hate assuage ;
    His innocence, to death pursued,
Must fully glut their utmost rage :
    Hark ! how they clamour for His blood !

6 " To us our own *Barabbas* give !
    Away with Him," (they loudly cry.)
" Away with Him, not fit to live,
    The vile Seducer crucify !"

7 Against his God the creature calls :
    Accused and sentenced by the breath
Himself inspired, their Maker falls ;
    The Lord of Life is doom'd to death.

* Compare Herbert, *The Sacrifice*, v. 46.

8 His sacred limbs they stretch, they tear,
    With nails they fasten to the wood ;
His sacred limbs—exposed, and bare,
    Or only cover'd with His blood.

9 See there ! His temples crown'd with thorns
    His bleeding hands extended wide,
His streaming feet, transfixt and torn !
    The fountain gushing from His side !

10 Where is the King of Glory now !
    The everlasting Son of God !
The' Immortal hangs His languid brow,
    The' Almighty faints beneath His load

11 Beneath *my* load He faints, and dies :
    I fill'd His soul with pangs unknown ;
I caused those mortal groans and cries,
    I kill'd the Father's only Son.

12 O, Thou dear suffering Son of God,
    How doth Thy heart to sinners move !
Help me to catch Thy precious blood,
    Help me to taste Thy dying love.

13 Give me to feel Thy agonies,
    One drop of Thy sad cup afford :
I fain with Thee would sympathise,
    And share the sufferings of my Lord.

14 The earth could to her centre quake,
    Convulsed, while her Creator died :
O, let my inmost nature shake,
    And die with Jesus crucified !

15 At Thy last gasp the graves display'd
    Their horrors to the upper skies :
O that my soul might burst the shade,
    And, quicken'd by Thy death, arise !

16 The rocks could feel Thy powerful death,
      And tremble, and asunder part :
    O, rend with Thine expiring breath
      The harder marble of my heart !

17 My stony heart Thy voice *shall* rent,
      Thou wilt, I trust, the veil remove.
    My inmost bowels shall resent
      The yearnings of Thy dying love.

18 The grace I surely shall receive,
      Thy death hath bought the grace for me :
    This is my whole desire, to live ;
      To live, and then to die in Thee.

DESIRING TO LOVE.

1 WHAT shall I do my God to love,
     My Saviour, and the world's, to praise ?
   Whose bowels of compassion move
     To me, and all the fallen race ;
   Whose mercy is divinely free
   For all the fallen race, and me.

2 I long to know, and to make known,
     The height and depth of love Divine,
   The kindness Thou to me hast shown,
     Whose every sin was counted Thine :
   My God for me resign'd His breath.
   He died to save my soul from death.

3 All souls are Thine : and Thou for all
     The ransom of Thy life hast given ;
   To raise the sinner from his fall,
     And bring him back to God and heaven ;

Thou all the world hast died to save.
And all may Thy salvation have.

4 How shall I thank Thee for the grace.
   On me, and all mankind bestow'd ?
O that my every breath were praise !
   O that my heart were fill'd with God !
My heart would then with love o'erflow.
And all my life Thy glory show.

5 See me, O Lord, athirst and faint,
   Me weary of forbearing see ;
And let me feel Thy love's constraint.
   And freely give up all for Thee ;
True in the fiery trial prove,
And pay Thee back Thy dying love.

ANOTHER.

1 O Love, I languish at Thy stay.
   I pine for Thee with lingering smart.
Weary and faint through long delay :
   When wilt Thou come into my heart ?
From sin and sorrow set me free.
And swallow up my soul in Thee !

2 Come, O Thou universal Good !
   Balm of the wounded conscience. come !
The hungry, dying spirit's food,
   The weary, wandering pilgrim's home.
Haven to take the shipwreck'd in.
My everlasting rest from sin.

3 Be Thou, O Love, whate'er I want;
    Support my feebleness of mind,
Relieve the thirsty soul, the faint
    Revive, illuminate the blind,
The mournful cheer, the drooping lead,
And heal the sick, and raise the dead.

4 Come, O my comfort and delight,
    My strength and health, my shield and sun,
My boast, and confidence, and might,
    My joy, my glory, and my crown,
My gospel-hope, my calling's prize,
My tree of life, my paradise.

5 The secret of the Lord Thou art,
    The mystery so long unknown,
Christ in a pure and perfect heart,
    The name inscribed in the white stone.
The Life Divine, the little leaven,
My precious pearl, my present heaven.

ANOTHER.

1 O Love Divine, what hast Thou done!
    The' immortal God hath died for me!
The Father's co-eternal Son
    Bore all my sins upon the tree:
The' immortal God for me hath died!
My Lord, my Love is crucified!

2 Behold Him, all ye that pass by,
    The bleeding Prince of Life and Peace!
Come, see, ye worms, your Maker die,
    And say, was ever grief like His?
Come, feel with me His blood applied:
My Lord, my Love is crucified!

3 Is crucified for me and you,
  To bring us rebels near to God;
Believe, believe the record true:
  We all are bought with Jesu's blood:
Pardon for all flows from His side;
My Lord, my Love is crucified!

4 Then let us sit beneath His cross,
  And gladly catch the healing stream,
All things for Him account but loss,
  And give up all our hearts to Him;
Of nothing speak or think beside,
"My Lord, my Love is crucified!"

SALVATION BY GRACE.

1 Jesu, Great Redeemer, hear
  A feeble sinner's cry;
Thou in my behalf appear,
  And bring salvation nigh:
To my Lord what shall I say?
  Saviour, I of Thee have need:
Take, O, take my sins away,
  And make me free indeed.

2 Thee, all-lovely as Thou art,
  Should I profess to love,
Surely my rebellious heart
  The falsehood would disprove:
Thee my heart cannot obey
  Till from every evil freed:
Take, O, take, &c.

3 Should I say, that aught in me
      Of good doth now abide,
   Self-condemn'd I now should be ;
      My all is self and pride.
   Guilty, guilty, must I say,
      Nothing, Lord, have I to plead :
   Take, O, take, &c.

4 No desire or will have I
      Thy mercy to embrace ;
   From Thine arms of love I fly,
      And slight Thy proffer'd grace :
   But Thou didst my ransom pay,
      But Thy blood for me was shed :
   Take, O, take, &c.

5 Thy salvation to obtain,
      Out of myself I go ;
   Freely Thou must heal my pain,
      Thy unbought mercy show ;
   For myself I cannot pray ;
      Let Thy Spirit intercede :
   Take, O, take, &c.

6 Not because I willing am,
      On me this grace be show'd ;
   But Thou art the' Atoning Lamb,
      Therefore apply Thy blood :
   Therefore, Lord, no more delay,
      Therefore heal my soul, and lead ;
   Take, O, take my sins away,
      And make me free indeed.

[The hymn " Before the Sacrament," which immediately follows
   this in the first edition, is transferred to a subsequent publication.]

AFTER A JOURNEY.

1 GLORY to God, whose gracious care
    Doth all my steps attend,
  Throughout the way my weakness bear.
    And bring me to the end.

2 Thou, Lord, hast saved both man and beast:
    How excellent Thy name !
  While underneath Thy wings I rest.
    Thy goodness I proclaim.

3 Still (for I put my trust in Thee)
    All evil turn aside,
  Cover my helpless head, and be
    Mine everlasting Guide.

4 Lead me, till my few evil years
    Of pilgrimage are o'er ;
  But ere I leave this vale of tears,
    O, bid me sin no more.

PSALM LI. 10. [P. B. V.]

" Make me a clean heart, O God."

1 O FOR an heart to praise my God, *
    An heart from sin set free !
  An heart that always feels Thy blood.
    So freely spilt for me !

2 An heart resign'd, submissive, meek.
    My dear Redeemer's throne.
  Where only Christ is heard to speak.
    Where Jesus reigns alone.

* In the final revision (1782) we find " a heart " throughout ;
" dear " in v. 2 is changed to " great ;" and " dearest " in v. 8
to " gracious ;" " self and." v. 6, line 4. into " every."

3 An humble, lowly, contrite heart,
    Believing, true, and clean,
Which neither life nor death can part
    From Him that dwells within.

4 An heart in every thought renew'd,
    And full of love Divine,
Perfect, and right, and pure, and good.
    A copy, Lord, of Thine.

5 Thy tender heart is still the same.
    And melts at human woe :
Jesu, for Thee distrest I am,
    I want Thy love to know.

6 My heart. Thou know'st, can never rest.
    Till Thou create my peace ;
Till, of my *Eden* repossest,
    From self and sin I cease.

7 Fruit of Thy gracious lips, on me
    Bestow that peace unknown,
The hidden manna, and the tree
    Of life, and the white stone.

8 Thy nature, dearest Lord, impart ;
    Come quickly from above ;
Write Thy new name upon my heart.
    Thy new, best name of Love.

A PRAYER FOR HUMILITY.

1 O MY heart, what must I do !
    Shall the self-admiring fiend
Still my helplessness pursue ?
    Shall his malice never end ?

Still the stubborn sin remains,
 Still the thorn is in my side,
Still I groan to feel my chains,
 Sorely buffeted by pride.

2 Vanity, the serpent-seed,
 Poisoning all my good I find :
Stealing on with silent tread
 Vanity lurks close behind ;
As the substance by the shade,
 Grace I find by pride pursued :
Grace is pride's occasion made,
 Evil ever cleaves to good.

3 Pleased in borrow'd plumes to shine.
 Nature arrogates a share,
Mixes in the work Divine,
 Bold the Godhead's form to wear :
Proudly in her beauty trusts,
 Heavenly charms as hers displays.
Falsely, blasphemously boasts,
 Varnish'd, deck'd, and *hid* by grace.

4 When the boasted grace is gone.
 Humbled in the dust I lie ;
Poor, forsaken, and alone,
 From the deep on God I cry.
Seeing there my loss of God.
 Proud I am my loss to see,
Proud to find that I am proud.
 Proud of my humility.

5 O the strength of inbred sin !
 Who can vanity subdue ?
From a creature all unclean
 Who can bring a creature new :

Jesu, Lord, all power is Thine,
 Nothing is too hard for Thee ;
Greater than this heart of mine.
 Surely Thou canst humble me.

6 O, begin ; the way prepare :
 Pride and unbelief confound :
Far away my fig-leaves tear,
 Throughly search my spirit's wound :
Cast me down, and keep me poor,
 All my weak supports remove.
Lay the deep foundation sure,
 Humble me by faith and love.

7 Take my broken reeds away,
 Every vain fallacious rest.
All on which my soul I stay,
 All that keeps me from Thy breast :
Strip me, empty me of all ;
 Joyless, cheerless would I be.
So I might on Jesus fall,
 Fall, and lose myself in Thee.

PSALM LV. 6. [P. B. V.]

" O that I had wings like a dove ! for then would I
flee away, and be at rest."

1 O THAT I had the silver wings
 Of the mild, holy dove,
To bear me far from earthly things.
 And every creature-love !

2 Then would I swiftly fly away
   To Christ, and be at rest;
On Him my fluttering spirit stay,
   And hide me in His breast.

3 Jesu, my hiding-place, to Thee
   I know not how to fly ;
Long have I struggled to be free,
   Nor found deliverance nigh.

4 Full oft in fruitless, fond desire
   I *to the desert* ran ;*
But could not from myself retire,
   Or 'scape the inner man.

5 I took the morning's wings, and fled
   For rest to worlds unknown ;
Sin found me in the secret shade,
   And claim'd me for its own.

6 O, who shall bid this self depart,
   This world of sin exclude ;
Empty, and make my peaceful heart
   An holy solitude ?

7 'Tis not the desert, or the cell,
   Can hide me from my pain ;
I carry with me my own hell,
   While self and pride remain.

8 Baffled, o'ercome, I yield at last.
   I yield to self-despair ;
My unavailing strife is past,
   And void returns my prayer.

9 I cannot pray, I cannot praise,
   For grace I cannot call,
I cannot *feel* my want of grace,
   My soul is stript of all.

* Compare Preface to Vol. I., p. xx.

10 A vile, unworthy worm, my eyes
    I dare not lift to heaven;
  Let Him who sees me from the skies
    Speak if I am forgiven.

11 Or let my Lord still hold His peace,
    And do as seems Him good,
  Forsake me in my last distress,
    And leave me in my blood.

12 If He can find it in His heart,
    His fury let Him pour
  On me, and from my soul depart,
    And never love me more.

13 I leave it all to Him alone;
    It lies within His breast;
  His will, His only will be done,
    Let me be curst or blest.

ANOTHER.

1 OMNISCIENT GOD, whose eyelids try
    The self-deceiving sons of men,
  To Thee how shall I dare draw nigh,
    A man of lips and heart unclean !
  Thou know'st I mean not what I say,
  Thou know'st I only seem to pray.

2 Doubtless Thou art of purer eyes
    Than to behold iniquity;
  And all my nature naked lies,
    And all my thoughts appear to Thee ;
  No fig-leaves from Thy sight can hide
  My filthiness of self and pride.

3 O my abominable heart !
       Its secrets all to Thee are known :
The sin from which I cannot part,
       The sin that claims me for its own :
Thou seest it all ; my nature's shame :
Thou seest, what I should die to name.

4 The foul reproach I groan to bear.
       And vainly struggle to get free :
Yet still I breathe a tainted air,
       (Tainted, alas ! by sin and me.)
And wish for wings to flee away.
And ever in the desert stay.

5 O that I had a cottage there
       To lodge a poor wayfaring man !
Far from the world of noise and care.
       Of grief, anxiety, and pain,
O, could I from my people roam,
And be where none but God could come.

6 Me as a bowl if now He turn,
       To foreign climes with violence tos-
I would not for a moment mourn
       My kindred, or my country's loss :
A voluntary exile. I
Would there consent to live and die.

   7 O, might I have my one request.
        My fond and foolish heart's desire.
   And get me hence, and be at rest.
        Into the deepest shades retire.
   Be clean forgot, and out of mind !
   O, where shall I the desert find ?

8 Can earth afford that secret place?
    Long have I sought it out in vain,
And fled before the human face,
    And dragg'd to distant worlds my chain:
Yet still I found the carnal mind,
I could not leave myself behind.

9 'Tis vain, I find, from self to flee
    For rest, to earth's remotest bound:
The deep cries out, 'Tis not in me!
    Happiness is not to be found,
Save only, Jesus, in Thy breast:
Thou art the soul's eternal rest.

10 But how shall I to Thee attain,
    Thee, whom I sinfully pursue;
Unprofitable I, and vain!
    Thy glory is not in my view:
What shall I say Thy grace to win?
My very prayer is turn'd to sin.

11 Nothing in me Thy grace can move,
    A wretched man of sin I am;
But Thou art good, but Thou art love,
    And Jesus is Thy healing name:
O, for Thy name and mercy's sake,
The sinner to Thy bosom take!

12 Do as Thou findest in Thy heart;
    Reject me, Saviour, or receive;
Bid me from Thee to hell depart,
    Or bid me come to Thee, and live:
I trust my soul to this alone,
Let all Thy will on me be done.

A POOR SINNER.

1   How happy is the man
      Who sees his misery,
Who ever feels his nature's chain,
      Nor murmurs to be free !

      Who waits in patient hope,
      And, languishing for home,
With cheerful confidence looks up,
      And says, " My Lord will come."

2   He neither hopes nor fears
      Evil or good below ;
But sighs for God, and lets his tears
      In secret silence flow.

      Stript of his joy, he grieves
      Quiet, and meek, and still :
The matter to his Father leaves,
      And bids Him work His will.

3   In calm, submissive grief
      He suffers his distress;
He cannot snatch undue relief,
      Or wish his misery less :

      " My Father's will is good,"
      (The patient mourner cries,)
" He never gives a stone for food,
      Or slights His children's sighs."

4   O that I thus resign'd
      Might bear my nature's load !
O that in me were such a mind
      To leave the whole to God !

With Him to trust my cause,
And quietly endure
Till He remove the hallow'd cross,
And all my sickness cure.

5   I would, (but Thou canst tell,)
I would be humble, Lord,
My burden every moment feel,
And tremble at Thy word:

I would be stript of all,
And calmly wait Thy stay;
Poor at Thy feet, and helpless fall,
And weep my life away.

6   I would be truly still,*
Nor set a time to Thee,
But act according to Thy will,
And speak, and think, and be.

I would with Thee be one;
And till the grace is given,
Incessant pray, Thy will be done
In earth, as 'tis in heaven.

JEREMIAH XVII. 9.

*" The heart is deceitful above all things, and desperately
wicked: who can know it ?"*

1 O my false, deceitful heart,
Desperately false thou art,
Foul as hell, when fair in show;
Who can all the mazes know?

The quiet irony in this verse and in the title is illustrated by
a reference to "The Journal of John Nelson," pp. 33—41, 66,
67. (Ed. 1806.)

He the stars may reckon o'er,
Tell the sands that bound the shore.
Count the drops that make the sea,
Comprehend eternity.

2 Foolish heart, unjust and vain !
Pride was never made for man ;
Glory dost thou still pursue ;
Glory all to God is due.
What hast thou whereof to boast?
God alone is good and just :
Only His be all the praise ;
What we are, we are by grace.

3 Wretched heart, with woes opprest !
Ever roving after rest :
Wilt thou still pretend to own
Bliss is found in God alone?
While thy foolish wishes go
After empty joys below,
False imaginary ease,
Dreams of creature happiness.

4 Stony heart, which nought can move !
Thou canst neither fear nor love :
Threats and promises are vain,
Give thee neither joy nor pain :
All alike, it seems, to thee
Perfect bliss or misery,
Joys or woes unspeakable,
Life or death, and heaven or hell.

5 Wavering, frail, inconstant heart.
O, how blind and weak thou art !
Weak as helpless infancy.
Blind thy helplessness to see,

To thine own corruptions blind,
More inconstant than the wind,
Wavering as a shaken reed,
Cold, and dark, and doubly dead.

6 Stubborn heart, ungrateful, hard.
With a red-hot iron sear'd !
Carnal heart, immersed in sin,
All a cage of birds unclean !
Downward all thy motions tend ;
Lust, the beast, or pride, the fiend.
Show thee, since thy total fall,
Earthly, sensual, devilish all.

7 Faithless heart ! be this thy grief,
Groan beneath thine unbelief :
Unbelief, the damning sin,
Keeps thee all unclean, unclean.
Aggravates thy heavy load,
Will not let thee come to God,
Suffers not His grace to move,
Robs Him of His truth and love.

8 Faithless heart ! to Jesus bow,
Suffer Him to save thee now.
No— thou wilt not now believe.
Wilt not take what God would give :
Thou refusest to be free,
All the hindrance is in thee ;
Through thy own rebellious will,
Bound thou art and faithless still.

9 O my Lord, what must I do?
Only Thou the way canst show,
Thou canst save me in this hour,
I have neither will nor power :

God if over all Thou art,
Greater than the sinful heart,
Let it now on me be shown,
Take away the heart of stone.

10　Take away my darling sin,
Make me willing to be clean ;
Make me willing to receive
What Thy goodness waits to give ;
Force me, Lord, with all to part ;
Tear these idols from my heart ;
All Thy power on me be shown,
Take away the heart of stone.

11　Jesu, mighty to renew,
Work in me to will and do ;
Turn my nature's rapid tide,
Stem the torrent of my pride,
Stop the whirlwind of my will,
Speak, and bid the sun stand still ;
Now Thy love almighty show,
Make even me a creature new.

12　Arm of God, Thy strength put on ;
Bow the heavens, and come down.
All mine unbelief o'erthrow,
Lay the' aspiring mountain low :
Conquer Thy worst foe in me.
Get Thyself the victory ;
Save the vilest of the race,
Force me to be saved by grace.

REVELATION III. 17.

*" Wretched, and miserable, and poor, and blind, and
naked."*

1　Rich, and increased with goods, I was,
　　Abundant in my virtuous store ;
In wisdom rich, and strength and grace ;
　　So rich I needed nothing more :
Alas ! my God, I could not see
That still I needed all in Thee.

2　Thanks to Thy grace, if I begin
　　My wretchedness at length to know :
If now, in part convinced of sin,
　　I groan beneath my weight of woe ;
Surely at last I more than see
That sin is perfect misery.

3　Stript of my boasted gifts, I fall
　　A beggar at Thy mercy's door :
I ask an alms : for grace I call ;
　　Poor, beyond all expression poor :
If one good thought Thy heaven could buy,
Alas ! not one good thought have I.

4　How dark and dreary is my heart !
　　Dark as the chambers of the grave :
So blind, till Thou Thy light impart,
　　I cannot see Thy power to save ;
Or know, till Thou the veil remove,
That I am sin, and God is love.

5　My fig-leaves now are cast aside,
　　The rags of my self-righteousness :

From Thee my shame I cannot hide,
　My spirit sinks in deep distress:
How shall I in Thy sight appear?
Or bear myself when Thou art near?

6　A monster to myself I am,
　　Self-loathing at Thy feet I lie :
How shall I bear this load of shame?
　How shall I meet Thy piercing eye?
I faint and sink, and die away
At Thy insufferable day.

7　Mountains and rocks, on you I call,
　　My nakedness of soul to screen ;
Fall, on my guilty nature fall,
　And hide me from the hell of sin !
Alas ! my soul, it cannot be :
The hell of sin remains in thee.

8　O God ! (but shall I dare to pray ?)
　　O Jesus ! Son of God and man,
Pity a sinful worm, and stay
　My grief, and mitigate my pain :
Cover my shame, remove my load
Of sin, for Thou hast blush'd in blood.

9　Or rather, if it be Thy will,
　　Conform me fully to Thy death ;
Now let me all my vileness feel,
　Now let me render up my breath,
And bow my head, and die with Thee,
For shame that Thou hast died for me.

ANOTHER.

1 WRETCHED, helpless, and distrest,
   Ah! whither shall I fly?
Ever gasping after rest,
   I cannot find it nigh:
Naked, sick, and poor, and blind,
Fast bound in sin and misery,
   Friend of sinners, let me find
     My help, my all in Thee.

2 Who my misery can relate,
   My depth of woe reveal?
I have left my first estate,
   In hapless *Adam* fell;
Driven out of my abode,
I now have lost my perfect bliss,
   Fallen, fallen out of God,
     And banish'd paradise.

3 I am all unclean, unclean,
   Thy purity I want;
My whole heart is sick of sin,
   And my whole head is faint:*
Full of putrefying sores,
Of bruises, and of wounds, my soul
   Looks to Jesus, help implores,
     And gasps to be made whole.

* This singular transposition of the Prophet's words, (Isaiah
i. 5,) though found in all the editions, must still be regarded as
an oversight.

4 In the wilderness I stray;
   My foolish heart is blind;
 Nothing do I know; the way
   Of peace I cannot find:
 Jesu, Lord, restore my sight,
And take, O, take the veil away:
   Turn my darkness into light,
     My midnight into day.

5 Naked of thine image, Lord,
   Forsaken and alone,
 Unrenew'd and unrestored
   I have not Thee put on:
 Over me Thy mantle spread,
Send down Thy likeness from above.
   Let Thy goodness be display'd,
     And wrap me in Thy love.

6 Poor, alas! Thou know'st I am,
   And would be poorer still,
 See my nakedness and shame,
   And all my vileness feel:
 No good thing in me resides,
My soul is all an aching void
   Till Thy Spirit here abides,
     And I am fill'd with God.

7 Jesus, full of truth and grace,
   In Thee is all I want;
 Be the wanderer's resting-place.
   A cordial to the faint.
 Make me rich, for I am poor:
In Thee may I my *Eden* find;
   To the dying health restore.
     And eyesight to the blind.

8 Clothe me with Thy holiness,
　　　Thy meek humility ;
　Put on me my glorious dress,
　　　Endue my soul with Thee.
　Let Thine image be restored,
　Thy name and nature let me prove ;
　With Thy fulness fill me, Lord,
　　　And perfect me in love.

A WELCOME TO THE CROSS.

1 ALL hail the Saviour's hallow'd cross,
　　　By which I daily die within !
　All things for Thee I count but loss :
　　　Enter my soul, and work out sin ;
　Here let Thy mortal virtue move,
　And crucify my creature-love.

2 Wither my strength, destroy my will,
　　　Stain all the glory of my pride,
　My appetites and passions kill,
　　　Be to my whole of self applied,
　Implunge me in the depth beneath,
　And speak to all my nature death.

3 O that I now with all could part,
　　　Cut off the hand, pluck out the eye :
　Jesus, Thou greater than my heart,
　　　Thine efficacious death apply ;
　Now for Thyself prepare the way ;
　Breathe, and the sinful *Adam* slay.

4 Thou know'st what keeps me out of Thee,
   Naked I in Thine eyes appear :
Reveal the thing I would not see,
   The' accursed thing that harbours here :
O, tear it hence, although the smart,
The killing anguish break my heart.

5 Thou seest, alas ! I am not dead,
   My nature's life in me is whole ;
Again the rebel lifts his head,
   And self bears down my struggling soul ;
This thorn, I feel it in my side,
The' unconquerable strength of pride.

6 Still do I live, not Christ, but I;
   The inbred sin I groan to bear ;
Jesu, with Thee I long to die,
   The suffering of Thy cross to share,
Sweet fellowship with Thee to have :
Bury me, Saviour, in Thy grave.

7 There let me lay my burden down
   In sweet forgetfulness of care :
The cross shall bring me to the crown,
   The dead Thy praises shall declare ;
When all renew'd in love I shine,
Partaker of a life Divine.

IN TEMPTATION.

1   Jesu, hear a sinner's prayer :
   Lo ! I flee Unto Thee,
     Cast on Thee my care.

2   If, O Lord, I have found favour
In Thy sight, Be my might,
    Be my loving Saviour.

3   To my soul in sore temptation
Let Thine aid Be convey'd,
    Show me Thy salvation.

4   Christ the tempted, hear my crying :
Sinner's Friend, Succour send,
    See, my soul is dying.

5   Lord, I cannot cease from sinning,
Till Thou art In my heart,
    Ending as beginning.

6   Every moment am I falling
Into hell, Till Thou seal
    My effectual calling.

7   Alpha and Omega, save me :
Enter in, Bid my sin,
    Bid my nature leave me.

8   Jesu, for Thy love I languish ;
Only love Can remove
    All my grief and anguish.

9   I shall all in Thee inherit ;
Thirst no more, If Thou pour
    Into me Thy Spirit.

10   Jesu's love than sin is stronger :
When I prove Jesu's love,
    I shall sin no longer.

11   Faithful to Thy Spirit's leading,
I shall rest On Thy breast,
    Find my long-sought *Eden.*

12   Neither life nor death shall sever:
    When Thou art In my heart,
      Thou art there for ever.*

ANOTHER.

1 Jesu, gentle, loving Lamb,
  Let me call Thee by Thy name :
  Saviour, I have need of Thee ;
  As Thou art so may I be.

2 Save me, Lord, from sin and fear,
  Bring the great salvation near :
  Bring into my soul Thy peace,
  Everlasting righteousness.

3 Me to save if Thou hast died,
  Save me from this self and pride :
  All the plague of sin remove,
  Cast it out by perfect love.

4 See me the reverse of Thee,
  Only sin and misery ;
  Make me willing to receive
  All the grace Thou hast to give.

5 O, supply my every want ;
  Feed a tender sickly plant ;
  Day and night my Keeper be,
  Every moment water me.

* The Wesleys at this time were " inclined to believe " that those who were perfected in love could not finally fall ; (Works. vol. i., p 427 ;) but soon saw abundant reason for a widely different opinion, which was stated and vindicated in a treatise on the subject : Works, vol. x., p. 284.

6 Hide me, dearest Saviour, hide ;
 Let me never leave Thy side :
 O, 'tis hell from Thee to part ;
 Press me closer to Thy heart.

7 When Thy love is my defence,
 Sin shall never pluck me thence ;
 When my heart with love runs o'er,
 Sin can never enter more.

8 Only love can end the strife ;
 Give me love, and take my life :
 Do not, Lord, my suit deny ;
 Give me love, and let me die.

LOOKING UNTO JESUS.

1 Lamb of God for sinners slain,
 To Thee I feebly pray :
 Heal me of my grief and pain,
 O, take my sins away !
 From this bondage, Lord, release ;
 No longer let me be opprest :
 Jesus, Master, seal my peace,
 And take me to Thy breast.

2 Hast Thou not invited all
 Who groan beneath their sin ?
 Weary, I obey Thy call,
 And come to be made clean :
 Give my burden'd conscience ease ;
 O, grant me now the promised rest :
 Jesus, Master, &c.

3 Wilt Thou cast a sinner out
    Who humbly comes to Thee?
No, my God, I cannot doubt
    Thy mercy is for me.
Let me then obtain the grace
And be of paradise possest:
    Jesus, Master, &c.

4 Full of pain and sin am I,
    I ever bear my shame,
Waiting till my Lord pass by,
    And call me by my name:
Surely now my pain He sees,
And I shall quickly be released!
    Jesus, Master, &c.

5 Worldly good I do not want,
    Be that to others given;
Only for Thy love I pant,
    My all in earth and heaven:
This the crown I fain would seize,
The good wherewith I would be blest:
    Jesus, Master, &c.

6 This delight I fain would prove,
    And then resign my breath;
Join the happy few, whose love
    Was mightier than death:
Let it not my Lord displease,
That I would die to be Thy guest:
    Jesus, Master, seal my peace,
    And take me to Thy breast.

IN DOUBT.

1 THE children to the birth are come;
  But, O ! they have not might
To burst the barriers of the womb,
  And struggle into light.

2 My feeble soul gives o'er the strife,
  Just as it sees the skies ;
Fails in the very gate of life,
  Sinks back again, and dies.

3 I saw the port of Jesu's breast ;
  But, while I enter'd in,
A whirlwind swept me from my rest,
  And plunged me into sin.

4 What shall I do, or whither turn?
  Despairing of relief,
I only can my ruin mourn
  With unavailing grief.

5 Ah, woe is me ! to evil sold,
  And fallen back from grace !
I never, never shall behold
  The dear Redeemer's face.

6 Better that I had never felt
  My Saviour's blood applied;
Less aggravated were my guilt,
  Had I in *Egypt* died.

7 Better that I had never known
  The way of righteousness,
Than to break off the course begun,
  And leave the' unfinish'd race.

8 Ah! wherefore did I ever take,
   If I must quit the field;
 Must shamefully at last turn back,
   And cast away my shield?

9 But shall I throw on God the blame?
   Or daringly complain
 Because I most unfaithful am,
   And make His mercies vain?

10 No, Lord, Thy truth and grace I clear;
    For years Thy Spirit strove,
 Faithful to me Thy mercies were,
    And infinite Thy love.

11 Far be it from my wretched heart
    To charge my death on Thee;
 To save me now Thou ready art,
    If saved I now would be.

12 Whether or no my heart of stone
    Will yield to be renew'd,
 Sufficient is Thy grace I own,
    I justify my God.

13 This record do I leave behind,
    Whether I stand or fall:
 Sinners, ye all His grace may find,
    His grace is free for all.

FOR THE SPIRIT OF PRAYER.

1 WHAT shall I do to 'scape the hell
   That burns me up within?
 Satan, and all his hosts, I feel
   In this indwelling sin.

2 It mocks my strength, prevents my flight,
　　Still intimately nigh :
　Impossible it is to fight,
　　Impossible to fly.

3 One only refuge there remains ;
　　But that I cannot find,
　So fast these grievous, fleshly chains
　　My slothful spirit bind.

4 Monster of sin ! How can it be
　　That I should still delay?
　Jesus I know would set me free,
　　Would I to Jesus pray.

5 He bids me ask, and I shall have :
　　I know it, and forbear;
　Assured He would the sinner save,
　　In answer to my prayer.

6 He pities now my sad estate,
　　And gladly would relieve ;
　But, O ! I cannot—will not— wait
　　Till He the blessing give.

7 He waits that He may gracious be,
　　To all His bowels move:
　Fury, O God, is not in Thee,
　　But all Thy heart is love.

8 Then help me to receive Thy word,
　　Help me on Thee to call ;
　Have patience with me, dearest Lord,
　　And I will pay Thee all.

9 On me for good this token show,
    Pronounce the *Ephphatha,*
  And let my heart in prayer o'erflow,
    And let me always pray.

10 A time to Thee I will not set,
    Nor charge Thee with delay;
  Do with me, Lord, as seems Thee meet,
    But let me always pray.

11 Thou art not slack touching Thy word:
    Content I am to stay,
  To wait the leisure of my Lord,
    But let me always pray.

12 Though in my flesh I feel the thorn,
    No more will I complain,
  Let me but in Thy bosom mourn,
    And tell Thee all my pain.

13 Come joy or grief, come life or death,
    For this I take no care ;
  But when I render up my breath,
    Let my last breath be prayer.

GOING INTO A PLACE OF DANGER.

1 O ! BUT must I, Lord, return
    Into the dreadful fight?
  Bear what is not to be borne,
    Again dragg'd out to light?
  I, a weak and helpless worm,
    Only shall Thy cause betray;
  Perish in temptation's storm,
    A final castaway.

2 Didst Thou only bid me leap
      Into a burning fire,
   Cast me down the threatening steep,
      Or now my soul require;
   Gladly would I now comply,
      Plunge into the depths beneath,
   Rush into the flames, and die
      To escape the second death.

3 O Almighty God of Love,
      Thy holy arm display;
   Send me succour from above
      In this my evil day;
   Arm my weakness with Thy power;
      Woman's Seed, appear within;
   Be my safeguard, and my tower
      Against the face of sin.

4 Could I of Thy strength take hold,
      And always feel Thee near,
   Steadfastly, divinely bold,
      My soul would scorn to fear:
   Nothing should my firmness shock:
      Though the gates of hell assail,
   Were I built upon the Rock,
      They never could prevail.

5 Rock of my salvation, haste,
      Extend Thy ample shade;
   Let it over me be cast,
      And screen my naked head:
   Save me from the trying hour,
      Thou my sure protection be,
   Shelter me from Satan's power,
      Till I am fix'd on Thee.

6 Set upon Thyself my feet,
    And make me surely stand ;
From temptation's rage and heat
    Cover me with Thy hand:
Let me in the cleft be placed,
    Never from my fence remove,
In Thine arms of love embraced,
    Of everlasting love.

FOR ONE CONVINCED OF INORDINATE AFFECTION.

1   WOE is me ! that wretched man
      More than my God I prize !
    Well I know them void and vain,
      Yet pant for earthly joys:
    Downward still my wishes move,
   Though fairer than earth's sons Thou art:
    Touch me, Jesus, with Thy love,
      And vindicate my heart.

2   " Happiness is not in me,"
      Though every creature cry.
    Still the airy form I see
      Where'er I turn mine eye:
    After shadows still I rove,
   Nor can I with my idols part:
    Touch me, Jesus, &c.

3   Burning with unhallow'd fires,
      Thou seest, my tortured breast
    Pines away with low desires,
      Stranger to joy and rest:

How shall I this death remove?
How tear away the' inrooted dart?
Touch me, Jesus, &c.

4   Poison now o'erflows my cup,
        Fills me with thrilling pain,
    Drinks my blood and spirits up,
        And throbs in every vein;
    Yet I fear Thy grace to prove,
    I dread for Thee with all to part:
        Touch me, Jesus, &c.

5   God, arise, Thou jealous God,
        And all Thy foes subdue;
    Claim the purchase of Thy blood,
        Create my soul anew;
    Let it now no longer rove,
    Now let me taste how good Thou art:
        Touch me, Jesus, &c.

6   Saviour, purify my soul,
        As Thou my God art pure;
    Make my wounded spirit whole,
        And all my sickness cure;
    From Thee never let me move,
    Thou my sufficient portion art:
        Touch me, Jesus, &c.

7   From all filthiness of flesh
        And spirit make me clean;
    Stamp Thine image, Lord, afresh,
        And purge me from all sin:
    Thee my God, my all I prove;
    Ah! never more from me depart;
        Fill, O Jesu, with Thy love
            My vindicated heart.

LET ME DIE WITH THE PHILISTINES.

[*Judges xvi.* 30.]

1 WHERE is my strength, my faith, my God.
    My confidence of boasting now?
Borne down by sin's revolting load,
    Beneath its iron yoke I bow,
Again indignantly I groan ;
My strength, my faith, my God is gone.

2 Departed is the Lord from me,
    Weak as another man I am ;
Spoil'd of my power and liberty,
    I bear my punishment and shame ;
The world their feeble foe despise,
Their god hath put out both mine eyes.

3 Into their hands by sin betray'd,
    (The sin I cherish'd in my breast,)
Low in the deepest dungeon laid,
    Fetter'd in brass. by guilt opprest,
A slave to Satan I remain,
And bite, but cannot burst, my chain.

4 Now to their idol's temple brought,
    A sport I am to fiends and men :
They set my helplessness at nought,
    They triumph in my toil and pain :
The' uncircumcised lift up their voice.
And *Dagon's* worshippers rejoice.

5 Remember me. O Lord. my God,
    If ever I could call Thee mine ;
Though now I perish in my blood.
    And all my hopes of heaven resign,

Yet listen to my latest call,
Nor suffer me alone to fall.

6 O, cast not out my dying prayer!
  Strengthen me with Thy Spirit's might
This only once: I pray Thee, hear;
  Avenge me for my loss of sight;
Avenge it on mine enemies,
For they have put out both mine eyes.

7 Blind as I am, with both my hands
  The pillars let me feel, and seize,
On which the house of *Dagon* stands,
  The pillars of self-righteousness:
'Tis done; with all my might I bow:
Help me, O God, and help me now.

8 Now let the ponderous ruin fall,
  And crush the world, and Satan's head:
O, let it now o'erwhelm us all:
  Since I must sink among the dead,
Since I can neither fight nor fly,
Let me with the *Philistines* die!

- - -

AFTER A RELAPSE INTO SIN.

1 Jesu, wherewith shall I draw near,
  What shall I for acceptance bring?
How in my Judge's sight appear
  A rebel 'gainst my God and King?
Loudly my sins for vengeance cry,
And justice wills that I should die.

2 Summon'd to answer at Thy 'bar,
  I come, but "Guilty, guilty" plead !
Did I not all Thy judgments dare ?
  On all Thy tender mercies tread ?
Death's sentence justly I receive ;
I am not worthy, Lord, to live.

3 Then let me every good resign,
  And give my forfeit blessings back :
My gifts and blessings were not mine ;
  Thou, only Thou, the glory take :
I might have heard Thy frequent call ;
I might have stood, though now I fall.

4 Long did Thy loving Spirit strive
  To win me over to my good ;
The spark of grace was kept alive
  For years amidst temptation's flood :
I now have sinn'd it all away,
And ended is my gracious day.

5 An alien from the life Divine,
  The covenant of promised grace.
Saviour, no more I call Thee mine ;
  An outcast from Thy blissful face.
Without or faith, or joy, or hope,
I give (but must I give) Thee up ?

6 Yes : with my shield of faith I part :
  My hope is lost in just despair :
Love is not in my stony heart.
  It cannot be, while sin is there ;
My vain pretensions sin disproves ;
He cannot sin who Jesus loves.

7 No choice, endeavour, or desire,
   Motion, or will have I to turn ;
Extinguish'd is the trembling fire
   Which once in me began to burn :
What have I now whereof to boast ?
My all is gone, my God is lost.

8 See then the sinner stript of all,
   A foe, and hater of his God ;
Despairing, self-condemn'd I fall,
   Of every spark of goodness void ;
I cannot now for mercy groan,
Or offer Thee an heart of stone.

9 My mouth is stopp'd, and guilty now
   Before my Judge I am become :
Lo ! at Thy judgment-seat I bow ;
   O God of love, pronounce my doom :
And, if Thy yearning heart permit,
Now, Saviour, slay me at Thy feet.

THE BACKSLIDER.

1 SURELY in the Lord we have
   Both strength and righteousness :
Jesus mighty is to save
   The sinner in distress.
Jesu's blood, on which we stay,
   Cleanses us from every stain ;
Takes the guilt of sin away,
   Nor lets the power remain.

2 Why then, O my Saviour, why
    (If mine indeed Thou art)
Am I thus? a sinner I,
    And still unclean of heart?
Why doth sin my heart divide?
    Whence this grievous tyranny,
All this hell of self and pride,
    If Thou hast sprinkled me?

3 Did I not believe and feel
    Through faith my sins forgiven?
Was I not caught up from hell,
    And strangely raised to heaven?
Yes! I once could call Thee mine,
    Felt my Saviour's blood applied;
Clothed in righteousness Divine,
    I once was justified.

4 What, alas! I once have been
    Nothing avails me now;
I the servant am of sin,
    While to its yoke I bow:
While the love of sin remains,
    Christ in me can never dwell;
Christ with *Belial* never reigns,
    Nor mixes heaven with hell.

5 Can unholy actions suit
    With one that is in Thee?
Jesu, Thou hast said, the fruit
    Must answer to the tree:
If the tree (the heart) were good,
    Evil thoughts it could not bear;
Could not be by sin subdued,
    If Thou, my God, wert there.

6 Can the self-same fountain yield
    Both bitter streams and sweet?
In a soul by Jesus fill'd
    Can Satan find a seat?
No, my Lord, I am not clean,
    Am not inwardly renew'd,
Am not, (for I still can sin,)
    I am not born of God.

7 See, I give up all at last,
    My boasted gifts disclaim;
Trust no more in graces past,
    But now condemn'd I am:
Nothing do I bring to Thee,
    That I may Thy mercy move;
No one spark remains in me
    Of faith, or hope, or love.

8 If but one good thought could buy
    Thy grace, and heaven win,
Lord, not one good thought have I;
    My all is self, and sin:
Full of guilt and misery,
    Saviour, at Thy feet I fall;
See, the unbeliever see,
    The sinner stript of all!

9 Let me never, never more
    My wretched soul deceive;
Dream that I have life, before
    I hear Thy voice and live:
Let me, humbled in the dust,
    Wait to taste how good Thou art;
See, and feel, but never trust
    My own deceitful heart.

10 O that I could truly wait
     The dictates of Thy will;
Calmly mourn my sinful state,
     Till Thou shalt say, " Be still :
The lost sheep to save I came,
     The backslider to restore ;
Sinners I do not condemn;
     Depart, and sin no more."

ANOTHER.

1   O, THE dire effects of sin !
     What tongue can fully tell
All that I have felt within,
     Since first from grace I fell?
Still Thou seest my stormy breast;
My soul is as the troubled sea ;
     Never, never can I rest,
     Till I believe in Thee.

2   O, the load my spirit bears,
     The mountain of my grief !
Full of cruel doubts and fears,
     Of racking unbelief :
Did I ever Thee behold?
Thee did I ever truly know?
     I can neither keep my hold,
     Nor let my Saviour go.

3   Did I not my soul deceive
     With groundless hopes of heaven?
Did I, Lord, indeed believe,
     And was I once forgiven ?

Still I ask, but no reply :
O, bid me, bid me come to Thee ;
Son of *David*, hear my cry,
  If mercy is for me.

4 Hear me still myself bemoan,
  A bullock to the yoke
Unaccustom'd I rush on ;—
  O that my heart were broke !
Long I after Thee have mourn'd.
And still unpitied I complain ;
  Turn me, and I shall be turn'd,
  And never sin again.

5 Me Thou wouldst not disregard,
  Were I indeed sincere ;
But my heart, alas ! is hard,
  And void of love and fear ;
Seldom can I lift mine eyes,
Or offer Thee an hearty groan :
  Take, if Thou wouldst have me rise,
  O, take away the stone.

ANOTHER.

PART I.

1 AH ! my dear, loving Lord,
  To Thee what shall I say ?
Behold, I tremble at Thy word,
  And scarce presume to pray :
Ten thousand wants have I ;
  Alas ! I all things want ;
And Thou hast bid me always cry,
  And never, never faint.

2   Yet now, Thou know'st, I fear,
       I fear to ask Thy grace ;
    So often have I, Lord, drawn near,
       And mock'd Thee to Thy face :

       With all pollutions stain'd,
       Thy hallow'd courts I trod,
    Thy name and temple I profaned,
       And dared to call Thee God.

3   Nigh with my lips I drew,
       My lips were all unclean ;
    Thee with my heart I never knew,
       My heart was full of sin:

       Far from the living God,
       As far as hell from heaven,
    Thy purity I still abhorr'd,
       Nor look'd to be forgiven.

4   My nature I obey'd,
       My own desire pursued ;
    And still a den of thieves I made
       The hallow'd house of God :

       The worship He approves,
       To Him I would not pay ;
    My selfish ends, and creature-loves,
       Had stole my heart away.

5   My sin and nakedness
       I studied to disguise ;
    Spoke to my soul a flattering peace,
       And put out mine own eyes :

In fig-leaves I appear'd,
　Nor with my form would part ;
But still retain'd a conscience sear'd,
　An hard, deceitful heart.

6　A goodly, formal saint
　I long appear'd in sight ;
By self and Satan taught to paint
　My tomb, my nature, white :

The *Pharisee* within
　Still undisturb'd remain'd ;
The strong man, arm'd with guilt of sin.
　Safe in his palace reign'd.

7　But, O ! the jealous God
　In my behalf came down ;
Jesus Himself the stronger show'd,
　And claim'd me for His own :

My spirit He alarm'd,
　And brought into distress ;
He shook and bound the strong man, arm'd
　In his self-righteousness.

8　Faded my virtuous show,
　My form without the power ;
The sin-convincing Spirit blew.
　And blasted every flower :

My mouth was stopp'd, and shame
　Cover'd my guilty face ;
I fell on the Atoning Lamb.
　And I was saved by grace.

PART II.

1   YET soon my wretched heart
      To folly turn'd again.
    How could I, Lord, from Thee depart,
        And make Thy mercy vain?

      'Twas pride my soul betray'd;
      I lost my poverty,
    An idol of Thy gifts I made,
        And loved them more than Thee.

2   Thy perfect comeliness,
      In which my soul did shine,
    Dazzled my eyes; Thy glorious dress
        I fondly counted mine:

      With sacrilegious boast
      I spread mine own renown,
    And in Thy beauty put my trust,
        And call'd it all my own.

3   I thought not of my God,
      Nor call'd to mind the day
    When naked, foul, and in my blood,
        And loathed of all, I lay:

      None cast a pitying eye,
      None could assistance give,
    Till Jesus graciously pass'd by,
        And bade the sinner live.

4   Why did I this forget,
      So soon return to sin?
    How weak my heart that could submit,
        And let the mischief in!

I fell, alas! through pride;
I needed not Thy blood,
As when I felt it first, and cried,
  "Thou art my Lord, my God!"

5   O that I once again
  "My Lord, my God" could cry:
Dost Thou not on my sin and pain
  Still cast a pitying eye?

  Thy mercy still is free;
  For aggravated guilt,
For sinners foul and black as me
  Thy precious blood was spilt.

6   Thou seest me lost in shame,
  But Thou canst still forgive;
Polluted in my blood I am,
  But Thou canst bid me live.

  O, speak the gracious word,
  Thy mercy let me prove;
Stand still, and look upon me, Lord,
  Make this the time of love.

7   Jesu, if Thou hast died
  My worthless soul to win,
Spread over me Thy skirt, and hide
  My nakedness and sin:

  Impute Thy righteousness,
  Wash away all my blood.
Adorn me now with every grace,
  And feed, and fill with God.

A PRAYER FOR RESTORING GRACE.

1 Jesu, Friend of sinners, hear,
  Yet once again I pray ;
From my debt of sin set clear,
  For I have nought to pay :
Speak, O, speak the kind release,
 A poor, backsliding soul restore ;
Love me freely, seal my peace,
  And bid me sin no more.

2 For my selfishness and pride,
  Thou hast withdrawn Thy grace :
Left me long to wander wide,
  An outcast from Thy face ;
But I now my sins confess,
 And mercy, mercy I implore :
Love me freely, &c.

3 Though my sins as mountains rise,
  And swell and reach to heaven,
Mercy is above the skies,
  I may be still forgiven :
Infinite my sins' increase,
 But greater is Thy mercy's store :
Love me freely, &c.

4 Sin's deceitfulness hath spread
  An hardness o'er my heart :
But if Thou Thy Spirit shed,
  The stony shall depart :
Shed Thy love, Thy tenderness,
 And let me feel the softening power :
Love me freely, &c.

5 From the' oppressive power of sin
  My struggling spirit free ;
 Perfect righteousness bring in,
  Unspotted purity :
 Speak, and all this war shall cease,
 And sin shall give its raging o'er :
  Love me freely, &c.

6 For this only thing I pray,
  And this will I require,
 Take the power of sin away,
  Fill me with chaste desire;
 Perfect me in holiness ;
 Thine image to my soul restore :
  Love me freely, seal my peace,
   And bid me sin no more.

ANOTHER.

1 O that I was as heretofore,
  When, warm in my first love,
 I only lived my Lord to' adore,
  And seek the things above !

2 Upon my head His candle shone :
  And, lavish of His grace,
 With cords of love He drew me on,
  And half unveil'd His face.

3 Butter and honey did I eat ;
  And, lifted up on high,
 I saw the clouds beneath my feet,
  And rode upon the sky.

4 Far, far above all earthly things
    Triumphantly I rode;
  I soar'd to heaven on eagle's wings,
    And found, and talk'd with God.

5 Where am I now? from what a height
    Of happiness cast down!
  The glory swallow'd up in night,
    And faded is the crown.

6 My first estate I could not keep;
    Fallen through pride I am;
  Implunged in sin's profoundest deep,
    And lost in guilty shame.

7 Forlorn, forsaken, and alone,
    Naked and void of God,
  My feeble soul can scarcely groan
    A dying *Ichabod!*

8 Ah! woe is me! my joy is fled,
    Vanish'd my glorious boast,
  My hope cut off, my life is dead,
    My paradise is lost!

9 Through the wide world of sin and woe,
    A banish'd man, I roam;
  But cannot find my rest below,
    But cannot wander home.

10 O God, Thou art my home, my rest,
    For which I sigh in pain:
  How shall I 'scape into Thy breast?
    My *Eden* how regain?

11 Vengeance Divine is always near;
    Where'er my steps I turn,
  I see the Cherubim appear,
    I see Thine anger burn.

12 When, longing oft to be restored,
    I would to *Eden* flee,
  Thine anger, as a flaming sword,
    Preserves the sacred tree.

13 What shall I do? 'Tis worse than death
    To live without Thy grace ;
  I yield, I yield Thee up my breath,
    So I may see Thy face.

14 A sinner in Thine hands I am ;
    No farther let me fly,
  But rush upon that sword of flame,
    And in Thy presence die.

15 Nothing, alas ! have I to plead,
    I am not fit to live :
  Yet if Thy justice strike me dead,
    Thy mercy shall revive.

16 This is the way to find my Lord ;
    Thyself hast made it known :
  Be it according to Thy word :
    On me Thy will be done.

17 Slay me, and I shall live indeed,
    With Thy dead men arise,
  From all the life of nature freed,
    In love's sweet paradise.

18 Now, Lord, Thy death, Thy life bring in.
    While at Thy feet I bow ;
  Enter at once, and cast out sin,
    Destroy, and save me now.

AFTER A RECOVERY.

1 Lord, and is Thine anger gone.
  And art Thou pacified?
After all that I have done,
  Dost Thou no longer chide?
Infinite Thy mercies are ;
Beneath the weight I cannot move :
  O! 'tis more than I can bear,
   The sense of pardoning love !

2 Let it still my heart constrain,
  And all my passions sway ;
Keep me, lest I turn again
  Out of the narrow way ;
Force my violence to be still,
Captivate my every thought;
  Charm, and melt, and change my will.
   And bring me down to nought.

3 If I have begun once more
  Thy sweet return to feel.
If even now I find Thy power
  Present my soul to heal,—
Still and quiet may I lie,
Nor struggle out of Thine embrace,
  Never more resist or fly
   From Thy pursuing grace.

4 To Thy cross, Thine altar, bind
  Me with the cords of love ;
Freedom let me never find
  From my dear Lord to move :

That I never, never more
　May with my much-loved Master part,
　To the posts of mercy's door,
　　O, nail my willing heart.

5　See my utter helplessness,
　　And leave me not alone ;
O, preserve in perfect peace,
　　And seal me for Thine own ;
More and more Thyself reveal,
Thy presence let me always find ;
　Comfort, and confirm, and heal
　　My feeble, sin-sick mind.

6　As the apple of an eye
　　Thy weakest servant keep ;
Help me at Thy feet to lie,
　　And there for ever weep :
Tears of joy mine eyes o'erflow,
That I have any hope of heaven ;
　Much of love I ought to know,
　　For I have much forgiven.

7　Now I seem to taste Thy love
　　As for a moment's space ;
But I cannot faithful prove
　　To Thy restoring grace ;
Cannot in temptation stand,
My own frail soul I cannot keep,
　If Thou once withdraw Thine hand
　　I sink into the deep.

8　Now, this instant now, if sin
　　Were knocking at my heart,
I should let the tempter in,
　　And bid my Lord depart ;

But Thou wilt not let me fall,
Thou wilt not from my weakness move,
Till I more than conquer all
Through Thy redeeming love.

ANOTHER.

1 Son of God, if Thy free grace
Again hath raised me up,
Call'd me still to seek Thy face,
And gave me back my hope :
Still Thy gracious help afford,
And all Thy lovingkindness show ;
Keep me, keep me, dearest Lord,
And never let me go.

2 Feebly if I now begin
After my fall to rise,
Save me from my bosom sin,
My worst of enemies :
Let me fully be restored,
And cause me all Thy power to know :
Keep me, keep me, &c.

3 By me, O my Saviour, stand
In sore temptation's hour ;
Save me with Thine outstretch'd hand,
And show forth all Thy power :
O, be mindful of Thy word,
Thine all-sufficient grace bestow :
Keep me, keep me, &c.

4 Give me, Lord, a holy fear,
And fix it in my heart,
That I may from evil near
With timely care depart :

Sin be more than hell abhorr'd,
Till Thou destroy the tyrant foe ;
Keep me, keep me, &c.

5   Never let me leave Thy breast,
From Thee, my Saviour, stray ;
Thou art my Support, and Rest,
My true and living Way ;
My exceeding great Reward,
In heaven above, and earth below :
Keep me, keep me, &c.

6   Never let me go, till I,
Upborne on wings of love,
Gain the regions of the sky,
And take my seat above ;
See Thee by all heaven adored,
And all Thy glorious fulness know :
Keep me, keep me, dearest Lord,
And never let me go.

GROANING FOR REDEMPTION.

PART I.

1 O Jesu, still, still shall I groan
Beneath the galling yoke of sin ?
Wilt Thou not claim me for Thine own,
And speak the word, and make me clean
My load is more than I can bear :
Where is the Friend of sinners ? where ?

2 Is there no balm in Thee to heal
The anguish of a sin-sick soul ?
Dost Thou not know the pangs I feel ?
Dost Thou not see the billows roll ?

My soul is all a troubled sea,
I cannot find my rest in Thee.

3 But wilt Thou let Thy foe devour
   And take me as his lawful prey?
But must I sink beneath the power
   Of sin, and fall a castaway?
Forbid it Love ! and save, (if Thou
Art Love indeed,) O, save me now !

4 'Tis not the punishment I dread ;
   Harden'd I seem, and cannot fear
Thy wrath abiding on my head,
   Or deprecate Thy judgments near :
But rescue me from Satan's power ;
Save me from sin, I ask no more.

5 I ask not sensible delight,
   The joy and comfort of Thy grace :
Still let me want Thy blissful sight,
   Let me go mourning all my days ;
With trembling awe Thy ways adore :
But save me, that I sin no more.

6 Rather than suffer me to sin,
   Now, Lord, my spotted soul require :
I know that I am all unclean,
   And Thou a sin-consuming fire ;
I cannot now in heaven appear ;
Nothing unclean shall enter there.

7 Yet now I choose to breathe my last,
   Rather than turn to sin again :
On Thee my soul unchanged I cast,
   And, foul with every sinful stain,
I plunge me in a sea unknown,
Without Thine utmost grace—undone !

8 Thou canst cut short the work, and heal
    The sinner in a moment's space ;
Be it according to Thy will ;
    I leave it to Thy secret grace ;
I venture all on this last hour,
And die, that I may sin no more.

PART II.

1 JESU, Thou know'st my simpleness,
    My faults are not conceal'd from Thee :
A sinner in my last distress,
    To Thy dear wounds I fain would flee.
And never, never thence depart,
Close shelter'd in Thy loving heart.

2 How shall I find the living way,
    Lost, and confused, and dark, and blind ?
Ah ! Lord, my soul is gone astray ;
    Ah ! Shepherd, seek my soul, and find,
And in Thine arms of mercy take,
And bring the weary wanderer back.

3 Weary and sick of sin I am ;
    I hate it. Lord, and yet I love :
When wilt Thou rid me of my shame ?
    When wilt Thou all my load remove ?
Destroy the fiend of inbred sin,
And speak the word of power, " Be clean"?

4 My Jesus, why dost Thou delay
    An helpless dying soul to heal ?
What shall I to my Jesus say ?
    Dost Thou not all my sufferings feel ?
Ah ! tell me if unmoved Thou art :
How dost Thou find it in Thy heart ?

5 What means this struggling in my breast,
    If Thine is steel'd against my prayer?
If Thou art deaf to my request,
    Why do I groan my sin to bear?
Surely it is Thy Spirit's groan ;
I do not grieve, or weep, alone.

6 I feel that Thou wouldst have me live,
    And waitest now Thy grace to show :
When I am willing to receive
    The grace, I all Thy life shall know ;
And Thou art striving now with me,
To get Thyself the victory.

7 O Lord, if I at last discern
    That I am sin, and Thou art love,
If now o'er me Thy bowels yearn,
    Give me a token from above,
And conquer my rebellious will,
And bid my murmuring heart " Be still."

8 Sin only let me not commit;
    (Sin never can advance Thy praise :)
And lo ! I lay me at Thy feet,
    And wait unwearied all my days,
Till my appointed time shall come,
And Thou shalt call Thine exile home.

9 Ah ! tell me that I shall not sin;
    Assured of this, I ask no more ;
The kingdom, when Thou wilt, bring in :
    Thine image, as Thou wilt, restore ;
But do not suffer sin to reign ;
Tell me I ne'er shall sin again.

10 Or if I ask I know not what,
    The knowledge of a future grace :
If this can only then be wrought,
    When pure in heart I see Thy face.
O pierce, and fill me now with fear
Of sin, and hell, for ever near.

11 O put Thy fear within my heart,
    That I may tremble at Thy word,
Nor ever from Thy paths depart,
    Or dare to sin against the Lord;
Till I the promised Seed receive,
Let *Ishmael* before Thee live.

12 I ask according to Thy will;
    O keep me till the grace is given,
Till I Thy holy law fulfil
    On earth, as angels do in heaven.
Thine uttermost salvation prove,
Made perfect in almighty love.

PART III.

1 BREAK, stubborn heart; and sigh no more
    To mock me with a show of good,
To make me think the conflict o'er,
    The strength of inbred sin subdued :
Or let me cease from every ill,
Or bear the nether mill-stone still.

2 Away my flattering hopes and fears,
    The transports of my short-lived grief;
Away my unavailing tears,
    Nor mock me with your vain relief !
Dissembling tears, 'tis past your art
To melt the marble of my heart.

3 My heart, which now to God aspires,
    The following moment cleaves to dust :
My firm resolves, my good desires,
    My holy frames—no more I trust.
Poor, feeble, broken reeds, to you ;
My goodness melts as morning dew.

4 Hardly convinced, I own at last
    No will to good abides in me :
My latest rag away I cast,
    The rag of my sincerity :
I bear my double sin, and shame ;
Beast, beast, and legion is my name.

5 Full of concupiscence and pride,
    Fit fuel for eternal fire,
With virtuous show I strive to hide
    The baseness of impure desire ;
Conceal'd it lies, yet not supprest :
The devil blushes for the beast.

6 I start from the contempt of men,
    But shameless in His sight appear
By whom my every thought is seen :
    My heart is harden'd from His fear,
Nor care I from His view to hide
My foulest filthiness of pride.

7 O what a loathsome hypocrite
    Am I ! A child of wrath and sin,
An heir of hell, a son of night,
    An outward saint, a fiend within,
A painted tomb, a whited wall,
A worm, a sinner stript of all !

8 Lay to Thine hand, O God of grace;
  O God, the work is worthy Thee;
See at Thy feet of all our race
  The chief, the vilest sinner see,
And let me all Thy mercy prove,
Thine utmost miracle of love.

9 Speak; and an holy thing and clean
  Shall strangely be brought out of me;
My *Ethiop* soul shall change her skin;
  Redeem'd from all iniquity,
I, even I, shall then proclaim
The wonders wrought by Jesu's name.

10 Thee I shall then for ever praise,
  In spirit and in truth adore,
While all I am declares Thy grace,
  And, born of God, I sin no more;
The pure and heavenly nature share,
And fruit unto perfection bear.

PART IV.

1 SAVIOUR from sin, I wait to prove
  That Jesus is Thy healing name,
To lose, when perfected in love,
  Whate'er I have, or can, or am;
I stay me on Thy faithful word,
The servant shall be as his Lord.

2 Answer that gracious end in me
  For which Thy precious life was given;
Redeem from all iniquity,
  Restore, and make me meet for heaven;

Unless Thou purge my every stain,
Thy suffering, and my faith, is vain.

3 'Tis not a bare release from sin,
     Its guilt and pain, my soul requires ;
I want a Spirit of power within;
     Thee, Jesus, Thee my heart desires,
And pants, and breaks to be renew'd,
And wash'd in Thine all-cleansing blood.

4 Didst Thou not in the flesh appear,
     Sin to condemn, and man to save?
That perfect love might cast out fear,
     That I Thy mind in me might have.
In holiness show forth Thy praise,
And serve Thee all my sinless days?

5 Didst Thou not die, that I might live
     No longer to myself, but Thee?
Might body, soul, and spirit give
     To Him who gave Himself for me?
Come, then, my Master and my God,
Take the dear purchase of Thy blood.

6 Thine own peculiar servant claim,
     For Thine own truth and mercy's sake :
Hallow in me Thy glorious name,
     Me for Thine own this moment take,
And change, and throughly purify :
Thine only may I live, and die.

HEBREWS IV. 15

*" We have not an High Priest which cannot be touched
with the feeling of our infirmities," &c.*

1 O COMPASSIONATE High-Priest,
    Full of truth and grace for me,
  Mark the heavings of my breast,
    See my sin and misery !
  Surely all to Thee is known,
    Though Thou dost not yet appear,
  Noted is my every groan,
    Counted is my every tear.

2 I have not a priest unmoved
    With the feeling of my woe,
  Who himself was never proved,
    Who my sufferings cannot know :
  Touch'd most sensibly Thou art
    With my soul's infirmities,
  Still the Saviour's gentle heart
    Doth with sinners sympathise.

3 Though He now triumphant reigns,
    Still, as in His days of flesh,
  All His agonies and pains
    In our souls He feels afresh :
  Though exalted to a throne,
    Thou dost in our sorrows share,
  Thou hast not forgot Thine own,
    Thine own flesh and blood we are.

4 Friend of Sinners, in Thy heart,
    Tell me, doth there not remain
  One unarm'd and tender part,
    Sensible of human pain?

Lord, I wait for the reply:
  Groan an answer from within:
Tell me, Comforter. that I,
  I shall be redeem'd from sin.

5 Hoping against hope, I wait
    For redemption in Thy blood;
  Help me in my lost estate,
    Take away my heavy load.
  Save me from this tyranny,
    O bring near the joyful hour;
  From all sin my spirit free,
    All the guilt. and all the power.

6 Grant, O grant my last request;
    Nothing do I ask beside,
  Only give my spirit rest,
    Rest from self, and rest from pride
  Bring into Thy perfect peace,
    Give me faith to enter in,
  Let me with Thy people cease
    From my own dead works of sin.

7 Power I want, a constant power
    My own evil to eschew,
  Till my heart can sin no more.
    Till I am a creature new;
  Let me in Thy wounds abide
    Till the perfect grace is given;
  Give me this, I ask beside
    Nothing or in earth or heaven.

A PRAYER FOR PERSONS JOINED IN FELLOWSHIP.

PART I.

1 TRY us, O God, and search the ground
    Of every sinful heart;
  Whate'er of sin in us is found,
    O bid it all depart.

2 When to the right or left we stray,
    Leave us not comfortless,
  But guide our feet into the way
    Of everlasting peace.

3 Help us to help each other, Lord,
    Each other's cross to bear;
  Let each his friendly aid afford,
    And feel his brother's care.

4 Help us to build each other up,
    Our little stock improve;
  Increase our faith, confirm our hope.
    And perfect us in love.

5 Up into Thee, our living Head,
    Let us in all things grow.
  Till Thou hast made us free indeed
    And sinless here below.

6 Then, when the mighty work is wrought,
    Receive Thy ready bride,
  Give us in heaven an happy lot
    With all the sanctified.

PART II.

1 JESU, all power is given to Thee;
    Command our inward parts;
  Turn, as the rivers of the sea,
    Our hard unyielding hearts.

2 Our hearts are to ourselves unknown,
   Till Thou the veil remove;
Open, enlarge, and melt them down
   By Thy victorious love.

3 Thee, at Thy word, we come to meet.
   And humbly to confess,
While lowly prostrate at Thy feet,
   Our utter sinfulness.

4 O let us faithfully obey
   The counsel of Thy will,
And each to each our faults display.
   Our every thought reveal.

5 Our fig-leaves all be cast aside;
   Let no self-soothing art
Conceal the lust, to' indulge the pride
   Of a foul hellish heart.

6 Open a window in our breast,
   That each our heart may see,
And let no secret be supprest,
   Since all are known to Thee.

7 Remove the sins which we declare.
   The burden of our soul,
And hear the mutual faithful prayer.
   Which makes the sinner whole.

8 To all, through faith which is in Thee,
   A perfect soundness give,
And let us, from all sin set free,
   The life of Jesus live.

PART III.

1 GOD of our life, at Thy command
      We now our sins confess,
  In nakedness of spirit stand,
      And show our sore disease.

2 God of our health, in Thy great name
      We now perform Thy will;
  Regard our prayer, admit our claim,
      Our sin-sick spirits heal.

3 Forgive the sins through which we groan,
      Which we no longer hide;
  Our filthiness of flesh we own,
      Our filthiness of pride.

4 The devilish and the brutal lust
      To Thee we now confess;
  Cleanse us, O faithful God and just,
      From all unrighteousness.

5 Then shall we to Thine only name
      The praise and glory give,
  The greatness of Thy power proclaim
      To us-ward who believe.

6 Then let or earth or hell oppose,
      We will assert Thy power,
  And witness to a world of foes
      That we can sin no more.

PART IV.

1 JESU, united by Thy grace,
      And each to each endear'd,
  With confidence we seek Thy face,
      And know our prayer is heard.

2 Still let us own our common Lord,
    And bear Thine easy yoke—
  A band of love, a threefold cord
    Which never can be broke.

3 Make us into one spirit drink,
    Baptize into Thy Name,
  And let us always kindly think,
    And sweetly speak the same.

4 Touch'd by the loadstone of Thy love,
    Let all our hearts agree,
  And ever towards each other move,
    And ever move towards Thee.

5 To Thee inseparably join'd,
    Let all our spirits cleave;
  O may we all the loving mind
    That was in Thee receive :

6 This is the bond of perfectness,
    Thy spotless charity;
  O let us (still we pray) possess
    The mind that was in Thee.

7 Grant this, and then from all below
    Insensibly remove;
  Our souls their change shall scarcely know,
    Made perfect first in love.

8 With ease our souls through death shall glide
    Into their paradise,
  And thence on wings of angels ride
    Triumphant through the skies.

9 Yet when the fullest joy is given
   The same delight we prove;
In earth, in paradise, in heaven,
   Our all in all is love.

AT WAKING.

1 GIVER and Guardian of my sleep,
   To praise Thy name I wake:
Still, Lord, Thy helpless servant keep,
   For Thy own mercy's sake.

2 The blessing of another day
   I thankfully receive:
O may I only Thee obey,
   And to Thy glory live.

3 Vouchsafe to keep my soul from sin ;
   Its cruel power suspend,
Till all this strife and war within
   In perfect peace shall end.

4 O respite me from self and pride,
   Curb and keep down my will,
My appetites and passions chide,
   And bid the sea be still.

5 Upon me lay Thy mighty hand,
   My words and thoughts restrain,
Bow my whole soul to Thy command.
   Nor let my faith be vain.

6 Prisoner of hope, I wait the hour
   Which shall salvation bring ;
When all I am shall own Thy power
   And call my Jesus King.

7 Thou wilt, I steadfastly believe
    Thou wilt, the captive free,
  Freedom, full perfect freedom, give,
    And more than victory.

8 Though now to every sin inclined,
    I shall be as Thou art;
  Lowly as Thine shall be my mind,
    And meek and pure my heart.

9 Anger and lust Thou wilt expel,
    And pride, by stronger grace;
  They can in me no longer dwell,
    When Jesus fills the place.

10 Thy presence, Lord, the place shall fill,
    My heart shall be Thy throne,
  Thy holy, just, and perfect will
    Shall in my flesh be done.'

11 I thank Thee for the future grace,
    And now in hope rejoice,
  In confidence to see Thy face
    And always hear Thy voice:

12 I have the things I ask of Thee;
    What shall I more require?
  That still my soul may restless be,
    And only Thee desire.

13 Or let me (if I more would have)
    This last desire submit,
  And lie, till Thou seest good to save,
    Expecting, at Thy feet.

14 Thy only will be done, not mine;
  But make me, Lord, Thy home:
Come *when* Thou wilt, I that resign;
  But, O my Jesus, come!

———

PSALM CX. 1.

1 THE Lord unto my Lord hath said,
  Sit Thou, in glory sit,
Till I Thine enemies have made
  To bow beneath Thy feet.

2 Jesu, my Lord, mighty to save.
  What can my hopes withstand,
When Thee my Advocate I have.
  Enthroned at God's right hand?

3 I fear nor earth, nor sin, nor hell.
  And death hath lost his sting;
In vain awhile Thy foes rebel,
  Thou, Jesus, art my King.

4 Nature is subject to Thy word.
  All power to Thee is given,
The uncontroll'd almighty Lord
  Of hell, and earth, and heaven.

5 And shall my sins Thy will oppose?
  Jesu, Thy right maintain;
O let not Thine usurping foes
  In me Thy servant reign.

6 Master, on Thee my soul is stay'd:
  Thou wilt not quit Thy claim;
Thou only hast my ransom paid,
  And only Thine I am.

7 Come then, and claim me for Thine own;
   Saviour, Thy right assert;
Come, gracious Lord, set up Thy throne.
   And reign within my heart.

8 The day of Thy great power I feel.
   And pant for liberty;
I loathe myself, deny my will,
   And give up all for Thee.

9 I hate my sins, no longer mine.
   For I renounce them too;
My weakness with Thy strength I join.
   Thy strength shall all subdue.

10 Our common foes. who Thee defied
   And would not own Thy sway.
Envy, and sloth, desire, and pride.
   And hate. and anger slay.

11 Thy enemies destroy in mine;
   Pronounce their speedy doom;
In vengeance speak. in brightness shine.
   The Man of Sin consume.

12 So shall I bless Thy pleasing sway.
   And. sitting at Thy feet.
Thy laws with all my heart obey.
   With all my soul submit.

13 So shall I do Thy will below.
   As angels do above.
The virtue of Thy passion show,
   The triumphs of Thy love.

14 Thy love the conquest more than gains:
  To all I shall proclaim,—
  Jesus the King, the Conqueror reigns,
  Bow down to Jesu's name.

15 To Thee shall earth and hell submit,
  And every foe shall fall,
  Till death expires beneath Thy feet,
  And God is all in all !

MATTHEW XI. 28.

*" Come unto Me, all ye that labour and are heavy
laden, and I will give you rest."*

1 O THAT my load of sin were gone !
  O that I could at last submit
At Jesu's feet to lay it down,
  To lay my soul at Jesu's feet !

2 When shall mine eyes behold the Lamb,
  The God of my salvation see ?
Weary, O Lord, Thou know'st I am;
  Yet still I cannot come to Thee.

3 Mark the hard travail of my soul,
  With pity view my labouring breast ;
O give me faith to make me whole,
  And speak my misery into rest.

4 Rest for my soul I long to find;
  Saviour of all, if mine Thou art,
Give me Thy meek and lowly mind,
  And stamp Thine image on my heart.

5 Break off the yoke of inbred sin,
    And fully set my spirit free:
  I cannot rest, till pure within,
    Till I am wholly lost in Thee.

6 Fain would I learn of Thee, my God,
    Thy light and easy burden prove,
  The cross all stain'd with hallow'd blood,
    The labour of Thy dying love;

7 This moment would I take it up,
    And after my dear Master bear,
  With Thee ascend to *Calvary's* top,
    And bow my head and suffer there.

8 I would: but Thou must give the power,
    My heart from every sin release:
  Bring near, bring near the joyful hour,
    And fill me with Thy perfect peace.

9 Come, Lord, the drooping sinner cheer,
    Nor let Thy chariot-wheels delay;
  Appear in my poor heart, appear;
    My God, my Saviour, come away.

10 One deep unto another cries,
    My misery, Lord, implores Thy grace;
  When wilt Thou hear, and bow the skies?
    When shall I see my Jesu's face?

11 The hireling longeth for his hire—
    But only punishment is mine:
  My merits are eternal fire—
    But heaven and happiness are Thine.

12 Give me Thy life; for Thou my death
    Hast swallow'd up in victory,
Quicken'd me with Thy latest breath.
    And died that I might live to Thee.

13 This, only this, is all my hope,
    And doth my sinking soul sustain;
Thy faithful mercies hold me up,
    My Saviour did not die in vain.

14 Answer Thy death's design in me;
    The guilt and power of sin remove.
Redeem from all iniquity,
    Renew, and perfect me in love.

I. TIMOTHY I. 15.

" This is a faithful saying, and worthy of all acceptation. that Christ Jesus came into the world to save sinners."

1 Jesu, Sin-atoning Lamb,
    Jesu, Lover of Thy foe,
Let me feel Thy sovereign name,
    Let me all its virtue know;
Hear my cry out of the deep,
    Haste and help a friendless soul,
Seek and save a wandering sheep,
    Make a sin-sick sinner whole.

2 Burden'd am I, and opprest,
    Till Thou dost remove my load;
Weary, till Thou give me rest;
    Guilty, till I feel Thy blood.

See me, a mere sinner see,
  Miserable, poor, and blind,
Till I lose my all in Thee,
  Till in Thee my all I find.

3 What have I Thy grace to move?
  Beast and devil is my name;
God I hate, and sin I love,
  Sin I love, and sin I am:
Yet I mean Thy grace to try;
  Sinners if Thou canst receive,
Here I am, their captain I;
  Wouldst Thou have me die or live?

4 Thou the Potter, I the clay,
  Nothing have I, Lord, to plead,
Nothing have I, Lord, to say:
  Bid me live, or strike me dead.
I cannot in judgment stand:
  Raise; or slay me with Thy breath:
Guilty, I shall feel Thine hand.
  Guilty of eternal death.

5 Trembling I expect my fate,
  If Thou as my Judge appear:
If Thou art my Advocate,
  Jesus, what have I to fear?
Jesus is the Sinners' Friend,
  Sinners Jesus came to save;
Jesus, I on Thee depend,
  Peace and power in Thee I have.

6 I the golden sceptre see,
  (Self-despairing as I was,)
Now, even now, reach'd out to me:
  I receive Thy pardoning grace.

Of Thy grace I cannot doubt;
    Sinners to Thy wounds who fly
Thou in no wise wilt cast out:
    Lo! I come, the sinner I!

7 Thou shalt make me white as snow,
    Though my soul be black as hell;
Never from Thy cross I go,
    Safe within Thy wounds I dwell.
Other refuge have I none,
    None do I desire beside;
Friend of Sinners, I am one;
    Save me, who for me hast died.

ACTS XVI. 31.

*" Believe on the Lord Jesus Christ, and thou shalt
be saved."*

1 WHAT shall I do, my God, my God?
    I ask in Jesu's name;
Unsanctified and unrenew'd,
    I still remain the same.

2 Sin, only sin, in me I find;
    I cannot subject be
To Thy command; my carnal mind
    Is enmity to Thee.

3 But Thou canst wash the leper clean,
    The stone to flesh convert,
Canst make the *Ethiop* change his skin.
    And purify my heart.

4 Then only, when by grace renew'd,
   My will with Thine shall suit :
O make the tree of nature good,
   And good shall be its fruit.

5 I strive in all I do to please,
   With endless grief and pain,
But cannot, Lord, from sinning cease,
   Till I am born again.

6 With Thee my virtue is but vice,
   My good is specious ill;
'Tis self, 'tis nature in disguise,
   And I am carnal still.

7 No work of mine, or word, or thought
   Thy judgment can abide :
Thy glory, Lord. I never sought,
   For all my soul is pride.

8 What have I then wherein to trust?
   How must I come to Thee?
Foul as I am, condemn'd and lost,
   Thy Son hath died for me.

9 Jesus hath died that I might live,
   Might live to God alone,
In Him eternal life receive,
   And be in spirit one.

10 Saviour, I thank Thee for the grace,
   The gift unspeakable,
And wait, with arms of faith to' embrace,
   And all Thy love to feel.

11 My soul breaks out in strong desire
        The perfect bliss to prove,
    My longing soul is all on fire
        To be dissolved in love.

12 Give me Thyself, from every boast,
        From every wish set free:
    Let all I am in Thee be lost;
        But give Thyself to me.

13 Thy gifts, alas! cannot suffice,
        Unless Thyself be given;
    Thy presence makes my paradise,
        And where Thou art is heaven.

THE WOMAN OF CANAAN.

[*Matthew xv. 22, &c.*]

1   LORD, regard my earnest cry,
        A potsherd of the earth;
    A poor guilty worm am I,
        A *Canaanite* by birth:
    Save me from this tyranny,
    From all the power of Satan save;
        Mercy, mercy upon me,
            Thou Son of *David*, have.

2   Still Thou answerest not a word
        To my repeated prayer;
    Hear Thine own disciples, Lord,
        Who in my sorrows share;

O let them prevail with Thee
To grant the blessing which I crave:
Mercy, mercy upon me,
  Thou Son of *David*, have.

3   Send, O send me now away
      By granting my request;
Still I follow Thee, and pray,
      And will not let Thee rest;
Ever crying after Thee,
Till Thou my helplessness relieve:
Mercy, mercy upon me,
  Thou Son of *David*, have.

4   To the sheep of *Israel's* fold
      Thou in Thy flesh wast sent,
But the Gentiles now behold
      In Thee their Covenant:
See me then, with pity see,
A sinner whom Thou camest to save;
Mercy, mercy upon me,
  Thou Son of *David*, have.

5   Still to Thee, my God, I come,
      And mercy I implore;
Thee, (but how shall I presume,)
      Thee trembling I adore,
Dare not stand before Thy face,
But lowly at Thy feet I fall;
Help me, Jesu; show Thy grace,
  Thy grace is free for all.

6   Still I cannot part with Thee,
      I will not let Thee go;
Mercy, mercy unto me,
  O Son of *David*, show;

Vilest of the sinful race,
  On Thee importunate I call,
    Help me, Jesu; show Thy grace,
      Thy grace is free for all.

7*   Nothing am I in Thy sight,
        Nothing have I to plead;
      Unto dogs it is not right
        To cast the children's bread:
      Yet the dogs the crumbs may eat,
    That from their master's table fall;
        Let the fragments be my meat,
          Thy grace is free for all.

8   Give me, Lord, the victory,
        My heart's desire fulfil;
      Let it now be done to me
        According to my will;
      Give me living bread to eat,
    And say, in answer to my call,
      " *Canaanite*, thy faith is great,
        My grace is free for all."

9   If Thy grace for all is free,
        Thy call *now* let *me* hear,
      Show this token upon me,
        And bring salvation near;
      Now the gracious word repeat,
    The word of healing to my soul,
      " *Canaanite*, thy faith is great,
        Thy faith hath made thee whole."

———

THE POOL OF BETHESDA.

[*John v. 2, &c.*]

1   JESU, take my sins away,
    And make me know Thy name :
Thou art now as yesterday,
    And evermore the same :
Thou my true *Bethesda* be :
I know within Thy arms is room,
  All the world may unto Thee,
    Their House of Mercy, come.

2   See the porches open wide !
    Thy mercy all may prove,
All the world is justified
    By universal love.
Halt and wither'd when they lie,
And sick, and impotent, and blind,
  Sinners may in Thee espy
    The Saviour of mankind.

3   See me lying at the pool,
    And waiting for Thy grace;
O come down into my soul,
    Disclose Thy angel-face !
If to me Thy bowels move,
If now Thou dost my sickness feel,
  Let the Spirit of Thy love
    The helpless sinner heal.

4   Sick of anger, pride, and lust,
    And unbelief I am ;
Yet in Thee for health I trust,
    In Jesu's sovereign name.

Were I taken into Thee,
Could I but step into the pool,
I from every malady
Should be at once made whole.

5   Persons Thou dost not respect;
Whoe'er for mercy call
Thou in no wise wilt reject,
Thy mercy is for all;
Thou wouldst freely all restore,
(Would all the gracious season find,)
Fill with goodness, love, and power,
And with an healthful mind.

6   Mercy then there is for me,
(Away my doubts and fears!)
Plagued with an infirmity
For more than thirty years;
Jesu, cast a pitying eye;
Thou long hast known my desperate case.
Poor and helpless here I lie,
And wait the healing grace.

7   Long hath Thy good Spirit strove
With my distemper'd soul,
But I still refused Thy love
And would not be made whole:
Hardly now at last I yield,
I yield with all my sins to part;
Let my soul be fully heal'd,
And throughly cleansed my heart.

8   Sin is now my sore disease;
But though I would be free,
When the water troubled is
There is no help for me:

Others find a cure, not I ;
In Thee they wash away their sin ;
    I, alas ! have no man nigh,
    To put my weakness in.

9   Pain and sickness, at Thy word,
    And sin and sorrow flies ;
    Speak to me, Almighty Lord,
    And bid my spirit rise ;
    Bid me take my burden up,
The bed on which Thyself didst lie.
    When on *Calvary's* steep top
    My Jesus deign'd to die.

10   Bid me bear the hallow'd cross
    Which Thou hast borne before.
    Walk in all Thy righteous laws,
    And go and sin no more,
    Lest the heaviest curse of all,
The vile apostate's curse. I prove :
    To the hottest hell they fall
    Who fall from pardoning love.

11   But Thou canst preserve from sin.
    And stablish me with grace,
    Keep my helpless soul within
    Thy arms through all my days :
    Jesu, I on Thee alone
For persevering grace depend ;
    Love me freely. love Thine own,
    And love me to the end.

THE GOOD SAMARITAN.

[Luke x. 30, &c.]

1   Woe is me ! what tongue can tell
    My sad afflicted state ?
  Who my anguish can reveal,
    Or all my woe relate ?
  Fallen among thieves I am,
And they have robb'd me of my God.
  Turn'd my glory into shame,
    And left me in my blood.

2   God was once my glorious dress,
    And I like Him did shine ;
  Satan of His righteousness
    Hath spoil'd this soul of mine ;
  By the mortal wound of sin,
'Twixt God and me the parting made :
  Dead in *Adam*, dead within,
    My soul is wholly dead.

3   I have lost the life Divine,
    And when this outward breath
  To the Giver I resign,
    Must die the second death.
  Naked, helpless, stript of God,
And at the latest gasp I lie :
  Who beholds me in my blood,
    And saves me ere I die ?

4   Lo ! the priest comes down in vain,
    And sees my sad distress,
  Sees the state of fallen man,
    But cannot give me ease :

Patriarchs and prophets old
Observe my wretched, desperate case:
Me expiring they behold,
But leave me as I was.

5   Lo! the *Levite* me espies,
And stops to view my grief,
Looks on me, and bids me rise.
But offers no relief.
All my wounds he open tears,
And searches them, alas! in vain;
Fill'd with anguish, griefs, and fears,
He leaves me in my pain.

6   O Thou Good *Samaritan,*
In Thee is all my hope;
Only Thou canst succour man.
And raise the fallen up.
Hearken to my dying cry,
My wounds compassionately see.
Me a sinner pass not by,
Who gasp for help to Thee.

7   Still Thou journey'st where I am.
And still Thy bowels move:
Pity is with Thee the same,
And all Thy heart is love.
Stoop to a poor sinner, stoop.
And let Thy healing grace abound:
Heal my bruises, and bind up
My spirit's every wound.

8   Saviour of my soul, draw nigh.
In mercy haste to me;
At the point of death I lie.
And cannot come to Thee.

Now Thy kind relief afford,
The wine and oil of grace pour in;
Good Physician, speak the word,
And heal my soul of sin.

9   Pity to my dying cries
       Hath drawn Thee from above,
Hovering over me with eyes
       Of tenderness and love :
Now, e'en now I see Thy face,
The balm of *Gilead* I receive ;
       Thou hast saved me by Thy grace,
       And bade the sinner live.

10   Surely now the bitterness
       Of second death is past :
O my Life, my Righteousness,
       On Thee my soul is cast.
Thou hast brought me to Thine inn,
And I am of Thy promise sure;
       Thou shalt cleanse me from all sin,
       And all my sickness cure.

11   Perfect then the work begun,
       And make the sinner whole ;
All Thy will on me be done.
       My body, spirit, soul.
Still preserve me safe from harms,
And kindly for Thy patient care;
       Take me, Jesu, to Thine arms,
       And keep me ever there.

———

GROANING FOR REDEMPTION.
PART I.

1 LORD, I confess my sins to Thee,
  My sins beyond expression great;
Fast bound in sin and misery,
  My spirit faints beneath the weight,
And struggles to throw off the load,
But cannot, cannot come to God.

2 O how shall I the anguish bear
  Of inbred sin's envenom'd dart?
The mischief hence I cannot tear;
  'Tis enter'd deep into my heart,
Its poison drinks my spirits up,
And quenches my last spark of hope.

3 O wretched man, what must I do?
  I neither can resist nor fly;
Hell, earth, and sin my soul pursue,
  I cannot find my Saviour nigh;
Unhappy, I shall one day fall,
Shall perish by the hand of *Saul.*

4 Me from perdition what can save?
  Justly my God His help denies:
No evil I abhor, and have
  No fear of God before my eyes;
Self-harden'd in my lost estate,
All sin I love, all good I hate.

5 Whither, ah whither shall I go?
  The snares of death my soul surround,
The floods of wickedness o'erflow,
  And desperate is my spirit's wound;
The worm that never dies I feel,
Arrested by the pains of hell.

6 O could I but escape away,
  And steal into the silent tomb,
Defraud the lion of his prey,
  And at my latest hour o'ercome,
That hour I now would present have,
Would now rejoice to find a grave.

7 O God, behold my troubled breast:
  Yet once again I Thee implore;
Indulge me in my last request,
  And let me die, and sin no more;
Now, let me now lay down my head.
From pain and sin for ever freed.

8 O God, regard my bitter cry,
  I groan to be redeem'd from sin;
To Thee I lift my weeping eye,
  Open Thine arms and take me in;
To Thee my labouring soul I bow;
Require it, O require it now.

9 I know it is not now renew'd,
  I am not fit Thy face to see,
But trust the virtue of Thy blood
  In my last hour shall work on me
Some miracle of grace unknown,
Without a miracle undone.

10 My God, I cannot let Thee go
  Without an answer to my prayer:
O tell me that it shall be so,
  I soon shall lose in death my care.
Where fiends and sins no more molest.
And weary spirits are at rest.

11 I doubt not, Lord, but there remains
    A rest from sin and sorrow *here*,
Thy people *here* are freed from pains,
    From troubles, doubts, and guilt, and fear :
But let me hence this moment fly,
Save me from sin, and let me die.

12 I only wait for this glad hour,
    'Tis all my business here below;
Send down into my soul the power,
    And let me die Thy love to know;
Renew me, and withdraw my breath;
Give power o'er sin and instant death.

PART II.

1 FORGIVE me, O long-suffering God,
    The hurry of my peevish grief;
Though fainting underneath my load,
    And staggering oft through unbelief.
Thee for my Lord I fain would own,
And say, Thine only will be done.

2 Forgive me then my follies past,
    The fond impatience of my prayers,
My rash complaints and eager haste,
    My faithless doubts and fruitless cares.
Thou know'st, till Thou Thy life bring in,
I cannot, cannot cease from sin.

3 The captive exile makes his moan,
    And hastens to be loosed from pain,
The pain through which I ever groan,
    The dread lest I should turn again,
Lest all my bread of life should fail,
And I sink down unchanged to hell.

4 That dreadful thought comes thundering back,
   And falls a mountain on my head :
Nor can, nor will I comfort take
   In hearing Satan's factors plead ;
I cannot hug, like them, my chain,
Or rest, if sin in me *remain.*

5 In vain they bid me blindly fly,
   And catch at Thy unknown decree ;
In vain they bid me dream that I
   Was chose from all eternity :
Alas ! I want election's seal,
For I am all unholy still.

6 Tell me no more, ye carnal saints,
   "The best must always strive with sin,
God will not answer *all* your wants,
   God will not make you *throughly* clean.
Sin *must* have *some* unhallow'd part,
Christ *cannot* fill up *all* the heart."

7 Can life and death together dwell ?
   Can Christ with Belial e'er agree,
Darkness with light, and heaven with hell ?
   Can both at once have place in me ?
Can I be Christ's and sin's abode,
A den of thieves and house of God ?

8 No, Jesus, no ! Thou Holy One,
   When Thou shalt come into my heart,
I know that Thou wilt reign alone,
   And sin for ever shall depart ;
Thy love shall cast out all my fear
Lest sin should come, when Thou art here.

9 In patient hope for this I wait,
   Till all old things are past away,
  Till Thou shalt all things new create,
   And I behold Thy perfect day,
  The mark of mine election show,
  And be in Christ a creature new.

PART III.

1 OMNISCIENT, Omnipresent King,
   The true, and merciful, and just,
  To Thee my last distress I bring,
   To Thee my desperate cause I trust:
  I give my fond complainings o'er,
  I set my God a time no more.

2 My time, O God, is in Thine hand,
   Thou know'st my feebleness of soul;
  Able Thou art to make me stand,
   Thou canst this moment speak me whole.
  Or keep me thus till my last hour,
  To show forth all Thy saving power.

3 I leave it all to Thee alone,
   Thy counsellor I cannot be;
  To Thee Thy every work is known,
   And secret things belong to Thee:
  Thy manner, and Thy time is best:
  But let me enter into rest.

4 The hireling longeth for his hire,
   The watcher for the break of day;
  But, O my restless heart's Desire,
   Let me not murmur at Thy stay!
  Be stopt my mouth, and fail my tongue,
  But let Thy Spirit groan, *How long!*

5 The thing Thou dost I know not now,
    But I shall know hereafter, Lord;
To Thy dread sovereign will I bow,
    Thy will be done, Thy name adored;
Act for the glory of Thy name;
Lo! in Thy gracious hands I am.

6 Act for Thine own and *Sion's* sake,
    And let Thy will in me be done;
If but one soul may comfort take
    By hearing me so deeply groan,
Still let me all my burden feel,
And groan, and weep, and suffer still.

7 If but one tempted soul may find
    Relief by my afflicted state,
I would be patient and resign'd,
    Still in the iron furnace wait;
Still let the sin, the grief, the pain,
The thorn in my weak flesh remain.

8 Still let my bleeding heart be torn,
    If other bleeding hearts it cheer;
Disconsolate for Thee I mourn,
    My nature's cross consent to bear,
To languish for my Lord's delay
And weep a thousand lives away.

PART IV.

1 BEHOLD, ye souls that mourn for God,
    And take ye comfort from my grief,
Be strengthen'd by my grievous load,
    Let my distress be your relief,
With mine your tears and sorrows join,
And lose by mixing them with mine

2 I am the man who long have known
    The strength and rage of inbred sin;
My soul is dead, my heart is stone,
    A cage of birds and beasts unclean,
A den of thieves, a dire abode
Of dragons, but no house of God.

3 I dare not speak, I cannot show
    The depths of Satan harbour'd there,
The horrors of infernal woe,
    The black and blasphemous despair;
Who can conceive, but those that feel
Indwelling sin, indwelling hell!

4 A stranger intermeddleth not
    With our inexplicable grief;
'Tis past the reach of human thought,
    The torture of this unbelief,
The struggling groan, the passion loud,
The heart that says, There is no God.

5 But will He not at last appear,
    And make His power and Godhead known?
Surely He shall the mourner cheer,
    And make the broken heart His throne:
Shall break it first, and then bind up:
In hope believe ye against hope.

6 Comfort, ye ministers of grace,
    Comfort My people, saith our God!
Ye soon shall see His smiling face,
    His golden sceptre, not His rod,
And own, when now the cloud's removed,
He only chasten'd whom He loved.

7 Who sow in tears in joy shall reap,
    The Lord shall comfort all that mourn;
Who now go on our way and weep,
    With joy we doubtless shall return
And bring our sheaves with vast increase,
And have our fruit to holiness.

8 Then let us patiently attend,
    And wait the leisure of our Lord:
Surely we all shall in the end
    Experience His abiding word,
Shall all His gracious power declare,
And fruit unto perfection bear.

MY LORD AND MY GOD.

[*John xx.* 28.]

1 O THOU whom fain my soul would love,
    Whom I would gladly die to know,
This veil of unbelief remove,
    And show me, all Thy goodness show:
Jesu, Thyself in me reveal,
Tell me Thy name, Thy nature tell.

2 Hast Thou been with me, Lord, so long?
    Yet Thee, *my* Lord, have I not known?
I claim Thee with a faltering tongue,
    I pray Thee in a feeble groan:
Tell me, O tell me who Thou art,
And speak Thy name into my heart.

3 If now Thou talkest by the way
      With such an abject worm as me,
   Thy mysteries of grace display,
      Open mine eyes that I may see,
   That I may understand Thy word,
   And now cry out, It is the Lord!

4 I know Him by those prints of love,
      His bleeding wounds are open wide;
   Through faith I handle Him, and prove,
      I thrust my hand into His side,
   I feel the sprinkling of His blood:
   Jesu, Thou art my Lord, my God!

PART II.

THE FIFTY-SECOND CHAPTER OF ISAIAH.

PART I.

1 AWAKE, *Jerusalem*, awake;
    No longer in thy sins lie down,
  The garment of salvation take,
    Thy beauty and thy strength put on.

2 By impious feet no longer trod,
    Thy God shall cleanse thy every stain;
  O holy city of thy God,
    Thou shalt not bear His name in vain.

3 Shake off the dust that blinds thy sight
    And hides the promise from thine eyes;
  Arise, and struggle into light;
    Thy great Deliverer calls, Arise!

4 Shake off the bands of sad despair,
    Sion, assert thy liberty;
  Look up, thy broken heart prepare,
    And God shall set the captive free.

5 For thus the Lord your God hath said,—
     Ye all have sold yourselves for nought;
   A ransom (not by you) is paid,
     Receive your liberty unbought.

6 My people have been long opprest;
     (No glory thence redounds to Me;)
   Long have I seen them sore distrest,
     Grieved at My people's misery.

7 They groan'd beneath the tyrant's chain,
     Sin ruled them with an iron rod,
   The suffering abjects howl'd for pain,
     They groan'd, but durst not groan to God.

8 The' oppressors with insulting boast
     My truth and saving power contemn'd;
   My worship and My praise was lost,
     My name was every day blasphemed.

9 For this My jealousy is stirr'd,
     And shall a great deliverance show;
   My people shall confess their Lord,
     My faithfulness and mercy know.

10 Surely they all shall know My name,
     They all My attributes shall prove;
   I am what I am call'd; I am
     Justice, and Truth, and Power, and Love.

PART II.

1 How beautiful His feet appear,
     High on the mountain-tops, who brings
   Glad tidings of salvation near,
     Salvation from the King of kings!

2 Who publishes the joyful sound,
      Proclaims a peace 'twixt earth and heaven.
   A ransom for the sinner found,
      God reconciled and man forgiven.

3 That says to *Israel's* mournful race,—
      Awake, arise, shake off thy chains,
   Believe the word of Gospel grace,
      Thy God, thy great Redeemer, reigns.

4 Thy watchmen shall the voice lift up,
      Shall sing with gladsome melody,
   Object of all their joy and hope,
      When eye to eye their Lord they see.

5 Him eye to eye shall they behold,
      Shall shout to see the Saviour come.
   To save a world redeem'd of old,
      To bring the weary captives home.

6 Break forth into joy, Your Comforter sing;
   Ye sinners, employ Your all for your King;
   Rejoice, ye waste places, Your Saviour proclaim.
   Bestow all your praises And lives on His name.

7 For Jesus the Lord Hath comforted man,
   The sinner restored, Nor suffer'd in vain;
   To bring us to heaven When raised from our fall.
   His life He hath given A ransom for all.

8 His arm He hath bared, His mercy and grace
   Hath pardon prepared For all the lost race;
   His absolute merit, Display'd in our sight,
   We all may inherit And claim as our right.

9 The *Gentiles* shall hear The life-giving call.
His grace shall appear And visit them all;
The common salvation To all doth belong,
To every nation, And people, and tongue.*

PART III.

1 DEPART, ye ransom'd souls, depart,
    The house of bondage quit; be clean :
Call'd to be saints, be pure in heart,
    Abhor the loathsome touch of sin.

2 Vessels of mercy, sons of grace,
    Be purged from every sinful stain ;
Be like your Lord; His word embrace.
    Nor bear His hallow'd name in vain.

3 For not as fugitives that try
    By hasty flight to' escape the foe,
Ye from the power of sin shall fly,
    But calmly in full triumph go.

4 The Lord shall in your front appear.
    And lead the pompous triumph on ;
His glory shall bring up the rear,
    And perfect what His grace begun.

5 Behold the Servant of My grace,
    My Son shall heavenly wisdom show.
Deal gently with the sin-sick race,
    And minister My life below.

* The four last verses were first published as one of the first
series of " Hymns on God's Everlasting Love," and are omitted
from that collection that they may stand in their proper place
here. The effect of the skilful change of metre is as beautiful as
it is obvious.

6 His mighty arm, His high right-hand,
 Still the pre-eminence shall have,
Shall bow the world to His command,
 And magnify His power to save.

7 Vilest of all the sons of men
 Him in His days of flesh they view'd,
His body mangled, torn with pain,
 His visage marr'd with tears and blood.

8 The world on Him they doom'd to die
 With fresh astonishment shall gaze,
Amazed their Saviour to descry,
 O'erpower'd with His stupendous grace.

9 The suffering, sin-atoning God
 Shall kindly raise them from their fall.
Sprinkle the nations with His blood,
 And tell them He hath died for all.

10 The nations shall receive His word,
 And kings to His command submit;
The lords of earth shall call Him Lord,
 And lay their crowns before His feet.

11 Fountain of power, when He is near
 The gods of earth are gods no more ;
Poor guilty worms, they bow, they fear,
 And fall, and silently adore.

12 Children of wrath and slaves of sin,
 They now shall see their lost estate ;
Shall see the blood that makes them clean.
 The power that makes them truly great.

13 Shall now, in Jesus taught to trust,
   Accept the grace on all bestow'd,
   This their best title and their boast,
   Servants of Christ, and sons of God.

WRESTLING JACOB.*

1 COME, O Thou Traveller unknown.
   Whom still I hold, but cannot see,
   My company before is gone,
   And I am left alone with Thee;
   With Thee all night I mean to stay.
   And wrestle till the break of day.

2 I need not tell Thee who I am,
   My misery or sin declare,
   Thyself hast call'd me by my name,
   Look on Thy hands, and read it there.
   But who, I ask Thee, who art Thou?
   Tell me Thy name, and tell me now.

* Genesis xxxii. 24, &c. In the obituary of Charles Wesley, inserted in the "Minutes of Conference," for 1788, his brother states that Dr. Watts did not scruple to say that "that single poem, *Wrestling Jacob*, was worth all the verses he himself had written." Montgomery reckons the poem among the author's "highest achievements; in which, with consummate art, he has carried on the action of a lyrical drama; every turn in the conflict with the mysterious Being against whom Jacob wrestles all night being marked with precision by the varying language of the speaker, accompanied by intense, increasing interest, till the rapturous moment of discovery, when he prevails, and exclaims, 'I know Thee, Saviour, who Thou art,' v. 11."—Christian Psalmist: Introductory Essay, p. xxiv., ed. 1828.

3 In vain Thou strugglest to get free,
  I never will unloose my hold;
Art thou the Man that died for me?
  The secret of Thy love unfold;
Wrestling I will not let Thee go
Till I Thy name, Thy nature know.

4 Wilt Thou not yet to me reveal
  Thy new, unutterable name?
Tell me, I still beseech Thee, tell;
  To know it now resolved I am;
Wrestling I will not let Thee go
Till I Thy name, Thy nature know.

5 'Tis all in vain to hold Thy tongue,
  Or touch the hollow of my thigh;
Though every sinew be unstrung,
  Out of my arms Thou shalt not fly;
Wrestling I will not let Thee go
Till I Thy name, Thy nature know.

6 What though my shrinking flesh complain,
  And murmur to contend so long,
I rise superior to my pain,
  When I am weak then I am strong;
And when my all of strength shall fail,
I shall with the God-man prevail.

7 My strength is gone, my nature dies,
  I sink beneath Thy weighty hand,
Faint to revive, and fall to rise;
  I fall, and yet by faith I stand,
I stand, and will not let Thee go,
Till I Thy name, Thy nature know.

8 Yield to me now; for I am weak.
    But confident in self-despair:
Speak to my heart, in blessings speak.
    Be conquer'd by my instant prayer;
Speak, or Thou never hence shalt move.
And tell me if Thy name is Love.

9 'Tis Love ! 'tis Love !   Thou diedst for me:
    I hear Thy whisper in my heart:
The morning breaks, the shadows flee:
    Pure UNIVERSAL LOVE Thou art;
To me. to all Thy bowels move;
Thy nature, and Thy name is Love.

10 My prayer hath power with God; the grace
    Unspeakable I now receive,
Through faith I see Thee face to face;
    I see Thee face to face, and live:
In vain I have not wept and strove:
Thy nature, and Thy name is Love.

11 I know Thee, Saviour, who Thou art,
    Jesus, the feeble sinner's Friend;
Nor wilt Thou with the night depart,
    But stay. and love me to the end:
Thy mercies never shall remove ;
Thy nature. and Thy name is Love.

12 The Sun of Righteousness on me
    Hath rose with healing in His wings:
Wither'd my nature's strength, from Thee
    My soul its life and succour brings;
My help is all laid up above;
Thy nature, and Thy name is Love.

13 Contented now upon my thigh
　　I halt, till life's short journey end;
All helplessness, all weakness, I
　　On Thee alone for strength depend,
Nor have I power from Thee to move;
Thy nature, and Thy name is Love.

14 Lame as I am, I take the prey,
　　Hell, earth, and sin with ease o'ercome;
I leap for joy, pursue my way,
　　And as a bounding hart fly home,
Through all eternity to prove,
Thy nature, and Thy name is Love

A THANKSGIVING.

1 O WHAT shall I do, My Saviour to praise,
So faithful and true, So plenteous in grace ;
So strong to deliver, So good to redeem
The weakest believer That hangs upon Him!

2 How happy the man Whose heart is set free,
The people that can Be joyful in Thee !
Their joy is to walk in The light of Thy face.
And still they are talking Of Jesus's grace.

3 Their daily delight Shall be in Thy name,
They shall as their right Thy righteousness claim :
Thy righteousness wearing, And cleansed by Thy
　　blood,
Bold shall they appear in The presence of God.

4 For Thou art their boast, Their glory and power;
  And I also trust To see the glad hour,
  My soul's new creation, A life from the dead,
  The day of salvation That lifts up my head.

5 For Jesus my Lord Is now my defence,
  I trust in His word, None plucks me from thence:
  Since I have found favour He all things will do,
  My King and my Saviour Shall make me anew.

6 Yes, Lord, I shall see The bliss of Thine own,
  Thy secret to me Shall soon be made known,
  For sorrow and sadness I joy shall receive,
  And share in the gladness Of all that believe.

ANOTHER.

1 O HEAVENLY King, Look down from above,
  Assist us to sing Thy mercy and love;
  So sweetly o'erflowing, So plenteous the store,
  Thou still art bestowing And giving us more.

2 O God of our life, We hallow Thy name;
  Our business and strife Is Thee to proclaim;
  Accept our thanksgiving For creating grace,
  The living, the living Shall show forth Thy praise.

3 Our Father and Lord, Almighty art Thou;
  Preserved by Thy word, We worship Thee now,
  The bountiful Donor Of all we enjoy;
  Our tongues to Thine honour And lives we employ.

4 But O, above all Thy kindness we praise,
  From sin and from thrall Which saves the lost race:
  Thy Son Thou hast given A world to redeem,
  And bring us to heaven Whose trust is in Him.

5 Wherefore of Thy love We sing and rejoice,
With angels above We lift up our voice;
Thy love each believer Shall gladly adore,
For ever and ever, When time is no more.

ANOTHER.

1 My Father, my God, I long for Thy love;
O shed it abroad, Send Christ from above;
My heart ever fainting He only can cheer,
And all things are wanting Till Jesus is there.

2 O when shall my tongue Be fill'd with Thy praise,
While all the day long I publish Thy grace,
Thy honour and glory To sinners forth show,
Till sinners adore Thee, And own Thou art true!

3 Thy strength and Thy power I now can proclaim,
Preserved every hour Through Jesus's name;
For Thou art still by me, And holdest my hand;
No ill can come nigh me, By faith while I stand.

4 My God is my guide, Thy mercies abound,
On every side They compass me round;
Thou savest me from sickness, From sin dost retrieve,
And strengthen my weakness, And bid me believe.

5 Thou holdest my soul In spiritual life,
My foes dost control And quiet their strife;
Thou rulest my passion, My pride and self-will;
To see Thy salvation Thou bidd'st me "Stand still!"

6 I stand and admire Thine outstretched arm,
I walk through the fire And suffer no harm;
Assaulted by evil, I scorn to submit,
The world and the devil Fall under my feet.

7 I wrestle not now, But trample on sin,
 For *with* me art Thou, And shalt be *within*.
 While, stronger and stronger In Jesus's power.
 I go on to conquer, Till sin is no more.

HYMN TO THE TRINITY.

1 God of unexhausted grace,
   Of everlasting love,
 Overpower'd before Thy face
   I fall. and dare not move.
 What hast Thou for sinners done.
   For so poor a worm as me?
 Thou hast given Thine only Son.
   To bring us back to Thee.

2 Suffering, sin-atoning God,
   Thy hallow'd name I bless;
 Jesus, lavish of Thy blood
   To buy the sinner's peace,
 Gushing from Thy sacred veins
   Let it now my soul o'erflow,
 Purge out all my sinful stains.
   And wash me white as snow.

3 Holy Ghost. set to Thy seal.
   The life of Jesus breathe ;
 The deep things of God reveal,
   Apply *my* Saviour's death:
 With the Father and the Son
   Soon as one in Thee I am.
 All my nature shall make known
   The glories of the Lamb.

4 Father, Son, and Holy Ghost,
    Thy Godhead we adore,
Join with the triumphant host
    Who praise Thee evermore;
Live, by heaven and earth adored,
    Three in One, and One in Three.
Holy, holy, holy Lord,
    All glory be to Thee!

ON HIS BIRTHDAY.

1 Oft have I cursed my natal day,
    While struggling in the legal strife.
And wish'd for wings to fly away.
    And murmur'd to be held in life:
But O, my blasphemies are o'er,
I curse my day, my God, no more.

2 His grace, which I abused so long,
    Hath this and all my sins forgiven;
I now have learnt a better song,
    I cheerfully look up to heaven,
With joy upon my head return,
And bless the day that I was born.

3 How could I, Lord, Thy goodness grieve?
    How could I do Thee such despite?
At last I thankfully receive
    The gift of Thy continued light;
No longer I Thy favours spurn,
But bless the day that I was born.

4 Fountain of life and all my joy,
  Jesu, Thy mercies I embrace;
The breath Thou givest for Thee employ,
  And wait to taste Thy perfect grace:
No more forsaken and forlorn,
I bless the day that I was born.

5 Since first I felt by grace removed
  My sin's intolerable load,
Long in the wilderness I roved,
  And groan'd to live without my God;
I cannot now as hopeless mourn,
But bless the day that I was born.

6 The tyranny of sin is past;
  And though the carnal mind remains,
My guiltless soul on Thee is cast,
  I neither hug, nor bite my chains:
Prisoner of hope, to Thee I turn,
And bless the day that I was born.

7 Preserved through faith by power Divine.
  A miracle of grace I stand,
I prove the strength of Jesus mine:
  Jesus, upheld by Thy right hand,
Though in my flesh I feel the thorn.
I bless the day that I was born.

8 Weary of life through inbred sin
  I was, but now defy its power;
When as a flood the foe comes in,
  My soul is more than conqueror,
I tread him down with holy scorn,
And bless the day that I was born.

9 Born from above, I soon shall praise
  Thy goodness with a thankful tongue,
Record the victory of Thy grace,
  And teach a listening world the song.
While many, whom to Thee I turn,
Shall bless the day that I was born.

10 Come, Lord, and make me pure within,
  O let me now be born of God,*
Live to declare I cannot sin!
  Or if I seal the truth with blood,
My soul, from out the body torn,
Shall bless the day that I was born.

JOB XIX. 25.

1 I KNOW that my Redeemer lives;
  He lives, and on the earth shall stand,
And though to worms my flesh He gives
  My dust lies number'd in His hand.

2 In this reanimated clay
  I surely shall behold Him near,
Shall see Him at the latter day
  In all His majesty appear.

See note, Vol. i., p. 370. The last verse of this glorious lyric, so full of the joy of faith, was improved by Wesley, who in the Hymn-Book of 1780 altered line 2 as follows: " And let me now be filled with God!" In the edition of 1809, and all following, line 3 reads better, thus: " Live to declare I'm saved from sin."

3 I feel what then shall raise me up,
    The' Eternal Spirit lives in me ;
This is my confidence of hope
    That God I face to face shall see.

4 Mine own and not another's eyes
    The King shall in His beauty view,
I shall from Him receive the prize,
    And wear the crown to victors due.

A FUNERAL HYMN.

(Used first for Mrs. Elizabeth Hooper.)*

1 COME, to the house of mourning come,
    The house of serious, solemn joy ;
Let us, till all are taken home,
    Our lives in songs of praise employ.

---

* Several interesting notices of her death and funeral are found in C. Wesley's Journal, May 1st to 8th, 1741. One is extracted as follows:—"I saw my dear friend again, in great bodily weakness, but strong in the Lord and in the power of His might. 'The Spirit,' said she, 'bears witness every moment with my spirit, that I am a child of God.' I spoke with her physician, who said he had but little hope of her recovery; 'only,' added he, 'she has no dread upon her spirits, which is generally the worst symptom. Most people die for fear of dying; but I never met with such people as yours. They are none of them afraid of death, but calm and patient and resigned to the last.' He had said to her, 'Madam, be not cast down;' she answered, smiling, 'Sir, I shall never be cast down.' . . . I hastened back and asked, 'How are you now?' Her answer was, ' Full, full of love.'"—Journal, i. 271 *et seq.*

2 Accomplish'd is our sister's strife,
    Her happier soul is gone before,
Her struggle for eternal life,
    Her glorious agony, is o'er.

3 The captive exile is released,
    Is with her Lord in paradise,
Of perfect paradise possest,
    And waiting for the heavenly prize.

4 In her no spot of sin remain'd,
    To shake her confidence in God;
The victory here she more than gain'd,
    Triumphant through her Saviour's blood.

5 She now the fight of faith hath fought,
    Finish'd and won the Christian race;
She found on earth the Lord she sought,
    And now beholds Him face to face.

6 She died in sure and steadfast hope,
    By Jesus wholly sanctified;
Her perfect spirit she gave up,
    And sunk into His arms, and died.

7 Thus may we all our parting breath
    Into the Saviour's hands resign:
O Jesu, let me die her death,
    And let her latter end be mine!

ANOTHER.

1 Draw near, ye strangers to our God,
    And taste with us the heavenly powers;
O that His love were shed abroad!
    O that your hearts were all like ours!

2 Come, see how Christians wail their dead ;
   Come, share in our mysterious bliss ;
 On Satan, sin, and death to tread,
   O what an happiness is this !

3 Though once ye intermeddled not
   With the strange madness of our joys,
 Ye all may be to *Eden* brought,
   And heighten our triumphant noise.

4 With tears of joy our eyes o'erflow,
   At parting with our dearest friend ;
 From us we gladly let her go
   To pleasures that shall never end.

5 We know in whom we have believed,
   Our faith in Jesus is not vain ;
 To all who have their Lord received
   To live is Christ, to die is gain.

6 Our sister's flesh shall turn to dust,
   Her sacred dust in hope shall sleep,
 The temple of the Holy Ghost
   The still indwelling God shall keep.

7 Triumphantly she laid it down,
   For time to waste, and worms devour ;
 In weakness and dishonour sown,
   Till raised in glory and in power.

8 A body natural it lies,
   A lifeless lump of mouldering clay ;
 But spiritual it soon shall rise,
   No more to perish or decay.

9 This corruptible body soon
    Shall all incorruptible be,
This mortal quickly shall put on
    Its robes of immortality.

10 The terrible, all-conquering king
    Shall then a final period have :
Say then, O death, where is thy sting?
    Where is thy victory, O grave ?

11 The sting of death, our sin, is gone,
    Scatter'd are all our guilty fears;
Thanks be to God, through Christ alone,
    Who makes us more than conquerors.

12 God only doth the victory give ;
    He shall our glorious flesh restore,
His many sons to heaven receive,
    Where time and death shall be no more.

ANOTHER.

1 *Thessalonians iv.* 13, *&c.*

1 LET the world lament their dead,
    As sorrowing without hope ;
When a friend of ours is freed,
    We cheerfully look up,
Cannot murmur or complain,
    For our dead we cannot grieve :
Death to them, to us, is gain ;
    In Jesus we believe.

2 We believe that Christ our Head
    For us resign'd His breath,
He was number'd with the dead,
    And dying conquer'd death ;

Burst the barriers of the tomb ;
  Death could Him no longer keep :
He is the Firstfruits become
  Of those in Him that sleep.

3 God, who Him to life restored,
  Shall all His members raise,
Bring them quicken'd with their Lord.
  The children of His grace.
We who then on earth remain
  Shall not sooner be brought home :
All the dead shall rise again
  To meet the general doom.

4 Jesus, faithful to His word,
  Shall with a shout descend ;
All heaven's host their glorious Lord
  Shall pompously attend ;
Christ shall come with dreadful noise,
  Lightnings swift, and thunders loud,
With the great archangel's voice,
  And with the trump of God.

5 First the dead in Christ shall rise :
  Then we who yet remain
Shall be caught up to the skies,
  And see our Lord again ;
We shall meet Him in the air,
  All wrapt up to heaven shall be,
Find, and love, and praise Him there
  To all eternity.

6 Who can tell the happiness
  This glorious hope affords !
Joy unutter'd we possess
  In these reviving words :

Happy while on earth we breathe,
  Mightier bliss ordain'd to know,
'Trampling down sin, hell, and death,
  To the third heaven we go.

ANOTHER.

1 BLESSING, honour, thanks, and praise,
  Pay we, gracious God, to Thee;
Thou in Thine abundant grace
  Givest us the victory :
True and faithful to Thy word,
  Thou hast glorified Thy Son;
Jesus Christ, our dying Lord,
  He for us the fight hath won.

2 Lo ! the prisoner is released;
  Lighten'd of his fleshly load,
Where the weary are at rest
  He is gather'd into God !
Lo ! the pain of life is past,
  All his warfare now is o'er,
Death and hell behind are cast,
  Grief and suffering are no more.

3 Yes, the Christian's course is run,
  Ended is the glorious strife,
Fought the fight, the work is done,
  Death is swallow'd up of life ;
Borne by angels on their wings,
  Far from earth the spirit flies,
Finds his God, and sits and sings
  Triumphing in paradise.

4 Join we then with one accord
      In the new, the joyful song ;
  Absent from our loving Lord
      We shall not continue long :
  We shall quit the house of clay,
      We a better lot shall share,
  We shall see the realms of day,
      Meet our happy brother there !

5 Let the world bewail their dead,
      Fondly of their loss complain :
  Brother, friend, by Jesus freed,
      Death to thee, to us, is gain :
  Thou art enter'd into joy :
      Let the unbelievers mourn,
  We in songs our lives employ,
      Till we all to God return.

ANOTHER.

1 HARK, a voice divides the sky !
      Happy are the faithful dead ;
  In the Lord who sweetly die,
      They from all their toils are freed.
  Them the Spirit hath declared
      Blest, unutterably blest :
  Jesus is their great Reward,
      Jesus is their endless Rest.

2 Follow'd by their works they go
      Where their Head had gone before,
  Reconciled by grace below :
      Grace had open'd mercy's door:

Justified through faith alone,
    Here they *knew* their sins forgiven,
Here they laid their burden down,
    Hallow'd, and made fit for heaven.

3 Who can now lament the lot
    Of a saint in Christ deceased?
Let the world, who know us not,
    Call us hopeless and unbless'd :
When from flesh the spirit freed
    Hastens homeward to return,
Mortals cry, " A man is dead !"
    Angels sing, " A child is born !"

4 Born into the world above,
    They our happy brother greet,
Bear him to the throne of love,
    Place him at the Saviour's feet :
Jesus smiles, and says, " Well done,
    Good and faithful servant thou,
Enter and receive Thy crown,
    Reign with Me triumphant now."

5 Angels catch the' approving sound,
    Bow, and bless the just award,
Hail the heir with glory crown'd,
    Now rejoicing with his Lord ;
Fuller joys ordain'd to know,
    Waiting for the general doom,
When the' archangel's trump shall blow,
    " Rise, ye dead, to judgment come."

———————

AFTER THE FUNERAL.

1 COME, let us who in Christ believe
    With saints and angels join,
  Glory, and praise, and blessing give.
    And thanks, to Love Divine.

2 Our friend in sure and certain hope
    Hath laid his body down ;
  He knew that Christ shall raise him up.
    And give the starry crown.

3 To all who His appearing love
    He opens paradise ;
  And we shall join the hosts above.
    And we shall grasp the prize.

4 Then let us wait to see the day,
    To hear the joyful word,
  To answer, Lo ! we come away,
    We die to meet our Lord.

A MIDNIGHT HYMN.

1 HEARKEN to the solemn voice,
    The awful midnight cry,
  Waiting souls, rejoice, rejoice,
    And see the Bridegroom nigh :
  Lo ! He comes to keep His word ;
    Light and joy His looks impart ;
  Go ye forth to meet your Lord,
    And meet Him in your heart.

2 Ye who faint beneath the load
    Of sin, your heads lift up ;
See your dear redeeming God,
    He comes, and bids you hope :
In the midnight of your grief,
    Jesus doth His mourners cheer,
Now He brings you sure relief ;
    Believe, and feel Him here.

3 Ye whose loins art girt, stand forth !
    Whose lamps are burning bright,
Worthy, in your Saviour's worth,
    To walk with Christ in light :
Jesus bids your hearts be clean,
    Bids you all His promise prove ;
Jesus comes to cast out sin,
    And perfect you in love.

4 Happiest souls. (if such are here,)
    Who have attain'd the prize,
Wait ye till your Lord appear,
    Descending from the skies :
Still forget the things behind,
    Toward your thrones of glory press ;
Stop not, till above ye find
    The crown of righteousness.

5 Wait we all in patient hope,
    Till Christ, the Judge, shall come :
We shall soon be all caught up
    To meet the general doom :
In an hour to us unknown,
    As a thief in deepest night.
Christ shall suddenly come down
    With all His saints in light.

6 Happy he whom Christ shall find
  Watching to see Him come;
Him the Judge of all mankind
  Shall bear triumphant home:
Who can answer to His word?
  Which of you dares meet His day?
Rise, and come to judgment!—Lord,
  I rise, and come away!

ANOTHER.

1 Oft have we pass'd the guilty night
  In revellings and frantic mirth;
The creature was our sole delight,
  Our happiness the things of earth;
But O! suffice the season past,
We choose the better part at last.

2 We will not close our wakeful eyes,
  We will not let our eyelids sleep,
But humbly lift them to the skies,
  And all a solemn vigil keep:
So many nights on sin bestow'd,
Can we not watch one hour for God?

3 We can, dear Jesu, for Thy sake,
  Devote our every hour to Thee:
Speak but the word, our souls shall wake,
  And sing with cheerful melody;
Thy praise shall our glad tongues employ,
And every heart shall dance for joy.

4 Dear Object of our faith and love,
  We listen for Thy welcome voice;
Our persons and our works approve,
  And bid us in Thy strength rejoice:

Now let us hear the midnight cry,
And shout to find the Bridegroom nigh.

5 Shout in the midst of us, O King
    Of saints, and let our joys abound ;
Let us rejoice, give thanks, and sing,
    And triumph in redemption found :
We ask for every waiting soul ;
O let our glorious joy be full !

6 O may we all triumphant rise !
    With joy upon our heads return,
And, far above these nether skies
    By Thee on eagles' wings upborne,
Through all yon radiant circles move,
And gain the highest heaven of love !

LORD, WHAT IS MAN ?

1 FATHER of uncreated light,
    Fountain of life, and Source of power,
We tremble at Thy glory's height,
    And, lost in silent praise, adore.

2 Truly Thou art a secret God,
    That hid'st Thee in the deepest shade :
Thy inaccessible abode
    Thou hast in cloud and darkness made.

3 Darkness and clouds surround Thy throne,
    And veil the brightness of Thy face ;
Still we revere a God unknown,
    A bottomless abyss of grace.

4 Who, who can all Thy counsel see,
    Thine uttermost perfection prove,
  Fathom the depths of Deity,
    The mystery of redeeming love!

5 Yet hast Thou in the Gospel glass
    The beamings of Thy glory shown;
  Before us made Thy goodness pass,
    And strongly stamp'd it on Thy Son.

6 Thy judgments all our thoughts transcend.
    Thy love is written on our heart.
  Thy love in part we comprehend.
    Love, only love, we know Thou art.

7 Angels, behold the bleeding Lamb.
    Your God for guilty sinners slain.
  Confess the power of Jesu's name ;
    Angels, bow down. and worship Man.

8 See where enthroned in Christ we sit,
    We, who the ransom'd nature share !
  Hell, earth, and heaven to man submit.
    To me; for I in Christ am there !

9 Amazing height of Jesu's love !
    Lord, what is man's distinguish'd race,
  Exalted in Thy flesh above,
    The angels that behold Thy face !

10 O when shall all Thy members rise,
     To perfect life in Thee restored.
   Caught up to meet Thee in the skies
     And be for ever with the Lord !

11 Who now our scanty offerings bring,
    And praise Thee with a stammering tongue,
We soon triumphantly shall sing
    The new, the everlasting song.

12 Come, Lord, we groan to see Thy day!
    Come, Son of Man, with glory crown'd!
The banner of Thy cross display;
    Descend, and bid the trumpet sound!

LUKE XII. 50.

*" I have a baptism to be baptized with ; and how
am I straitened till it be accomplished !"*

1 An inward baptism, Lord, of fire,
    Wherewith to be baptized, I have ;
"Tis all my longing soul's desire;
    This, only this, my soul can save.

2 Straiten'd I am till this be done :
    Kindle in me the living flame,
Father, in me reveal Thy Son,
    Baptize me into Jesu's name.

3 Transform my nature into Thine,
    Let all my powers Thine impress feel,
Let all my soul become Divine,
    And stamp me with Thy Spirit's seal.

4 Deferr'd my hope, and sick my heart,
    O when shall I Thy promise prove,
Set to my seal that true Thou art,
    Thy nature, and Thy name is Love !

5 Love, mighty Love, my heart o'erpower ;
    Ah ! why dost Thou so long delay ?
  Cut short the work, bring near the hour,
    And let me see Thy perfect day.

6 Behold, for Thee I ever wait,
    Now let in me Thine image shine ;
  Now the new heavens and earth create,
    And plant with righteousness Divine.

7 If with the wretched sons of men
    It still be Thy delight to live,
  Come, Lord, beget my soul again,
    Thyself, Thy quickening Spirit give.

8 With me He dwells, and bids Thee come :
    Answer Thine own effectual prayer,
  Enter my heart, and fix Thine home,
    Thine everlasting presence there.

THE GOOD FIGHT.

[1 *Timothy* vi. 12.]

1 OMNIPOTENT LORD, My Saviour and King,
  Thy succour afford, Thy righteousness bring ;
  Thy promises bind Thee Compassion to have :
  Now, now let me find Thee Almighty to save.

2 Rejoicing in hope, And patient in grief,
  To Thee I look up For certain relief;
  I fear no denial, No danger I fear,
  Nor start from the trial, While Jesus is near.

3 I every hour In jeopardy stand ;
   But Thou art my power, And holdest my hand ;
   While yet I am calling Thy succour I feel,
   It saves me from falling, Or plucks me from hell.

4 O who can explain This struggle for life,
   This travail and pain, This trembling and strife ?
   Plague, earthquake, and famine, And tumult, and war
   The wonderful coming Of Jesus declare.

5 For every fight Is dreadful and loud,
   The warrior's delight Is slaughter and blood.
   His foes overturning Till all shall expire ;
   But this is with burning, And fuel of fire.

6 Yet God is above Men, devils, and sin ;
   My Jesus's love The battle shall win ;
   So terribly glorious His coming shall be,
   His love all-victorious Shall conquer for me.

7 He all shall break through ; His truth and His grace
   Shall bring me into The plentiful place :
   Through much tribulation, Through water and fire,
   Through floods of temptation And flames of desire.

8 On Jesus, my power, Till then I rely,
   All evil before His presence shall fly :
   When I have my Saviour, My sin shall depart,
   And Jesus for ever Shall reign in my heart.

HABAKKUK III. 17, 18, 19.

1 Away, my unbelieving fear !
   Fear shall in me no more have place :
   My Saviour doth not yet appear,
   He hides the brightness of His face ;

But shall I therefore let Him go,
  And basely to the tempter yield?
No, in the strength of Jesus, no!
  I never will give up my shield.

2 Although the vine its fruit deny,
   Although the olive yield no oil,
 The withering fig-tree droop and die.
    The field elude the tiller's toil,
 The empty stall no herd afford,
    And perish all the bleating race;
 Yet will I triumph in the Lord,
    The God of my salvation praise.

3 Barren although my soul remain,
   And no one bud of grace *appear*,
 No fruit of all my toil and pain,
    But sin and only sin is here;
 Although, my gifts and comforts lost,
    My blooming hopes cut off I see,
 Yet will I in my Saviour trust,
    And glory that He died for me.

4 In hope, believing against hope,
   Jesus my Lord and God I claim;
 Jesus my Strength shall lift me up,
    Salvation is in Jesu's name:
 To me He soon shall bring it nigh;
    My soul shall then outstrip the wind.
 On wings of love mount up on high,
    And leave the world and sin behind.

———————

AFTER A RELAPSE INTO SIN.

1 God of my salvation, hear,
    And help me to believe ;
Simply do I now draw near,
    Thy blessing to receive :
Full of guilt, alas ! I am,
But to Thy wounds for refuge flee ;
    Friend of sinners, spotless Lamb,
        Thy blood was shed for me.

2 Standing now as newly slain,
    To Thee I lift mine eye ;
Balm of all my grief and pain,
    Thy blood is always nigh :
Now as yesterday the same
Thou art, and wilt for ever be:
    Friend of sinners, &c.

3 Full of truth and grace Thou art.
    And here is all my hope :
False and foul as hell, my heart
    To Thee I offer up ;
Thou wast given to redeem
My soul from all iniquity :
    Friend of sinners, &c.

4 Nothing have I, Lord, to pay,
    Nor can Thy grace procure ;
Empty send me not away,
    For I, Thou know'st, am poor :
Dust and ashes is my name,
My all is sin and misery :
    Friend of sinners, &c.

5 Without money, without price,
    I come Thy love to buy;
  From myself I turn my eyes,
    The chief of sinners, I :
  Take, O take me as I am,
 And let me lose myself in Thee :
    Friend of sinners, &c.

6 No good work, or word, or thought
    Bring I to gain Thy grace ;
  Pardon I accept unbought,
    Thy proffer I embrace,
  Coming as at first I came
 To take, and not bestow on Thee :
    Friend of sinners, &c.

7 Jesu, unto Thee my sin
    I quietly confess,
  Till Thy blood shall wash me clean
    From all unrighteousness,
  From the slightest touch of blame
 My spirit, soul, and body free :
    Friend of sinners, &c.

8 Saviour, from Thy wounded side
    I never will depart ;
  Here will I my spirit hide
    When I am pure in heart :
  Till my place above I claim,
 This only shall be all my plea,—
    Friend of sinners, spotless Lamb,
     Thy blood was shed for me.

ANOTHER.

1 Long have I labour'd in the fire,
 And spent my life for nought;
With pride, and anger, and desire,
 In nature's strength I fought.

2 Baffled, I still my foes defied,
 And rose with courage new;
All which the Lord commands, I cried,
 I now resolve to do.

3 But O, how soon from glory driven
 Down to profoundest hell!
As Lucifer cast down from heaven,
 From all my hopes I fell.

4 I fell, and sunk in self-despair
 I gave up all at last;
On Jesus then I cast my care,
 On Him my anchor cast.

5 With sin I strove, alas! too long;
 But now I to the Lamb
Look, and am saved; in weakness strong,
 While arm'd with Jesu's name.

6 Jesu, to Thee I now can fly,
 On whom my help is laid;
Oppress'd by sins, I lift mine eye,
 And see the shadows fade.

7 Soon as I find myself forsook,
 The grace again is given;
A sigh will reach Thy heart, a look
 Will bring Thee down from heaven.

8 Believing on my Lord, I find
   A sure and present aid;
 On Thee alone my constant mind
   Is every moment stayed.

9 Whate'er in me seems wise, or good,
   Or strong, I here disclaim ;
 I wash my garments in the blood
   Of the atoning Lamb.

10 Jesus, my Strength, my Life, my Rest.
    On Thee will I depend,
 Till summon'd to the marriage-feast,
    Where faith in sight shall end.

IN DOUBT.

1 My Father, O my Father, hear
   Thy weakest child's imperfect call !
 Now as a servant I appear,
   And yet Thou know'st me heir of all :
 O make me know as I am known ;
 Speak, Father; am I not Thy son ?

2 Allured by unresisted grace,
   Thy footsteps why did I pursue ?
 Why did I ever seek Thy face ?
   What secret power my spirit drew
 After I knew not whom to run ?
 Speak, Father ; am I not Thy son ?

3 From whom have all my blessings flow'd ?
   Who gave me these enlarged desires ?
 Who made me restless after God,
   And burnt me up with inward fires ?

O let the Author now be shown,
Speak, Father; am I not Thy Son?

4 Who held my fleeting soul in life,
    And turn'd aside the fatal hour?
Who, when I oft gave o'er the strife,
    Preserved me from the adverse power,
Removed the death I would not shun?
Speak, Father; am I not Thy son?

5 When twice ten thousand times I fell,
    Who was it raised the sinner up,
The sinner sinking into hell?
    How came I by this spark of hope?
Who quicken'd me, a lifeless stone?
Speak, Father; am I not Thy son?

6 If Thou didst see me in my blood,
    And bid the dying sinner live,
If freely I am counted good,
    O let me all Thy life receive,
O do not leave Thy work undone:
Speak, Father; am I not Thy son?

7 Led through the howling wilderness,
    If now I view the promised land,
Here let my weary wanderings cease;
    Divide the waves with Thy right hand.
Bid me through *Jordan's* stream go on:
Speak, Father; am I not Thy son?

8 Or if in my forlorn estate
    Thy will appoints me to remain,
Behold me still content to wait
    In doubt and fear, in grief and pain;

Only, when all my hope is gone,
Speak, Father; am I not Thy son?

9 Alas! I know not how to pray,
   But all my wants are known to Thee;
Father, instruct me what to say,
   Or intercede Thyself for me:
Then hearken to Thy Spirit's groan:
Speak, Father; am I not Thy son?

10 If now the bowels of Thy love
   Yearn over such a worm as me,
Send down Thy Spirit from above,
   And make me clean, and set me free;
The promised Comforter send down:
Speak, Father; am I not Thy son?

11 If now Thou knockest at my heart,
   Now open to Thyself the door;
The gift unspeakable impart,
   The kingdom to my soul restore;
Call home, call home Thy banish'd one:
Speak, Father; am I not Thy son?

12 Hast Thou not made me willing, Lord?
   Do I not now my sins confess?
Be just and faithful to Thy word,
   Cleanse me from all unrighteousness;
Finish the work Thou hast begun:
Speak, Father; am I not Thy son?

13 Hath not my Saviour died to make
   The child of wrath a child of God?
Hast Thou not pardon'd for His sake
   The soul for which He shed His blood?

And died He not for *me* to' atone ?
Speak, Father ; am I not Thy son ?

14 I cannot rest, till pure within :
    Though He hath wash'd away my stains.
Removed the guilt and power of sin.
    Yet while the carnal mind remains
I still must make my ceaseless moan :
Speak, Father ; am I not Thy son ?

15 Or if my endless groans and sighs
    Thy kind compassion cannot move.
Be deaf to all *my* prayers and cries,
    But hear my Advocate above,
Hear Him who pleads before Thy throne,—
" Speak, Father ; is he not Thy son ?"

ISAIAH XXXII. 2.

" And a man shall be as an hiding-place from the wind.
*   and a covert from the tempest : as rivers of water*
*   in a dry place, as the shadow of a great rock in a*
*   weary land."*

1   To the haven of Thy breast,
       O Son of Man, I fly :
    Be my refuge and my rest ;
       For O, the storm is high !
    Save me from the furious blast.
A covert from the tempest be :
    Hide me, Jesu, till o'erpast
       The storm of sin I see.

2   Welcome as the water-spring
       To a dry, barren place,
     O descend on me, and bring
       Thy sweet refreshing grace;
     O'er a parch'd and weary land
   As a great rock extends its shade,
       Hide me, Saviour, with Thy hand,
         And screen my naked head.

3   In the time of my distress
       Thou hast my succour been,
     In my utter helplessness
       Restraining me from sin ;
     O how swiftly didst Thou move
   To save me in the trying hour !
       Still protect me with Thy love,
         And shield me with Thy power.

4   First and Last, in me perform
       The work Thou hast begun,
     Be my shelter from the storm,
       My shadow from the sun ;
     Sprinkle still the mercy-seat,
   And bring Thy Father's anger down :
       Screen me, Jesu, from the heat
         And terror of His frown.

5   Let Thy merit as a cloud
       Still interpose between ;
     Plead the' atonement of Thy blood
       Till I am cleansed from sin :
     Weary, parch'd with thirst, and faint,
   Till Thou the' abiding Spirit breathe,
       Every moment, Lord, I want
         The merit of Thy death.

6 Never shall I want it less
　　When Thou the gift hast given,
Fill'd me with Thy righteousness,
　　And seal'd the heir of heaven;
I shall hang upon my God,
Till I Thy perfect glory see,
　　Till the sprinkling of Thy blood
　　Shall speak me up to Thee.

A POOR SINNER.

1　　Jesu, my Strength, my Hope,
　　On Thee I cast my care;
With humble confidence look up,
　　And know Thou hear'st my prayer.

　　Give me on Thee to wait
　　Till I can all things do,
On Thee, almighty to create,
　　Almighty to renew.

2　　I rest upon Thy word,
　　The promise is for me;
My succour and salvation, Lord,
　　Shall surely come from Thee.

　　But let me still abide,
　　Nor from my Hope remove,
Till Thou my patient spirit guide
　　Into Thy perfect love.

3　　I want a sober mind,
　　A self-renouncing will,
That tramples down and casts behind
　　The baits of pleasing ill;

A soul inured to pain,
To hardship, grief, and loss;
Bold to take up, firm to sustain,
The consecrated cross.

4   I want a godly fear,
A quick-discerning eye,
That looks to Thee when sin is near,
And sees the tempter fly;
A spirit still prepared,
And arm'd with jealous care,
For ever standing on its guard,
And watching unto prayer.

5   I want an heart to pray,
To pray and never cease;
Never to murmur at Thy stay,
Or wish my sufferings less.
This blessing above all,
Always to pray, I want,
Out of the deep on Thee to call,
And never, never faint.

6   I want a true regard,
A single steady aim
(Unmoved by threatening or reward)
To Thee and Thy great name;
A jealous, just concern
For Thine immortal praise;
A pure desire that all may learn
And glorify Thy grace.

7   I want with all my heart
Thy pleasure to fulfil,
To know myself, and what Thou art,
And what Thy perfect will.

I want I know not what,
I want my wants to see,
I want,—alas! what want I not.
When Thou art not in me!

A PRAYER FOR HUMILITY.

1 O my Father and my God,
    Look upon Thine helpless child !
Thou hast laid aside Thy rod,
    Thou in Christ art reconciled :
Hear me then, my Father, hear,
    Good and gracious as Thou art.
Fill me with an holy fear,
    Give me, Lord, an humble heart.

2 O ! 'tis all I want below,
    Jesus and myself to feel ;
Only sin and grace to know,
    All the good and all the ill.
Show me, Father, what I am ;
    Show me what in Christ Thou art.
All my glory, all my shame ;
    Give me, Lord, an humble heart.

3 Listen to my ceaseless cries ;
    Mean and little may I be,
Base and vile in my own eyes,
    Grieved at my own misery.
Show, and then my sickness cure ;
    Make me know as I am known,
Wound my spirit, make me poor,
    Break, O break this heart of stone.

4 Dust and ashes is my name;
     Sinful dust and ashes, I
  Back return from whence I came,
     Earth to earth I sink, and die.
  Abject I, yet haughty too,
     Nothing of my own possess,
  Nothing of myself can do,
     Proud of sin and proud of grace.

5 O the curse, the plague I feel,
     By the demon Pride pursued!
  Proud to see I merit hell,
     Proud I am that God is good,
  Proud that Thou my works hast wrought.
     Proud that I was justified,
  Proud in every word and thought:
     All my fallen soul is pride.

6 My own glory still I seek,
     Still I covet human praise,
  Still in all I do, or speak,
     Thee I wrong, and rob Thy grace:
  Nature will usurp a share,
     Fondly of Thy graces boast,
  Needlessly Thy gifts declare,
     Needlessly declared and lost.

7 And must that which is so good
     Evil prove to helpless me?
  Poison shall I draw from food,
     Sin from grace, and pride from Thee?
  O forbid it, humble love;
     Hide me, O my Father, hide:
  Far away this snare remove,
     Save me from the demon Pride.

8 Wean my soul, and keep it low;
  Do not with Thy gifts destroy;
Lowliness of heart bestow,
  Give me this, or take my joy
If with me Thou wilt not stay,
  Let my comfort all depart;
Take my joy and peace away,
  Leave me but an humble heart.

9 Father, hear; to Thee I cry,
  Thee in Jesu's name conjure,
With my one request comply,
  Make me humble, make me poor:
This of all Thy gifts impart:
  When I am of this possest,
When Thou giv'st an humble heart,
  If Thou canst, withhold the rest.

A THANKSGIVING.

1 LORD, and am I yet alive,
  Not in torments, not in hell!
Still doth Thy good Spirit strive,
  With the chief of sinners dwell!
Yes; I still lift up my eyes,
  Will not of Thy love despair,
Still in spite of sin I rise,
  Still to call Thee mine I dare.

2 O the length and breadth of love!
  Jesu, Saviour, can it be?
All Thy mercy's height I prove,
  All its depth is seen in me!

O the miracle of grace !
  Tell it out to sinners, tell ;
Fiends, and men, and angels, gaze.
  I am, I am out of hell !

3 Turn aside, a sight to' admire,
  I the living wonder am !
See a bush that burns with fire,
  Unconsumed amidst the flame !
See a stone that hangs in air !
  See a spark in oceans dwell !
Kept alive, with death so near,
  I am, I am out of hell !

FOR THE SPIRIT OF PRAYER.

1 FATHER, in the mighty name
    Of Thy well-beloved Son,
One of all Thy gifts I claim,
    All my wants I speak in one ;
Let me for the promise stay,
Only give me power to pray.

2 Sensible delights on me,
    Peace or joy, if Thou bestow.
Thankful I receive from Thee ;
    Or let all my comforts go.
Take Thine other gifts away.
Only give me power to pray.

3 See Thy poor afflicted child.
    Patient and resign'd in pain ;
Let me wander o'er the wild.
    Never more will I complain :

Here for ever let me stay,
Only give me power to pray.

4 Let the pangs that fill my breast
　　Fully all to Thee be known,
Griefs that cannot be exprest
　　Let me tell Thee in a groan ;
Haste to help me, or delay,
Only give me power to pray.

5 Grant me comfort, or deny ;
　　Visit, or from me depart :
Only let Thy Spirit cry,
　　Abba, Father, in my heart ;
Abba, Father, would I say,
Only give me power to pray.

SUBMISSION.

1 WHEN, my Saviour, shall I be
Perfectly resign'd to Thee !
Poor and vile in my own eyes,
Only in Thy wisdom wise ;—
Only Thee content to know,
Ignorant of all below,
Only guided by Thy light,
Only mighty in Thy might.

2 Take my nature's strength away,
Every comfort, every stay,
Every hindrance of Thy love,
All *my* power to act or move ;

Fain I would be truly *still*,
Fain I would be without will,
Simple, innocent, and free,
Free from all that is not Thee.

3 Weaken, bring me down to nought.
Captivate my every thought;
Take the future from my view,
All Thy love intends to do ;
Let me to Thy goodness leave
When and what Thou art to give:
All Thy works to Thee are known,
Let Thy blessed will be done.

4 Is it not enough that I
Now can "Abba, Father," cry ?
I am now a child of God,
Bought and sprinkled with Thy blood
Lord, it doth not yet appear
What I surely shall be here,
When Thou shalt unfold the word :
Only make me as my Lord.

5 So I may Thy Spirit know,
Let Him as He listeth blow :
Let the manner be unknown.
So I may with Thee be one,
Fully in my life express
All the heights of holiness,
Sweetly in my spirit prove
All the depths of humble love.

FOR A SICK FRIEND.

1 SEE, gracious Lord, with pitying eyes,
Beneath Thy hand a sufferer lies,
Thy mercy not Thine anger proves ;
And sick he is whom Jesus loves.

2 His to Thine own afflictions join,
Accept, exalt, and count them Thine ;
Thy passion which remains fulfil,
And suffer in Thy members still.

3 His sickness feel, endure his pain,
His burden bear, his cross sustain ;
Grieve in his griefs, and sigh his sighs.
And breathe his wishes to the skies.

4 Enter his heart, possess him whole,
Inspire and actuate his soul ;
Himself no longer let it be
That suffers, or that lives—but Thee.

5 Thyself, through sufferings perfect made.
Conform him thus to Thee his Head :
Refine, and raise his virtue higher,
When tried, and purified by fire.

6 So when his eyes behold Thee near,
And Thou, his hidden life, appear,
Bright in Thy likeness shall he shine.
And glorious all, and all Divine.*

----

* In the first edition there follows a paraphrase of part of
Psalm ciii., which will be inserted in its place among the Psalms.

AFTER A RECOVERY FROM SICKNESS.

Isaiah xxxviii. 17, 18, &c.

1 GLORY to God, whose gracious power
      Is in His creature's weakness show'd,
   Who turns aside the mortal hour,
      And bids me live to praise my God !

2 To praise my God I only live ;
      To Him my residue of days,
   His own continued gift, I give ;
      I only live my God to praise.

3 In love and pity to my soul,
      Thou, Lord, hast snatch'd me from the grave,
   Thy powerful touch hath made me whole :
      O, who can as my Saviour save ?

4 Jesu, the Saviour of mankind,
      How shall I magnify Thy grace,
   Which cast my every sin behind,
      And brought me to Thy Father's face !

5 Here I rejoice to bless Thy name,
      Thy goodness here I live to see :
   The grave cannot Thy praise proclaim,
      The dead can call no souls to Thee.

6 The living, he shall praise Thy love ;
      The living, he Thy truth shall own,
   As I this day delight to prove,
      And make Thy faithful mercies known.

7 Let future times Thy name confess,
      In which I sure salvation have,
   And learn from me their God to bless,
      So ready and so strong to save.

8 The Lord hath saved my soul from death ;
   Then let us sing my grateful songs,
And render with our latest breath
   The praise that to my Lord belongs.

RECEIVING A CHRISTIAN FRIEND.

1 WELCOME friend, in that great name
   Whence our every blessing flows,
Enter, and increase the flame
   Which in all our bosoms glows.

2 Sent of God, we thee receive :
   Hail the providential guest !
If in Jesus we believe,
   Let us on His mercies feast.

3 Jesus is our common Lord,
   He our loving Saviour is ;
By His death to life restored,
   Misery we exchange for bliss :

4 Bliss to carnal minds unknown,
   O 'tis more than tongue can tell,
Only to believers known,
   Glorious and unspeakable !

5 Christ, our Brother and our Friend,
   Shows us His eternal love ;
Never let our triumphs end,
   Till we join the host above.

6 Let us walk with Christ in white,
   For our bridal day prepare,
For our partnership in light,
   For our glorious meeting there!

THE SALUTATION.

1 PEACE be on this house bestow'd,
   Peace on all that here reside!
Let the unknown peace of God
   With the man of peace abide!
Let the Spirit now come down,
   Let the blessing now take place;
Son of peace, receive thy crown,
   Fulness of the Gospel grace.

2 Christ, my Master and my Lord,
   Let me Thy forerunner be;
O be mindful of Thy word,
   Visit them, and visit me:
To this house, and all herein,
   Now let Thy salvation come;
Save our souls from inbred sin,
   Make them Thine eternal home.

3 Let us never, never rest
   Till the promise is fulfill'd,
Till we are of Thee possest,
   Wash'd, and sanctified, and seal'd:
Till we all, in love renew'd,
   Find the pearl that *Adam* lost,
Temples of the living God,
   Father, Son, and Holy Ghost.

AT THE MEETING OF CHRISTIAN FRIENDS.

1 GLORY be to God above,
    God, from whom all blessings flow :
Make we mention of His love,
    Publish we His praise below ;
Call'd together by His grace,
    We are met in Jesu's name,
See with joy each other's face,
    Followers of the bleeding Lamb.

2 Let us then sweet counsel take
    How to make our calling sure,
Our election how to make
    Past the reach of hell secure ;
Build we each the other up,
    Pray we for our faith's increase.
Lasting comfort, steadfast hope,
    Solid joy, and settled peace.

3 More and more let love abound :
    Never, never may we rest,
Till we are in Jesus found,
    Of our paradise possest.
He removes the flaming sword.
    Calls us back. from *Eden* driven :
To His image here restored,
    Soon He takes us up to heaven.

4 Jesu, Lord, for this we wait,
    Till Thine image we regain :
Wilt Thou not our souls create?
    Saviour, shall our faith be vain ?

If we do in Thee believe,
  Now the second gift impart,
Now the' abiding witness give,
  Give us now the perfect heart.

5 Surely He will not delay
  If we patiently endure,
Will not empty send away
  Sinners hungry, mournful, poor.
Jesus wept, and still doth weep,
  Human misery to behold,
Pities now His wandering sheep,
  Longs to bring us to His fold.

6 "Children, have you aught to eat?"
  (Kindly asks our careful God;)
Jesu's flesh indeed is meat,
  Drink indeed is Jesu's blood:
Drink and eat, my well-beloved;
  Lean, He cries, upon my breast.
Till ye all, from earth removed,
  Share with Me the marriage-feast.

AT PARTING.

1 BLEST be the dear, uniting love,
  That will not let us part;
Our bodies may far off remove,
  We still are join'd in heart.

2 Join'd in one Spirit to our Head,
  Where He appoints we go,
And still in Jesu's footsteps tread,
  And do His work below.

3 O let us ever walk in Him,
    And nothing know beside,
Nothing desire, nothing esteem,
    But Jesus crucified.

4 Closer and closer let us cleave
    To His beloved embrace;
Expect His fulness to receive,
    And grace to answer grace.

5 While thus we walk with Christ in light.
    Who shall our souls disjoin?
Souls, which Himself vouchsafes to' unite
    In fellowship Divine !

6 We all are one who Him receive,
    And each with each agree;
In Him the One, the Truth, we live,
    Blest point of unity !

7 Partakers of the Saviour's grace,
    The same in mind and heart,
Nor joy, nor grief, nor time, nor place,
    Nor life, nor death can part:

8 But let us hasten to the day
    Which shall our flesh restore,
When death shall all be done away,
    And bodies part no more.

THE COMMENDATION.

1 Let the world lament and grieve
    At parting with a friend ;
Thee we back to Jesus give,
    We cheerfully commend

Thee to His preserving grace:
  Go, in full assurance go!
Heavenward set thy steadfast face,
  And only Jesus know.

2 Jesus, and Him crucified,
  For ever bear in mind;
Shelter in His bleeding side
  Be confident to find;
Let His truth and faithfulness
  Still thy shield and buckler prove.
Keep thy soul in perfect peace
  And everlasting love.

3 Love the dear atoning Lamb,
  And us for Jesu's sake;
Let us each, in Jesu's name,
  Of others mention make;
Present through the Spirit's prayer.
  Absent when in flesh thou art;
To the throne of grace we bear,
  We bear thee on our heart.

4 To the Source of all our good
  Thy soul we now commend;
Jesu, sprinkle with Thy blood.
  And love him to the end:
Faithfully on Thee we call,
  Perfect him and us in one:
With us, by us, in us all
  Thy only will be done.

THOUGH ABSENT IN BODY, YET PRESENT IN SPIRIT.

1 CHRIST, our Head, and common Lord,
　　See the souls that wait on Thee;
Hear us all with one accord
　　Sweetly in Thy praise agree:
Parted though in flesh we are,
　　Join'd to Thee, our Corner-stone,
We are intimately near,
　　Present, and in spirit one.

2 Let us now to Thee aspire,
　　Who Thy life begin to know;
Let the circulating fire
　　Now in every bosom glow:
Let the incense of our vows
　　From Thy golden censer rise,
Fragrant through the higher house,
　　Well-accepted sacrifice.

3 Come, ye absent souls who love
　　Jesus with a simple heart;
Seek with us the things above,
　　Never from the work depart:
Never let us cease to sing
　　The great riches of His grace,
Till we all behold our King
　　Eye to eye, and face to face.

4 Quickly we shall all appear
　　At the judgment-seat above;
We shall see our Jesus near,
　　Him whom now unseen we love:

We, His dear, peculiar ones,
  Sharers of our Master's bliss,
We shall sit upon our thrones,
  We shall see Him as He is.

5 Partners of this heavenly hope,
   Travel on and meet us there;
We shall surely be caught up,
   Meet the Saviour in the air:
Yes; eternity 's at hand,
   We shall soon be taken home,
With the Lamb on *Sion* stand—
   Come, Desire of nations, come!

ENTERING INTO THE CONGREGATION.

1 FOUNTAIN of Life, to all below
   Let Thy salvation roll;
Water, replenish, and o'erflow
   Every believing soul.

2 Into that happy number, Lord,
   Us weary sinners take;
Jesu, fulfil Thy gracious word
   For Thy own mercy's sake.

3 Turn back our nature's rapid tide,
   And we shall flow to Thee,
While down the stream of time we glide
   To our eternity.

4 The Well of life to us Thou art,
   Of joy the swelling flood;
Wafted by Thee, with willing heart
   We swift return to God.

5 We soon shall reach the boundless sea.
  Into Thy fulness fall,
Be lost and swallow'd up in Thee.
  Our God, our all in all.

ANOTHER.

1 O Thou whom all Thy saints adore.
  We now with all Thy saints agree.
And bow our inmost souls before
  Thy glorious, awful Majesty.

2 Thee, King of nations, we proclaim:
  Who would not our great Sovereign fear?
We long to' experience all Thy name,
  And now we come to meet Thee here.

3 We come. great God, to seek Thy face.
  And for Thy lovingkindness wait:
And O! how dreadful is this place!
  'Tis God's own house, 'tis heaven's gate.

4 Tremble our hearts to find Thee nigh,
  To Thee our trembling hearts aspire;
And lo! we see descend from high
  The pillar and the flame of fire!

5 Still let it on the' assembly stay,
  And all the house with glory fill;
To *Canaan's* bounds point out our way.
  And bring us to Thy holy hill.

6 There let us all with Jesus stand.
  And join the general church above,
And take our seats at Thy right hand.
  And sing Thine everlasting love.

7 Come, Lord, our souls are on the wing,
  Now on Thy great white throne appear,
And let *my* eyes behold *my* King,
  And let *me* see *my* Saviour there !

HYMN FOR THE DAY OF PENTECOST.

1 REJOICE, rejoice, ye fallen race,
    The day of Pentecost is come :
  Expect the sure descending grace,
    Open your hearts to make Him room.

2 Our Jesus is gone up on high,
    For us the blessing to receive:
  It now comes streaming from the sky:
    The Spirit comes, and sinners live.

3 To every one whom God shall call
    The promise is securely made;
  To you far off, He calls you all;
    Believe the word which Christ hath said.

4 " The Holy Ghost, if I depart,
    The Comforter, shall surely come,
  Shall make the contrite sinner's heart
    His loved, His everlasting home."

5 Lord, we believe to us and ours
    The apostolic promise given:
  We wait to taste the heavenly powers,
    The Holy Ghost sent down from heaven.

6 Ah ! leave us not to mourn below,
    Or long for Thy return to pine:
  Now, Lord, the Comforter bestow,
    And fix in us the Guest Divine.

7 Assembled here with one accord,
    Calmly we wait the promised grace,
The purchase of our dying Lord—
    Come, Holy Ghost, and fill the place !

8 If every one that asks may find,
    If still Thou art to sinners given,
Come as a mighty rushing wind,
    To shake our earth come down from heaven.

9 Behold, to Thee our souls aspire,
    And languish Thy descent to meet;
Kindle in each Thy living fire,
    And fix in every heart Thy seat.

10 Wisdom and strength to Thee belongs ;
    Sweetly within our bosoms move,
Now let us speak with other tongues
    The new strange language of Thy love.

11 Spirit of faith, within us live,
    And strike the crowd with fixed amaze;
Open our mouths, and utterance give
    To publish our Redeemer's praise:

12 To testify the grace of God,
    To-day as yesterday the same,
And spread through all the earth abroad
    The wonders wrought by Jesu's name.

ANOTHER.

1 FATHER of our dying Lord,
    Remember us for good,
O fulfil His faithful word,
    And hear His speaking blood;

Give us that for which He prays,
　　Father, glorify Thy Son ;
Show His truth, and power, and grace,
　　And send THE PROMISE down.

2 True and faithful Witness Thou,
　　O Christ, Thy Spirit give:
Hast Thou not received Him now,
　　That we might now receive?
Art Thou not our living Head?
　　Life to all Thy limbs impart,
Shed Thy love, Thy Spirit shed,
　　In every waiting heart.

3 Holy Ghost, the Comforter,
　　The gift of Jesus, come :
Glows our heart to find Thee near,
　　And swells to make Thee room:
Present *with* us Thee we feel ;
　　Come, O come, and *in* us be,
With us, in us live and dwell
　　To all eternity.

ANOTHER.

1　　SINNERS, your hearts lift up,
　　　Partakers of your hope !
This the day of Pentecost,
　　Ask, and ye shall all receive;
Surely now the Holy Ghost
　　God to all that ask shall give.

2　　　Ye all may freely take
　　　The grace for Jesu's sake;

He for every man hath died,
    He for all hath rose again;
Jesus now is glorified,
    Gifts He hath received for men.

3   He sends them from the skies
    On all His enemies;
By His cross He now hath led
    Captive our captivity:
We shall all be free indeed,
    Christ the Son shall make us free.

4   Blessings on all He pours
    In never-ceasing showers;
All He waters from above,
    Offers all His joy and peace,
Settled comfort, perfect love,
    Everlasting righteousness.

5   All may from Him receive
    A power to turn and live;
Grace for every soul is free,
    All may hear the' effectual call,
All the light of life may see,
    All may feel He died for all.

6   Drop down in showers of love,
    Ye heavens, from above;
Righteousness, ye skies, pour down;
    Open, earth, and take it in;
Claim the Spirit for your own,
    Sinners, and be saved from sin.

7   Father, behold we claim
    The gift in Jesu's name!

Him, the promised Comforter,
  Into all our spirits pour:
Let Him fix His mansion here,
  Come, and never leave us more.

A THANKSGIVING.

1 O GOD of my salvation hear,
  And help a sinner to draw near
    With boldness to the throne of grace:
  Help me Thy benefits to sing,
  And smile to see me feebly bring
    My humble sacrifice of praise.

2 I cannot praise Thee as I would;
  But Thou art merciful and good,
    I know Thou never wilt despise
  The day of small and feeble things,
  But bear me till on eagle's wings
    To all the heights of love I rise.

3 I thank Thee for that gracious taste,
  (Which pride would not permit to last,)
    That touch of love, that pledge of heaven.
  Surely on me my Father smiled,
  And once I knew Him reconciled,
    And once I felt my sins forgiven.

4 My Lord and God I then could see,
  My Saviour who had died for me,
    To bring the rebel near to God:
  Thou didst, Thou *didst*, Thy peace impart,
  Pardon was written on my heart
    In largest characters of blood.

5 When I had forfeited my peace,
My manners in the wilderness,
    Infinite Love, how didst Thou bear !
Thou wouldst not give the sinner up,
My heart retain'd a feeble hope,
    And could not, durst not, yet despair.

6 Assail'd with doubt, and fear, and grief,
I stagger'd oft through unbelief ;
    Yet still Thou wouldst not let me yield :
When stronger souls their Lord denied,
And fell in heaps on every side,
    I never cast away my shield.

7 Vilest of all the sons of men,
When I to folly turn'd again,
    And sinn'd against Thy light and love,
Grace did much more than sin abound,
Amazed I still forgiveness found,
    And thank'd my Advocate above.

8 Saviour, for this I thank Thee now ;
My Saviour to the utmost, Thou
    Hast snatch'd me from the gates of hell,
That I to all mankind may prove
Thy free, Thine everlasting love,
    Which all mankind with me may feel.

9 The boundless love that found out me
For every soul of man is free,
    None of Thy mercy need despair ;
Patient, and pitiful, and kind,
Thee every soul of man may find,
    And freely saved Thy grace declare.

10 A vile, backsliding sinner, I
  Ten thousand deaths deserve to die,
    Yet still by sovereign grace I live;
  Saviour, to Thee I still look up,
  I see an open door of hope,
    And wait Thy fulness to receive.

11 How shall I thank Thee for the grace,
  The trust I have to see Thy face
    When sin shall all be purged away!
  The night of doubts and fears is past,
  The Morning Star appears at last,
    And I shall see Thy perfect day.

12 I soon shall hear Thy quickening voice,
  Shall always pray, give thanks, rejoice;
    (This is Thy will and faithful word;)
  My spirit meek, my will resign'd,
  Lowly as Thine shall be my mind,
    The servant shall be as his Lord.

13 Already, Lord, I feel Thy power,
  Preserved from evil every hour,
    My great Preserver I proclaim:
  Safety and strength in Thee I have,
  I find, I find Thee strong to save,
    And know that Jesus is Thy name.

14 By faith I every moment stand;
  Strangely upheld by Thy right hand,
    I my own wickedness eschew:
  A sinner, I am kept from sin;
  And Thou shalt make me pure within,
    And Thou shalt form my soul anew.

15 I thank Thee, whose atoning blood
     Each moment intercedes with God,
          Sprinkling my every word and thought;
     God hears Thy blood for mercy cry,
     And passes all my follies by;
          He sees, but He imputes them not.

16 I sin in every breath I draw,
     Nor do Thy will, nor keep Thy law
          On earth as angels do above;
     But still the Fountain open stands,
     Washes my feet, and head, and hands,
          Till I am perfected in love.

17 Come then, and loose my stammering tongue,
     Teach me the new, the joyful song,
          And perfect in a babe Thy praise:
     I want a thousand lives to' employ
     In publishing the sounds of joy,
          The gospel of Thy general grace.

18 Come, Lord! Thy Spirit bids Thee come:
     Give me Thyself, and take me home,
          Be now the glorious earnest given;
     The counsel of Thy grace fulfil,
     Thy kingdom come, Thy perfect will
          Be done on earth as 'tis in heaven.

A DIALOGUE OF ANGELS AND MEN.

1 *A.* YE worms of earth, our God admire,
     The God of angels praise:
   M. Praise Him for us, ye heavenly choir,
     His earth-born sons of grace.

2 *A.* His image view in us display'd,
    His nobler creatures view:
  M. Lower than you our souls He made,
    But He redeem'd us too.

3 *A.* As gods we did in glory shine,
    Before your world began :
  M. Our nature too becomes Divine,
    And God Himself is Man.

4 *A.* He clothed us in these robes of light,
    The shadow of His Son:
  M. We, with transcendent glory bright,
    Have Christ Himself put on.

5 *A.* Spirits like Him He made us be,
    A pure ethereal flame:
  M. Join'd to the Lord, one spirit we
    With Jesus are the same.

6 *A.* We see Him on His dazzling throne,
    Crowns He to us imparts:
  M. To us the King of kings comes down,
    And reigns within our hearts.

7 *A.* Pure as He did at first create,
    We angels never fell:
  M. He saves us from our lost estate,
    He rescues man from hell.

8 *A.* When others fell we faithful proved,
    His love preserved us true:
  M. Yet own that we are more beloved,
    He never died for you.

9 *A.* Worms of the earth, to you, we own,
    The nobler grace is given:
  M. Then praise with us the great Three-One,
    Till we all meet in heaven.

ANOTHER.

1 To Father, Son, and Holy Ghost,
    Glory above be given:
  We 'll vie with the celestial host,
    And earth shall rival heaven.

2 Ye angels that in strength excel,
    To God your voices raise;
  In tenements of clay we dwell,
    Yet humbly chant His praise.

3 To Him ye Hallelujah cry,
    Loud as the thunder's noise;
  As many waters we reply,
    And echo back the voice.

4 Ten thousand times ten thousand, sing
    Ye your Creator's name;
  We claim Jehovah for our King,
    And we extol the Lamb.

5 Ye cast your crowns before His throne,
    And dare no longer gaze;
  We, prostrate at His footstool, own
    The wonders of His grace.

6 Thus let us all for ever lie,
    In songs or silence join
  To' adore the Majesty on high,
    The depth of love Divine.*

* In the first edition there follows a paraphrase of Psalm cxxxiii., which will be inserted in its place among the Psalms.

DAVID AND GOLIATH.

[1 *Samuel xvii.*]

1 WHO is this gigantic foe,
 That proudly stalks along;
Overlooks the crowd below,
 In brazen armour strong?
Loudly of his strength he boasts,
 On his sword and spear relies,
Meets the God of *Israel's* hosts,
 And all their force defies.

2 Tallest of the earth-born race,
 They tremble at his power,
Fly before the monster's face,
 And own him conqueror:
Who this mighty champion is
 Nature answers from within,
He is my own wickedness,
 My own besetting sin.

3 In the strength of Jesu's name
 I with the monster fight;
Feeble and unarm'd I am,
 But Jesus is my might:
Mindful of His mercies past,
 Still I trust the same to prove,
Still my helpless soul I cast
 On His redeeming love.

4 From the bear and lion's paws
 He hath deliver'd me;
He shall still maintain my cause,
 And still my Helper be;

God in my defence shall stand,
  Jesus on my side I have,
From the proud *Goliath's* hand
  He now my soul shall save.

5 With my sling and stone I go
    To fight the Philistine;
  God hath said, It shall be so,
    And I shall conquer sin:
  On the promise I rely,
    Trust in an Almighty Lord,
  Sure to win the victory,
    For He hath spoke the word.

6 In the strength of God I rise,
    I run to meet my foe;
  Faith the word of power applies,
    And lays the giant low;
  Faith in Jesu's conquering name
    Slings the sin-destroying stone,
  Points the word's unerring aim,
    And brings the monster down.

7 See the promise-word takes place,
    And smites the giant's head;
  See, he falls upon his face,
    He falls, and sin is dead!
  Now I more than conquer it,
    Trample on *Goliath* slain;
  Slain he lies beneath my feet,
    Never to rise again.

8 Willing now to be made free
    From my own sin I am,
  Saved from all iniquity,
    From every touch of blame:

Thou hast made me willing, Lord,
  Thou alone hast turn'd my heart.
Now I with *Goliath's* sword
  His head and body part.

9 Sin, my strongest sin, is dead,
  Goliath is o'erthrown;
Yes, he now has lost his head,
  The love of sin is gone:
Fallen is their boasted chief,
  Scatter'd are the Philistines.
Scatter'd by a true belief
  Are all my meaner sins.

10 Rise, ye men of *Israel*, rise,
  Your routed foe pursue;
Shout His praises to the skies
  Who conquers sin for you:
Jesus doth for you appear,
  He His conquering grace affords.
Saves you, not with sword and spear.
  The battle is the Lord's.

11 Every day the Lord of Hosts
  His mighty power displays,
Stills the proud Philistine's boasts,
  The threatening *Gittite* slays:
Israel's God let all below
  Conqueror over sin proclaim:
O that all the earth might know
  The power of Jesu's name!

12 Sin hath tyrannized too long
  O'er *Israel's* chosen race,
Dared defy the feeble throng.
  And all their armies chase :

Armies of the living God,
 Basely they to sin did yield;
Sin can never be destroy'd
 Till *David* takes the field.

13 Love alone can match in fight,
 And conquer every foe;
Saul, with all his strength and might,
 Can never sin o'erthrow;
Saul may vex, (the law restrain,)
 David takes the giant's head,
Love will never turn again
 Till every sin is dead.

ROMANS X. 6, &c.

1 OFT I in my heart have said,
 Who shall ascend on high,
Mount to Christ my glorious Head,
 To bring Him from the sky?
Borne on contemplation's wing,
 Surely I should find Him there
Where the angels praise their King,
 And gain the Morning Star.

2 Oft I in my heart have said,
 Who to the deep shall stoop,
Sink with Christ among the dead,
 From thence to bring Him up?
Could I but my heart prepare
 By unfeign'd humility,
Christ would quickly enter there,
 And ever dwell with me.

3 But the righteousness of faith
    Hath taught me better things ;
" Inward turn thine eyes," (it saith,
    While Christ to me it brings,)
" Christ is ready to impart
    Life to all for life who sigh ;
In thy mouth, and in thy heart,
    The word is ever nigh."

4 Jesu, I in Thee believe,
    My faith in Thee confess ;
Gladly do I now receive
    The offers of Thy grace :
Now Thy merits are applied,
    I from all my sins am free ;
I am clear, since Thou hast died
    And rose again for me.

5 Unto righteousness I still
    Believe on Thee, my Lord,
With my heart believe, and feel
    Thee faithful to Thy word ;
Unto full salvation Thee
    With my mouth I still confess,
Till the utmost heights I see
    Of perfect holiness.

6 Wherefore should I longer doubt ?
    I every whit am clean ;
My salvation is wrought out,
    I now am saved from sin.
Author of eternal grace
    Unto all who Thee obey,
I shall see Thee face to face :
    My Jesus, come away !

REJOICING IN HOPE.

[*Romans xii.* 12.]

1 I KNOW that my Redeemer lives,
   And ever prays for me;
 A token of His love He gives,
   A pledge of liberty.

2 I find Him lifting up my head,
   He brings salvation near,
 His presence makes me free indeed.
   And He will soon appear.

3 With confidence I now look up.
   His promised aid implore;
 Sweetly revives my blasted hope,
   And I can doubt no more.

4 Far spent is the Egyptian night
   Of fear, and pain, and grief;
 And lo! I see the morning light
   That brings assured relief.

5 The dreadful, dire, oppressive hour
   Of tyrant sin is past;
 My soul defies its rage and power,
   My soul on Christ is cast.

6 The power of hell, the strength of sin.
   My Jesus shall subdue;
 His healing blood shall wash me clean.
   And make my spirit new.

7 He will perform the work begun :
   Jesus, the sinner's Friend,
 Jesus, the Lover of His own,
   Will love me to the end.

8 No longer am I now afraid;
   The promise must take place,
Perfect His strength in weakness made,
   Sufficient is His grace.

9 Unto salvation kept I am,
   Through faith, by power Divine,
Ready His nature, with His name.
   To be reveal'd in mine.

10 He wills that I should holy be:
   Who can withstand His will?
The counsel of His grace in me
   He surely shall fulfil.

11 Confident now of faith's increase,
   I all its fruits shall prove—
Substantial joy, and settled peace,
   And everlasting love.

12 Yes, Lord, I put my trust in Thee.
   On Thee my soul I stay;
I know that Thou wilt come to me.
   And I shall see Thy day.

13 *With* me, I know. Thy Spirit dwells.
   Nor ever shall depart,
Till *in* me He Himself reveals
   And purifies my heart.

14 He tells me He will quickly come
   And seal me His abode;
He now marks out His future home,
   The temple of my God.

15 Jesu, I hang upon Thy word;
   I steadfastly believe
Thou wilt return, and claim me. Lord.
   And to Thyself receive.

16 Joyful in hope, my spirit soars
　　To meet Thee from above,
　Thy goodness thankfully adores,
　　And sure I taste Thy love.

17 Thy love I soon expect to find
　　In all its depth and height,
　To comprehend the' eternal Mind,
　　And grasp the Infinite.

18 When Thou dost in my heart appear,
　　And love erects its throne,
　I then enjoy salvation here,
　　And heaven on earth begun.

19 When God is mine, and I am His,
　　Of paradise possest,
　I taste unutterable bliss
　　And everlasting rest.

20 The bliss of those that fully dwell,
　　Fully in Thee believe,
　'Tis more than angel tongues can tell,
　　Or angel minds conceive.

21 Thou only know'st, who didst obtain,
　　And die to make it known:
　The great salvation now explain,
　　And perfect us in one.

22 May I, may all who humbly wait,
　　The glorious joy receive;
　Joy above all conception great,
　　Worthy of God to give.

23 Lord, I believe and rest secure
　　In confidence Divine;
　Thy promise stands for ever sure,
　　And all Thou art is mine.

ANOTHER.

1   Ye happy sinners, hear
      The prisoner of the Lord.
  And wait till Christ appear
      According to His word;
Rejoice in hope, rejoice with me.
We shall from all our sins be free.

2   The Lord our Righteousness
      We have long since received,
  Salvation nearer is
      Than when we first believed;
Rejoice in hope, rejoice with me,
We shall from all our sins be free.

3   Let others hug their chains,
      For sin and Satan plead,
  And say from sin's remains
      They never can be freed;
Rejoice in hope, rejoice with me,
We shall from all our sins be free.

4   In God we put our trust:
      If we our sins confess,
  Faithful He is, and just,
      From all unrighteousness
To cleanse us all, both you and me;
We shall from all our sins be free.

5   Surely in us the hope
      Of glory shall appear;
  Sinners, your heads lift up,
      And see redemption near;
Again I say, rejoice with me,
We shall from all our sins be free.

6   Who Jesu's sufferings share,
        My fellow-prisoners now,
    Ye soon the wreath shall wear
        On your triumphant brow;
    Rejoice in hope, rejoice with me,
    We shall from all our sins be free.

7   The word of God is sure,
        And never can remove;
    We shall in heart be pure,
        And perfected in love;
    Rejoice in hope, rejoice with me,
    We shall from all our sins be free.

8   Then let us gladly bring
        Our sacrifice of praise;
    Let us give thanks, and sing,
        And glory in His grace;
    Rejoice in hope, rejoice with me,
    We shall from all our sins be free.

ROMANS VI.

1 Away, vain thoughts that stir within,
      Nor further can proceed!
  How shall I longer live in sin,
      Who unto sin am dead?

2 Baptized into my Saviour's name,
      I of His death partake;
  Buried with Jesus Christ I am,
      And I with Him awake.

3 He burst the barriers of the tomb,
    Rose, and regain'd the skies;
  And lo! from nature's grave I come,
    And lo! with Christ I rise.

4 A new, a living life I live;
    And, fashion'd to His death,
  His resurrection's power receive,
    And by His Spirit breathe.

5 Now the old *Adam* is, I know,
    With Jesus crucified;
  Sin, vanquish'd by its passive foe,
    Kill'd my dear Lord—and died.

6 Its body was destroy'd, when nail'd
    With Jesus to the tree;
  My dying Surety then prevail'd,
    And I was then set free.

7 Dead with my gracious Lord and God,
    With Him by faith I live;
  The power He purchased with His blood
    I over sin receive.

8 Sin shall not have dominion now,
    Or in my body reign;
  Beneath its yoke I scorn to bow,
    And all its force disdain.

9 Under the law no more enslaved,
    No more I groan and grieve;
  By grace I am redeem'd and saved,
    And under grace I live.

10 I live to God, who from the dead
    Hath me to life restored,
  That I, from sin's oppression freed,
    Might only serve my Lord.

11 Jesus I serve, to Him alone
　　My thankful homage pay;
　My only Master, Christ I own,
　　And Him will I obey.

12 To Him my body I present,
　　Which He will not refuse;
　The meanest, basest instrument
　　His glory deigns to use.

13 Servant of sin too long I was,
　　But Christ hath set me free;
　Glory to His victorious grace
　　Which freely ransom'd me.

14 For ever be His name adored
　　For what I have received;
　I have embraced the Gospel word,
　　And with my heart believed.

15 Faith freed me from the iron yoke,
　　The strength of sin subdued,
　From off my soul the fetters broke,
　　And now I serve my God.

16 Jesus can to the utmost save:
　　On Jesus I depend;
　My fruit to holiness I have,
　　And all in heaven shall end.

THE FOURTH CHAPTER OF ISAIAH.

1 Jesu, fulfil the Gospel word,
　　In us, Thou beauteous Branch, arise;
　Arise, Thou Planting of the Lord,
　　Be glorious in Thy people's eyes.

2 O Root Divine, in this our earth
   Spring up, and yield a fair increase,
The graces of our second birth,
   The goodly fruits of righteousness.

3 'Scaped from the world of pride and lust,
   If now we in Thy sight remain,
O make us holy, good, and just,
   O let us not believe in vain.

4 Our names among the living write,
   Whose hearts are fix'd on things above,
Worthy who walk with Thee in white,
   Unblameable in spotless love.

5 Out of our inmost souls expel
   The filth and stain of inbred sin.
(In us it shall not always dwell,
   For Thou hast said, Ye shall be clean.)

6 O that the grace were now applied !
   Bring in, dear Lord, a purer flood ;
Open the fountain of Thy side,
   And purge out all our tainted blood.

7 *Adam* descended from above,
   The virtue of Thy blood impart,
And cleanse from every creature-love,
   And make, O make us pure in heart.

8 The judging, burning Spirit inspire ;
   O let Him to His temple come,
And sit as a refiner's fire,
   And all our sins condemn, consume.

9 Sin shall not in our flesh remain ;
   The sanctifying word is sure,
We shall be purged from every stain,
   And pure as God Himself is pure.

10   Then only can we fall no more,
         Freed from the stumbling-block within;
     Come, Thou Divine, Almighty Power,
         And save us from indwelling sin.

11   Keep us through faith to that Thy day,
         And mark us out for Thine abode;
     Thy glory over us display,
         And guard the future house of God.

12   Till Thou from all our sins shalt cleanse,
         And perfectly renew our heart,
     Thy glory be our sure defence,
         Nor ever from our souls depart.

13   On every dwelling-place of Thine
         Create a cloud and smoke by day;
     And let the fiery pillar shine
         By night, and on the' assembly stay.

14   Through the long night of doubts and fears,
         The day of fierce temptation, guide;
     And let us, till Thy face appears,
         O let us in Thy wounds abide;

15   Secure beneath Thy shadow sit,
         In Thee a tabernacle find,
     A refuge from the rain and heat,
         A covert from the storm and wind.

16   Lead us till all our toil is past,
         Till all Thy faithfulness we prove,
     And gain the promised land at last,
         The *Canaan* of Thy perfect love.

THE TWELFTH CHAPTER OF ISAIAH.

1 Happy soul who sees the day,
    The glad day of Gospel grace !
Thee, my Lord, (Thou then wilt say,)
    Thee will I for ever praise.

2 Though Thy wrath against me burn'd.
    Thou dost comfort me again ;
All Thy wrath aside is turn'd,
    Thou hast blotted out my sin.

3 Me, behold, Thy mercy spares;
    Jesus my salvation is :
Hence my doubts, away my fears,
    Jesus is become my peace.

4 Jah, Jehovah is my Lord,
    Ever merciful and just ;
I will lean upon His word,
    I will on His promise trust.

5 Strong I am, for He is strong.
    Just in righteousness Divine ;
He is my triumphal song.
    All He has, and is, is mine.

6 Mine; and yours, whoe'er believe:
    On His name whoe'er shall call
Freely shall His grace receive :
    He is full of grace for all.

7 Therefore shall ye draw with joy
    Water from salvation's well;
Praise shall your glad tongues employ.
    While His streaming grace ye feel.

8 Each to each ye then shall say,
   Sinners, call upon His name;
O rejoice to see His day,
   See it, and His praise proclaim.

9 Glory to His name belongs,
   Great, and marvellous, and high;
Sing unto the Lord your songs,
   Cry, to every nation cry.

10 Wondrous things the Lord hath done,
   Excellent His name we find;
This to all mankind is known,
   Be it known to all mankind.

11 *Sion*, shout thy Lord and King,
   Israel's Holy One is He!
Give Him thanks, rejoice, and sing :
   Great He is, and dwells in thee.

12 O the grace unsearchable !
   While eternal ages roll,
God delights in man to dwell,
   Soul of each believing soul.

ISAIAH XXVI. 13, 14.

1 O Lord, my God, with shame I own
   That other lords have sway'd,
Have in my heart set up their throne,
   And abject I obey'd.

2 Thy enemies usurp'd the place,
   And robb'd Thee of Thy due;
A slave to every vice I was,
   And only evil knew.

3 With sin I joyfully complied,
    I yielded unconstrain'd;
  Passion, and appetite, and pride,
    And self, and nature reign'd.

4 But ended is the shameful hour.
    The' usurper's reign is past,
  Blasted their strength, o'erturn'd their power.
    And I am saved at last.

5 Thy love, by which redeem'd I am.
    For ever be adored;
  I now shall live to bless Thy name,
    And call my Jesus Lord.

6 Those other lords no more are mine.
    No more their slave am I ;
  I tread them down with strength Divine.
    I all my sins defy.

7 Freed am I now, for ever freed
    From their destructive power;
  Nail'd to the cross, they all are dead.
    And shall revive no more.

8 The glorious presence of my God
    Hath all the tyrants slain ;
  Their name, their memory is destroy'd.
    When I am born again.

AFTER A RECOVERY FROM SICKNESS.

1 Thy will be done, Thy name be blest !
    I am not, gracious Lord, my own ;
  Whate'er Thy wisdom sends is best,
    Thy name be praised, Thy will be done.

2 Earnest of benefits behind,
       Of all Thy bounty waits to give,
   Pledge of a sound and healthful mind,
       My life I at Thy hands receive.

3 Snatch'd from the death of sin, my soul
       Shall never see corruption's grave ;
   Surely Thy love shall make me whole,
       Thy love can to the utmost save.

4 Thy love hath cast out servile fear,
       No longer can I doubt or mourn ;
   To the black dungeon of despair
       I never, never shall return.

5 Sin shall not have dominion now.
       Or in my mortal body reign ;
   Jesus, my Lord, my Saviour Thou,
       Thou hast the lawless tyrant slain.

6 Still, O my God, Thy power display,
       Thy kingdom to my soul restore ;
   Those other lords persist to slay,
       And suffer them to rise no more.

7 If now I have acceptance found
       With Thee, or favour in Thy sight,
   With Thine omnipotence surround,
       And arm me with Thy Spirit's might.

8 O may I hear His warning voice,
       And timely fly from danger near ;
   With reverence unto Thee rejoice,
       And love Thee with a filial fear.

9 Still hold my soul in second life,
       And suffer not my feet to slide ;
   Support me in the glorious strife,
       And comfort me on every side.

10 O give me faith and faith's increase,
    Finish the work begun in me;
Preserve my soul in perfect peace,
    That stays, and waits, and hangs on Thee.

11 O let Thy gracious Spirit guide,
    And bring me to the promised land,
Where righteousness and peace reside,
    And all submit to love's command.

12 A land where milk and honey flow,
    And springs of pure delights arise ;
Delights which I shall shortly know :
    I shall regain my paradise.

13 I see it now from *Pisgah's* top,
    Pleasant, and beautiful, and good ;
In all the confidence of hope,
    I claim the purchase of Thy blood.

14 Of righteousness Divine possest,
    O let me grasp the prize so nigh.
Enter into the promised rest,
    Enjoy Thy perfect love, and die.

[Seven Hymns for Children, which in the first edition follow the above, were transferred by the Author to a subsequent publication, and will be reprinted in a later Volume.]

AVENGE ME OF MINE ADVERSARY.

Luke xviii. 3.

1   JESU, Thou hast bid us pray,
    Pray always, and not faint ;
With the word a power convey
    To utter our complaint.

Quiet shalt Thou never know,
Till we from sin are fully freed :
    O avenge us of our foe,
        And bruise the Serpent's head.
2   We have now begun to cry,
        And we will never end
Till we find salvation nigh,
        And grasp the sinner's Friend ;
Day and night we 'll speak our woe.
With Thee importunately plead :
    O avenge us, &c.

3   Speak the word, and we shall be
        From all our bands released;
Only Thou canst set us free,
        By Satan long opprest ;
Now Thy power Almighty show,
Arise the woman's conquering Seed :
    O avenge us, &c.

4   To destroy his work of sin,
        Thyself in us reveal :
Manifest Thyself within
        Our flesh, and fully dwell
With us, *in* us, here below ;
Enter, and make us free indeed :
    O avenge us, &c.

5   Stronger than the strong man, Thou
        His fury canst control ;
Cast him out by entering now,
        And keep our ransom'd soul ;
Satan's kingdom overthrow,
On all the powers of darkness tread :
    O avenge us, &c.

6   Shall he still the souls enthral
       For whom Thy life was given ?
    Hast Thou not beheld him fall
       As lightning out of heaven ?
    Hitherto allow'd to go,
  He now no farther shall proceed :
    O avenge us, &c.

7   To the never-ceasing cries
       Of Thine elect attend;
    Send deliverance from the skies,
       Thy mighty Spirit send ;
    Though to man Thou seemest slow,
  Our cries Thou seemest not to heed :
    O avenge us, &c.

8   Come, O come, all-gracious Lord,
       No longer now delay;
    With Thy Spirit's two-edged sword
       The crooked serpent slay ;
    Bare Thine arm, and give the blow.
  Root out and kill the hellish seed :
    O avenge us, &c.

9   High enthroned at God's right hand,
       Thou dost in glory sit,
    Till whoe'er Thy sway withstand
       Indignantly submit ;
    Yes, they all shall be brought low,
  They all shall be Thy footstool made :
    O avenge us, &c.

10   Jesu, hear Thy Spirit's call,
       Thy bride who bids Thee come :
    Come, Thou righteous Judge of all,
       Pronounce the tempter's doom ;

Doom him to infernal woe,
For him and for his angels made;
Now avenge us of our foe,
For ever bruise his head.

COME, LORD JESUS!

1 WHEN, dearest Lord, when shall it be
That I shall find my all in Thee?
The fulness of Thy promise prove,
The seal of Thine eternal love?

2 A poor, blind child, I wander here,
If haply I may feel Thee near;
O dark, dark, dark (I still must say)
Amidst the blaze of Gospel day!*

3 Thee, only Thee, I fain would find,
I cast the world and flesh behind;
Thou, only Thou, to me be given,
Of all Thou hast in earth or heaven.

4 All earthly comforts I disdain;
They shall not rob me of my pain,
Or make me senseless of my load,
Or less disconsolate for God.

5 Rather let all the creatures take
Their miserable comforts back,
With every vain relief depart,
And leave me to my broken heart.

6 Leave me, my friends, the mourner leave;
For God, and not for you, I grieve;

* Compare *Samson Agonistes*, line 80, " O dark, dark, dark.
amid the blaze of noon."

My weakness, O ye strong, despise,
My foolish ignorance, ye wise.

7 Let all my father's children be
Still angry, still displeased with me,
Disclaim, dishonour, and disown ;
I would be poor, forlorn, alone.

8 A child, a fool, a thing of nought,
Abhorr'd, neglected. and forgot,
Contemn'd, abandon'd, and distrest,
Till I from mortal man have ceased.

9 When from the arm of flesh set free,
Jesu, my soul shall fly to Thee ;
Jesu, when I have lost my all,
My soul shall on Thy bosom fall.

10 When man forsakes Thou wilt not leave.
Ready the outcasts to receive,
Though all my simpleness I own,
And all my faults to Thee are known.

11 Ah ! wherefore did I ever doubt ?
Thou wilt in no wise cast me out,
An helpless soul that comes to Thee
With only sin and misery.

12 Lord, I am sick ; my sickness cure :
I want ; do Thou enrich the poor :
Under Thy mighty hand I stoop :
O lift the abject sinner up !

13 Lord, I am blind ; be Thou my sight :
Lord, I am weak ; be Thou my might :
An Helper of the helpless be,
And let me find my all in Thee.

THE SAME.

1 JESU, what hast Thou bestow'd
    On such a worm as me !
What compassion hast Thou show'd,
    To draw me after Thee !
Perfect then the work begun,
    All Thy goodness let me prove,
All Thy will in me be done,
    Till all my soul is love.

2 Not by my own righteousness,
    Or works that I have wrought,
Am I saved ; but by Thy grace,
    Surpassing human thought.
Nothing have I, nothing am,
    Nothing I deserve but hell;
Yet I glory in Thy name,
    Yet ! Thy mercy feel.

3 Thou a spark of hallow'd fire
    To me, even me, hast given :
Glows for Thee my whole desire,
    My life, my inward heaven :
Dreams of happiness below
    Never more will I pursue,
Jesus only will I know,
    Whose love is ever new.

4 Thou Thine hand on me hast laid,
    And calm'd my stormy will,
Nature's rapid tide hast stayed,
    And bid my heart be still :

Stablish Thou my heart in peace,
 Meek and lowly may I be,
Fill with all Thy gentleness
 The soul that hangs on Thee.

5 Oft Thou visitest my breast;
 But O, how short Thy stay,
As the memory of a guest
 That tarrieth but a day!
Come, and all Thy foes expel,
 Fix in me Thy constant home,
With Thy Father in me dwell;
 Lord Jesus, quickly come!

WAITING FOR CHRIST THE PROPHET.

1 PROPHET, sent from God above
 To teach His perfect will,
Lo! I wait to learn Thy love,
 I tremble, and am still;
To Thy guidance I submit,
 All my soul to Thee I bow;
See me sitting at Thy feet:
 Speak, Lord, I hear Thee now.

2 From the idle babbler, man,
 Behold I turn away,
Trample on the fairest plan
 That human wit can lay:
Foolish am I still, and blind,
 Till the Truth itself impart,
Chase the darkness from my mind,
 And shine within my heart.

3 What avails the creature's strife,
    When Thou, and only Thou,
Hast the words of endless life !
    (O could I hear them now !)
Mighty Thou in word and deed,
    Thou my only Teacher be ;
Thou, by Thine anointing, lead
    A soul that seeks to Thee.

4 I from outward things withdraw,
    No help in them is found ;
At Thy mouth I seek the law,
    I listen for the sound
Which shall all my griefs control,
    Empty me at once and fill,
Calm the tempest in my soul,
    And bid the sea be still.

5 Ah ! my Lord, if Thou art near
    And knockest at the door,
Let me now my Prophet hear,
    And keep Thee out no more :
Be reveal'd, Thou heavenly Guest,
    To consume the Man of Sin ;
Take possession of my breast,
    Come in, my Lord, come in.

THE SAME.

1 CHRIST, my hidden life, appear,
    Soul of my inmost soul ;
Light of life, the mourner cheer,
    And make the sinner whole.

Now in me Thyself display,
  Surely Thou in all things art ;
I from all things turn away,
  To seek Thee in my heart.

2 Open, Lord, my inward ear,
  And bid my heart rejoice,
Bid my quiet spirit hear
  Thy comfortable voice,
Never in the whirlwind found,
  Or where earthquakes rock the place :
Still and silent is the sound,
  The whisper of Thy grace.

3 From the world of sin, and noise,
  And hurry, I withdraw;
For the small and inward voice
  I wait with humble awe :
Silent am I now, and still,
  Dare not in Thy presence move ;
To my waiting soul reveal
  The secret of Thy love.

4 Thou hast undertook for me,
  For me to death wast sold :
Wisdom in a mystery
  Of bleeding love unfold;
Teach the lesson of Thy cross,
  Let me die with Thee to reign,
All things let me count but loss
  So I may Thee regain.

5 Show me, as my soul can bear,
  The depth of inbred sin;
All the unbelief declare,
  The pride that lurks within :

Take me, whom Thyself hast bought;
    Bring into captivity
Every high aspiring thought
    That would not stoop to Thee.

6 Lord, my time is in Thy hand,
    My soul to Thee convert;
Thou canst make me understand,
    Though I am slow of heart.
Thine, in whom I live and move,
    Thine the work, the praise is Thine;
Thou art wisdom, power, and love,
    And all Thou art is mine.

THE SAME.

1 I WILL hearken what my Lord
    Shall say concerning me:
Hast Thou not a gracious word
    For one that waits on Thee?
Speak it to my soul, that I
    May in Thee have peace and power,
Never from my Saviour fly,
    And never grieve Thee more.

2 How have I Thy Spirit grieved,
    Since first with me He strove !
Obstinately disbelieved,
    And trampled on Thy love !
I have sinn'd against the light,
    I have broke from Thy embrace ;
No, I would not, when I might,
    Be freely saved by grace.

3 After all that I have done
    To drive Thee from my heart,
Still Thou wilt not leave Thine own,
    Thou wilt not yet depart,
Wilt not give the sinner o'er :
    Ready art Thou now to save,
Bidd'st me come, as heretofore,
    That I Thy life may have.

4 O Thou meek and gentle Lamb,
    Fury is not in Thee ;
Thou continuest the same,
    And still Thy grace is free;
Still Thy arms are open wide,
    Wretched sinners to receive;
Thou hast once for sinners died,
    That all may turn and live.

5 Lo ! I take Thee at Thy word,
    My foolishness I mourn;
Unto Thee, my bleeding Lord,
    However late, I turn :
Yes; I yield, I yield at last,
    Listen to Thy speaking blood,
Me with all my sins I cast
    On my atoning God.

6 Freely am I justified,
    And till my heart is pure
In Thy wounds will I abide,
    From hell and sin secure ;
What of sin in me remains
    I believe Thou wilt remove,
Throughly wash out all my stains,
    And perfect me in love.

DANIEL IN THE DEN OF LIONS.

[Daniel vi.]

1 God of *Daniel*, hear my prayer,
    And let Thy power be seen;
Stop the lion's mouth, and bear
    Me safe out of his den :
Save me in this dreadful hour ;
    Earth, and hell, and nature join,
All stand ready to devour
    This helpless soul of mine.

2 No way to escape, I see
    The sure-approaching death ;
Vain are all my hopes to flee
    Out of the lion's teeth ;
In the mire of sin I lie,
    In the dungeon of despair;
Hear my lamentable cry,
    O God of *Daniel*, hear !

3 Thee I serve, my Lord, my God,
    In me Thy power display,
Save me, save me, and defraud
    The lion of his prey :
Angel of the Covenant,
    Jesus mighty to retrieve,
Let Him to my help be sent ;
    In Jesus I believe.

4 Save me for Thine own great name,
    That all the world may know
Daniel's God is still the same,
    And reigns supreme below.

Him let all mankind adore,
  Spread His glorious name abroad;
Tremble all, and bow before
  The great, the living God.

5 Absolute, unchangeable,
    O'er all His works He reigns;
His dominion cannot fail,
    But undisturb'd remains;
His dominion standeth fast,
    Is when time no more shall be,
Still shall His dominion last
    Through all eternity.

6 He delivers by His love,
    He rescues souls from death ;
Signs He works in heaven above,
    And signs in earth beneath ;
Daniel He doth every hour
    From the lion's paw retrieve:
I am saved from Satan's power,
    And lo ! by grace I live.

THE THREE CHILDREN IN THE FIERY FURNACE.

[*Daniel iii.*]

1 God of *Israel's* faithful Three,
    Who braved a tyrant's ire,
Nobly scorn'd to bow their knee,
    And walk'd unhurt in fire ;
Breathe their faith into my breast.
    Arm me in this fiery hour,
Stand, O Son of Man, confest
    In all Thy saving power.

2 Lo! on dangers, deaths, and snares
      I every moment tread,
   Hell without a veil appears,
      And flames around my head;
   Sin increases more and more,
      Sin in all its strength returns,
   Seven times hotter than before
      The fiery furnace burns.

3 But while Thou, my Lord, art nigh,
      My soul disdains to fear,
   Sin and Satan I defy
      Still impotently near;
   Earth and hell their wars may wage;
      Calm I mark their vain design,
   Smile to see them idly rage
      Against a child of Thine.

4 Unto Thee, my help, my hope,
      My safeguard, and my tower,
   Confident I still look up,
      And still receive Thy power;
   All the alien's hosts I chase,
      Blast, and scatter with mine eyes:
   Satan comes; I turn my face,
      And lo! the tempter flies!

5 Sin in me, the inbred foe,
      Awhile subsists in chains;
   But Thou all Thy power shalt show,
      And slay its last remains:
   Thou hast conquer'd my desire;
      Thou shalt quench it with Thy blood,
   Fill me with a purer fire,
      And change me into God.

A THANKSGIVING.

1   'Tis of Thy mercies, Lord,
        That I am not consumed,
    By God and men abhorr'd,
        To endless torments doom'd :
    Thy tender mercies never fail,
    And therefore I am not in hell.

2   In vain was Tophet moved
        To meet me from beneath,
    For Jesu's sake beloved
        I 'scape the second death :
    Thy tender mercies never fail,
    And therefore I am not in hell.

3   Within its mouth I was,
        And there I lay asleep ;
    Its mouth it could not close,
        My soul it could not keep :
    Thy tender mercies never fail,
    And therefore I am not in hell.

4   Thy mercies found out me,
        To me they first did stoop;
    From depths of misery
        Thy mercies brought me up :
    Thy tender mercies never fail,
    And therefore I am not in hell.

5   Thy dear preserving grace
        Each moment I receive,
    And trust to see Thy face,
        And without sin to live :
    Thy tender mercies never fail,
    And I shall never be in hell.

HE THAT LOSETH HIS LIFE FOR MY SAKE SHALL FIND IT.

[*Matthew* x. 39.]

1 BE it according to Thy word;
    This moment let it be!
  O that I now, my dearest Lord,
    Might lose my life for Thee!

2 Now, Jesu, let Thy powerful death
    Into my being come;
  Slay the old *Adam* with Thy breath,
    The Man of Sin consume.

3 Whate'er I have, or can, or am,
    I now would fain resign,
  And lose my nature and my name,
    O God, to purchase Thine.

4 Withhold whate'er my flesh requires,
    Poison my pleasant food,
  Spoil my delights, my vain desires,
    My all of creature good.

5 My old affections mortify,
    Nail to the cross my will,
  Daily and hourly bid me die,
    Or altogether kill.

6 Passion and appetite destroy;
    Tear, tear this pride away;
  And all my boast, and idle joy,
    And all my nature, slay.

7 Jesu, my life, appear within,
  And bruise the serpent's head;
Enter my soul, extirpate sin,
  Cast out the cursed seed.

8 Thou wilt, I know Thou wilt, appear,
  And end this inward strife;
Thy harbinger proclaims Thee near,
  And death makes way for life.

9 Hast Thou not made me willing, Lord?
  Would I not die this hour?
Then speak the killing, quickening word.
  Slay, raise me by Thy power.

10 Slay me, and I in Thee shall trust,
  With Thy dead men arise,
Awake, and sing from out the dust
  Soon as this nature dies.

11 O let it now make haste to die,
  The mortal wound receive:
So shall I live; and yet not I,
  But Christ in me shall live.

12 Be it according to Thy word;
  This moment let it be!
The life I lose for Thee, my Lord,
  I find again in Thee.

WATCH IN ALL THINGS.
[2 *Timothy* iv. 5.]

1 Jesu, my Saviour, Brother, Friend,
  On whom I cast my every care,
On whom for all things I depend,
  Inspire, and then accept my prayer.

2 If I have tasted of Thy grace,
    The grace that sure salvation brings,
If with me now Thy Spirit stays,
    And, hovering, hides me in His wings.

3 Still let Him with my weakness stay,
    Nor for a moment's space depart,
Evil and danger turn away,
    And keep till He renews my heart.

4 When to the left or right I stray,
    His voice behind me may I hear:
" Return, and walk in Christ thy way,
    Fly back to Christ, for sin is near."

5 His sacred unction from above
    Be still my comforter and guide,
Till all the stony He remove,
    And in my loving heart reside.

6 Jesu, I fain would walk in Thee,
    From nature's every path retreat ;
Thou art my way, my Leader be,
    And set upon the rock my feet.

7 Uphold me, Saviour, or I fall;
    O reach me out Thy gracious hand :
Only on Thee for help I call,
    Only by faith in Thee I stand.

8 Pierce, fill me with an humble fear,
    My utter helplessness reveal ;
Satan and sin are always near,
    Thee may I always nearer feel.

9 O that to Thee my constant mind
    Might with an even flame aspire :
Pride in its earliest motions find,
    And mark the risings of desire.

10 O that my tender soul might fly
    The first abhorr'd approach of ill.
Quick as the apple of an eye
    The slightest touch of sin to feel.

11 Till Thou anew my soul create,
    Still may I strive, and watch, and pray.
Humbly and confidently wait,
    And long to see Thy perfect day.

12 My whole regard still may I place
    On the faint ray of opening light.
(The sure prophetic word of grace,)
    That glimmers through my nature's night.

13 Here let my soul's sure anchor be.
    Here let me fix my wishful eyes.
And wait till I exult to see
    The Day-star in my heart arise.

14 My Lord, Thou wilt not long delay;
    This inward calm proclaims Thee near:
Sorrow and doubt are fled away,
    My Lord shall in my heart appear.

15 Jesu, my Saviour, Brother, Friend.
    As I believe, so let it be ;
O make me patient to the end,
    And then reveal Thyself in me.

A PRAYER FOR HOLINESS.

1　Ever fainting with desire,
　　For Thee, O Christ, I call;
　Thee I restlessly require,
　　I want my God, my all;
　Jesu, dear redeeming Lord,
I wait Thy coming from above :
　Help me, Saviour, speak the word,
　　And perfect me in love.

2　Wilt Thou suffer me to go
　　Lamenting all my days?
　Shall I never, never know
　　Thy sanctifying grace?
　Wilt Thou not Thy light afford,
The darkness from my soul remove?
　Help me, Saviour, &c.

3　Wretched, naked, poor, and blind,
　　Afflicted and distrest,
　Settled peace I cannot find,
　　Uninterrupted rest,
　Till my spirit is restored,
And fix'd my heart on things above :
　Help me, Saviour, &c.

4　Gifts, alas ! cannot suffice,
　　And comforts all are vain ;
　While one evil thought can rise,
　　*I am not born again ;**
　Still I am not as my Lord,
Thy holy will I do not prove :
　Help me, Saviour, &c.

* See Note, Vol. 1., p. 370. and reference there.

5 Why hast Thou on me bestow'd
     Thy free, preventing grace?
  Why beheld me in my blood,
     And call'd to seek Thy face?
  Thou hast not my soul abhorr'd,
  But still with me Thy Spirit strove:
     Help me, Saviour, &c.

6 Why didst Thou my ransom pay,
     The work of faith begin?
  Surely Thou hast purged away
     The guilt of all my sin;
  All the guilt 's on Thee transferr'd:
  And wilt Thou not the power remove?
     Help me, Saviour, &c.

7 Lord, if I on Thee believe,
     The second gift impart;
  With the' indwelling Spirit give
     A new, a loving heart:
  If with love Thy heart is stored,
  If now o'er me Thy bowels move,
     Help me, Saviour, &c.

8 Let me gain my calling's hope,
     O make the sinner clean;
  Dry corruption's fountain up,
     Cut off the' entail of sin : *
  Take me into Thee, my Lord,
  And I shall then no longer rove :
     Help me, Saviour, &c.

i. e., That which has been entailed on me by the transgression of the first man. Some exaggerated expectations which have sought shelter under these words were expressly disowned. See Wesley's Works, vol. xi., p. 400.

9 Thou my life, my treasure be,
  My portion here below;
 Nothing would I seek but Thee,
  Thee only would I know,
 My exceeding great reward,
My heaven on earth, my heaven above:
 Help me, Saviour, &c.

10 Grant me now the bliss to feel
  Of those that are in Thee;
 Son of God, Thyself reveal,
  Engrave Thy name on me;
 As in heaven be here adored,
And let me now the promise prove:
 Help me, Saviour, speak the word,
  And perfect me in love.

LET THIS MIND BE IN YOU, WHICH WAS ALSO IN CHRIST JESUS.

[*Philippians ii.* 5.]

1 Jesu, shall I never be
 Firmly grounded upon Thee?
 Never by Thy work abide,
 Never in Thy wounds reside?

2 O how wavering is my mind,
 Toss'd about with every wind!
 O how quickly doth my heart
 From the living God depart!

3 Easily I fall away,
 Never am I at one stay;

Strong in faith I seem this hour,
Stripp'd the next of all my power.

4 Faith is lost in unbelief,
Joy is swallow'd up of grief,
Hope, my latest hope, expires,
God, my angry God, retires.

5 Vanishing out of my sight,
Jesus leaves me sunk in night;
Where shall I my Jesus find,
Helpless I, and dark, and blind?

6 Seek, O seek me, Lord, again;
Let not all Thy gifts be vain;
Comfort to my soul restore;
Come, and never leave me more.

7 Jesu, let my nature feel
Thou art God unchangeable;
Jah, Jehovah, great I am,
Speak into my soul Thy name.

8 Fruit that I may bear, ordain;
That my fruit may still remain,
Make my heart, and keep it, true;
After God my soul renew.

9 Grant that every moment I
May believe, and feel Thee nigh;
Steadfastly behold Thy face,
'Stablish'd with abiding grace.

10 Plant, and root, and fix in me
All the mind that was in Thee;
Settled peace I then shall find;
Jesu's is a quiet mind.

11 When it doth in me appear,
I shall nothing covet here;

I shall cast the world behind;
Jesu's is an heavenly mind.

12 Then the' accursed lust of praise
Shall in me no more have place;
Pride no more my soul shall bind;
Jesu's is an humble mind.

13 Anger I no more shall feel,
Always quiet, always still,
Meekly on my God reclined;
Jesu's is a gentle mind.

14 I shall suffer and fulfil
All my Father's gracious will,
Be in all alike resign'd;
Jesu's is a patient mind.

15 When 'tis deeply rooted here
Perfect love shall cast out fear;
Fear doth servile spirits bind:
Jesu's is a noble mind.

16 When I feel it fix'd within
I shall have no power to sin;
How should sin an entrance find?
Jesu's is a spotless mind.

17 I shall nothing know beside
Jesus and Him crucified;
I shall all to Him be join'd:
Jesu's is a loving mind.

18 I shall triumph evermore,
Gratefully my God adore,—
God so good, so true, so kind;
Jesu's is a thankful mind.

19 Lowly, loving, meek, and pure,
I shall to the end endure,

Be no more to sin inclined;
Jesu's is a constant mind.
20 I shall fully be restored
To the image of my Lord.
Witnessing to all mankind
Jesu's is a perfect mind.

I. JOHN I. 9.

" *If we confess our sins, He is faithful and just to
forgive us our sins, and to cleanse us from* ALL
unrighteousness."

1 FATHER of my dying Lord,
To whom I sue for peace,
Trusting in Thy faithful word,
Lo! I my sins confess.
For Thy truth and mercy's sake,
Grant the blessing which I claim;
Cast my sins behind Thy back:
I ask in Jesu's name.

2 Hast Thou not reversed my doom?
Thou hast, and I believe:
Yet I still a sinner come,
That Thou mayst still forgive;
Wretched, miserable, blind,
Poor, and naked, and unclean,
Still, that I may mercy find,
I bring Thee nought but sin.

3 I have always equal need
Of Thy forgiving love;
Still do I the promise plead, .
That I Thy truth may prove.

Just and faithful as Thou art,
    Hear me now my sins confess,
Hear, and purify my heart
    From all unrighteousness.

4 Lord, I look to be made clean
    From every sinful blot,
All unrighteousness and sin,
    In deed, and word, and thought;
Evil shall not here abide,
    Sin shall have no place in me,
From the' iniquity of pride
    And self I shall be free.

5 I shall be redeem'd from all,
    Unless Thy word is vain;
Here recover from my fall,
    My *Eden here* regain;
Jesus shall His image *here*
    Perfectly in me restore;
God shall in my flesh appear,
    And sin subsist no more.

THEY THAT WAIT ON THE LORD SHALL RENEW THEIR STRENGTH.

[*Isaiah xl.* 31.]

1 LORD, I believe Thy every word,
    Thy every promise, true;
And lo ! I wait on Thee, my Lord,
    Till I my strength renew.

2 If in this feeble flesh I may
        Awhile show forth Thy praise,
    Jesu, support the tottering clay,
        And lengthen out my days.

3 If such a worm as I can spread
        The common Saviour's name,
    Let Him who raised Thee from the dead
        Quicken my mortal frame.

4 Still let me live Thy blood to show,
        Which purges every stain;
    And gladly linger out below
        A few more years in pain.

5 My time and life are in Thy hand;
        No more for death I groan,
    Still let the ruinous mansion stand
        Till all Thy will be done.

6 My life I know Thou canst repair,
        And give a stronger thread;
    But, Lord, of this I take no care,
        For O my soul is dead !

7 Health I shall have, if that be best ;
        But what is health to me?
    Alas ! my spirit cannot rest,
        Till it is whole with Thee.

8 The spirit of an healthful mind :
        For this I wait in pain,
    This precious pearl I long to find,
        And to be born again.

9 Spare me till I my strength of soul,
        Till I Thy love, retrieve ;
    Till faith shall make my spirit whole,
        And perfect soundness give.

10 Faith to be heal'd Thou know'st I have,
  From sin to be made clean;
Able Thou art from sin to save,
  From all indwelling sin.

11 Surely Thou canst, I do not doubt,
  Thou wilt Thyself impart,
The bond-woman's base son cast out,
  And take up all my heart.

12 I shall my ancient strength renew;
  Thy excellence Divine
(If Thou art good, if Thou art true)
  Throughout my soul shall shine.

13 I shall, a weak and helpless worm,
  Through Jesus strengthening me,
Impossibilities perform,
  And live from sinning free.

14 For this in steadfast hope I wait:
  Now, Lord, my soul restore;
Now the new heavens and earth create,
  And I shall sin no more.

THE THINGS WHICH ARE IMPOSSIBLE WITH MEN ARE POSSIBLE TO GOD.

[Luke xviii. 27.]

1 WHAT a mystery am I,
  A mystery of sin,
Full of all iniquity,
  Unholy and unclean!

Every thought of all our hearts
  Only evil always is;
Now I know my inward parts
  Are very wickedness.

2 Stripp'd of every boasted grace,
  Of every show of good,
Still I am but what I was,
  Unchanged and unrenew'd.
Dust and ashes is my name;
  Sinful dust and ashes, I,
Bearing all my sin and shame,
  At Jesu's feet I lie.

3 From a thing like me unclean,
  A clean and holy thing
Who of all the sons of men
  Can ever hope to bring?
All our strife at last must cease,
  All our strength and wisdom fail;
Such a work we must confess
  With man impossible.

4 But shall human weakness dare
  To limit strength Divine;
Teach almighty Wisdom where
  To lay the measuring line?
Yes; we give our God the lie,
  Trample on the' all-cleansing blood;
From *all* sin to save, we cry,
  This is too hard for God.

5 Still we listen to our foe,
  His other gospel hear:
" No perfection is below;
  No love that casts out fear:

Fear and sin must still remain,
    Still in you maintain their seat;
Sin *sometimes* will always reign,
    And force you to submit."

6 Soon as Satan gives the word,
    His advocates for sin
Witness with their lying lord,—
    " Ye never can be clean
From all sin, while here below;
    Do not you the word receive;
God's own word may tell you so,
    But do not you believe !"

7 Flesh and blood cry out amain:
    " It cannot, cannot be !
All my faith and hope is vain,
    From sin to be set free;
I with only evil fraught,
    Full of desperate wickedness,
I who sin in every thought,
    Can I from sinning cease ? "

8 World, and sin, and Satan, go
    And ask my faithful Lord ;
Surely I the truth shall know,
    For He hath spoke the word:
Whether every perfect one
    Shall not as his Master be,
Thou shalt shortly make it known,
    Shalt answer, Lord, for me.

LET GOD BE TRUE, AND EVERY MAN
A LIAR.

[*Romans iii.* 4.]

1 God of all power, and truth, and love,
    I act my faith on Thee,
Expect Thy promises to prove
    Accomplish'd all in me.

2 In hope believing against hope,
    Thy faithfulness I plead;
Assured that Thou shalt lift me up,
    And make me free indeed.

3 Thou shalt on me Thy Spirit pour,
    And make the sinner clean;
In confidence I wait the hour
    When I shall cease from sin.

4 I trust that to the life Divine
    Thou wilt my soul restore,
And I shall in Thine image shine,
    And I shall sin no more.

5 Though Satan all Thy truths deny,
    He shall no more deceive;
I cannot give my God the lie,
    For I shall surely live.

6 Though men blaspheme the liberty,
    The power they never knew,
Let every man a liar be,
    So God alone be true.

7 Though nature fail, and flesh and blood
    Would from the promise start,
God shall His word accomplish, God
    Is greater than my heart.

8 Through unbelief I stagger not;
  Though now my soul is dead,
Quicken'd in Christ, from every thought
  Of sin I shall be freed.

9 I shall be perfected in love;
  For Thou hast spoke the word,
The servant cannot be above,
  But shall be as, his Lord.

10 The glory of Thy truth and grace
  To Thee, O God, I give;
The vilest of the sinful race,
  I without sin shall live.

THY WILL BE DONE IN EARTH, AS IT IS IN HEAVEN.

[*Matthew* vi. 10.]

1 Jesu, the Life, the Truth, the Way,
  In whom I now believe,
As taught by Thee, in faith I pray,
  Expecting to receive.

2 Thy will by me on earth be done
  As by the choirs above,
Who always see Thee on Thy throne,
  And glory in Thy love.

3 I ask in confidence the grace
  That I may do Thy will
As angels who behold Thy face,
  And all Thy words fulfil.

4 Surely I shall, the sinner I,
    Shall serve Thee without fear;
  My heart no longer gives the lie
    To my deceitful prayer.

5 Thee I shall serve without constraint,
    Shall every moment please:
  Those blessed spirits never faint,
    Nor from Thy service cease.

6 When Thou the work of faith hast wrought
    I shall be pure within,
  Nor sin in deed, or word, or thought;
    For angels never sin.

7 From Thee no more shall I depart,
    No more unfaithful prove,
  But love Thee with a constant heart:
    For angels always love.

8 Tell me no more it cannot be,
    Ye sons of earth and hell;
  The things impossible to me
    To God are possible.

9 The world of liars and their god
    In vain deny Thee, Lord;
  I listen not to flesh and blood,
    I hearken to Thy word.

10 The thing for which thou bidd'st me pray
    Thou promisest to give;
  And I shall perfectly obey,
    I without sin shall live.

11 I all Thy holy will shall prove;
    I, a weak sinful worm,
  When Thee with all my heart I love,
    Shall all Thy law perform.

12 The graces of my second birth
    To me shall all be given;
And I shall do Thy will on earth
    As angels do in heaven.

THE WORD OF OUR GOD SHALL STAND FOR EVER.

[*Isaiah xl. 8.*]

1 PRISONERS of hope, lift up your heads;
    The day of liberty draws near;
Jesus, who on the serpent treads,
    Shall soon in your behalf appear:
The Lord shall to His temple come;
Prepare your hearts to make Him room.

2 We all shall find, (whom in His word
    Himself hath caused to put our trust,)
The Father of our dying Lord
    Is ever to His promise just;
Faithful, if we our sins confess,
To cleanse from all unrighteousness.

3 Lord, we confess our sins to Thee;
    In sin we were conceived and born:
Plunged in the depth of misery,
    We never can to Thee return,
Till Thou our fallen souls convert,
And give the new, believing heart.

4 Now, if Thou canst, withhold the grace
    From sinners hungry, mournful, poor,
Who ask Thy love, who seek Thy face,
    Who ever knock at mercy's door,

    At Jesu's feet who humbly lie,
    Resolved at Jesu's feet to die.

5 Yes, Lord, we must believe Thee kind.
    Thou never canst unfaithful prove;
  Surely we shall Thy mercy find;
    Who ask, shall all receive Thy love;
  Nor canst Thou it to me deny;
  I ask, the chief of sinners, I!

6 'Tis done; my prayer hath pierced the skies.
    Hath reach'd my gracious Father's ear;
  He hears, He answers to my cries;
    My God shall in my heart appear;
  He hath to me a token given—
  This inward peace, this taste of heaven.

7 Wherefore of Him I make my boast,
    I triumph in His truth and grace,
  I in His faithful mercies trust,
    I shall with joy behold His face,
  I shall be soon His fix'd abode—
  A temple of the living God.

8 O ye of fearful hearts, be strong!
    Your downcast hands and eyes lift up!
  Ye shall not be forgotten long;
    Hope to the end, in Jesus hope!
  Tell Him ye wait His grace to prove.
  And cannot fail, if God is love!

9 Prisoners of hope, be strong, be bold:
    Cast off your doubts, disdain to fear!
  Dare to believe; on Christ lay hold!
    Wrestle with Christ in mighty prayer;
  Tell Him, We will not let Thee go
  Till we Thy name, Thy nature know.

10 Hast Thou not died to purge our sin,
      And rose, Thy death for us to plead ;
   To write Thy law of love within
      Our hearts, and make us freed indeed ?
   That we our *Eden* might regain,
   Thou diedst, and couldst not die in vain.

11 Lord, we believe, and wait the hour
      Which all Thy great salvation brings;
   The Spirit of love, and health, and power
      Shall come, and make us priests and kings;
   Thou wilt perform Thy faithful word,—
   The servant shall be as his Lord.

12 The promise stands for ever sure,
      And we shall in Thine image shine,
   Partakers of a nature pure,
      Holy, angelical, Divine;
   In Spirit joined to Thee the Son,
   As Thou art with Thy Father one.

13 Faithful and True, we now receive
      The promise ratified by Thee:
   To Thee the when and how we leave,
      In time and in eternity;
   We only hang upon Thy word,—
   The servant shall be as his Lord.

ZECHARIAH IV. 7, &c.

1 O GREAT mountain, who art thou,
      Immense, immovable ?
   High as heaven aspires thy brow,
      Thy foot sinks deep as hell !

Thee, alas! I long have known,
   Long have felt thee fix'd within ;
Still beneath thy weight I groan :
   Thou art Indwelling Sin.

2 Thou art darkness in my mind,
   Perverseness in my will ;
Love inordinate and blind,
   Which always cleaves to ill ;
Every passion's wild excess,
   Anger, lust, and pride thou art ;
Self, and sin, and sinfulness,
   And unbelief of heart.

3 Not by human might or power
   Canst thou be moved from hence :
But thou shalt flow down before
   Divine Omnipotence :
My *Zerubbabel* is near ;
   I have not believed in vain :
Thou, when Jesus doth appear,
   Shalt sink into a plain.

4 Christ, the Head, the Corner-Stone,
   Shall be brought forth in me :
Glory be to Christ alone !
   His grace shall set me free :
I shall shout my Saviour's name,
   Him I evermore shall praise,
All the work of grace proclaim,
   Of sanctifying grace.

5 Christ hath the foundation laid,
   And Christ shall build me up :
Surely I shall soon be made
   Partaker of my hope :

Author of my faith He is,
 He its Finisher shall be;
Perfect love shall seal me His
 To all eternity.

THE SAME.

1 O GREAT mountain, who art thou,
 That darest my God defy?
Thou shalt tremble, stoop, and bow,
 When Jesus but draws nigh:
When He to my heart comes in,
 Thou shalt there no longer be;
From that hour, Indwelling Sin,
 Thou hast no place in me.

2 As a grain of mustard-seed
 If faith in Christ I have,
From all sin I shall be freed;
 I know my Lord will save
Me from all iniquity;
 Faith shall move the mountain load,
Cast it out into the sea
 Of His all-cleansing blood.

3 Who hath slighted or contemn'd
 The day of feeble things?
I shall be by grace redeem'd,
 'Tis grace salvation brings:
Ready now my Saviour stands;
 Him I now rejoice to see
With the plummet in His hands,
 To build and finish me.

4 I right early shall awake,
    And see the perfect day:
  Soon the Lamb of God shall take
    My inbred sin away:
  When to me my Lord shall come,
    Sin for ever shall depart;
  Jesus takes up all the room
    In a believing heart.

5 Son of God, arise, arise,
    And to Thy temple come;
  Look, and with Thy flaming eyes
    The Man of Sin consume;
  Slay him with Thy Spirit, Lord,
    Reign Thou in my heart alone;
  Speak the sanctifying word,
    And seal me all Thine own.

WAITING FOR THE PROMISE.

1 DROOPING soul, shake off thy fears;
    Fearful soul, be strong, be bold;
  Tarry till the Lord appears,
    Never, never quit thy hold :
  Murmur not at His delay,
    Dare not set thy God a time,
  Calmly for His coming stay,
    Leave it, leave it all to Him.

2 Fainting soul, be bold, be strong;
    Wait the leisure of thy Lord:*
  Though it seem to tarry long,
    True and faithful is His word.

* This remarkable expression occurs first in Coverdale's version
of Psalm xxvii. 16, and has been perpetuated by means of the
P. B. V.

On His word my soul I cast;
  (He cannot Himself deny;)
Surely it shall speak at last;
  It shall speak, and shall not lie.

3 Every one that seeks shall find;
    Every one that asks shall have;
  Christ. the Saviour of mankind,
    Willing, able, all to save:
  I shall His salvation see;
    I in faith on Jesus call;
  I from sin shall be set free,
    Perfectly set free from all.

4 Lord, my time is in Thine hand;
    Weak and helpless as I am,
  Surely Thou canst make me stand:
    I believe in Jesu's name;
  Saviour, in temptation Thou,
    Thou hast saved me heretofore;
  Thou from sin dost save me now,
    Thou shalt save me evermore.

5 Wherefore should I doubt the grace
    Which I every moment prove?
  Sin and Satan must give place,
    Both must yield to stronger love.
  Sin and Satan rage their hour;
    But Thou all-sufficient art,
  Thou art infinite in power,
    Thou art greater than my heart.

6 Gladly therefore will I boast
    Of my soul's infirmities;
  I a sinner, helpless, lost,
    I cannot from sinning cease;

Yet the power on me doth rest.
  Now it doth from sin secure:
When it sinks into my breast,
  Pure I am as God is pure.

THE SAME.

1 O Jesu, full of truth and grace,
  O all-atoning Lamb of God,
I wait to see Thy lovely face,
  I seek redemption through Thy blood.

2 In Thee, who hast redeem'd of old
  Mine and the souls of all mankind,
Though once to sin and Satan sold,
  Surely I shall redemption find.

3 Hold of Thy righteousness I take;
  Thou hast exchanged it for my sin;
Thy spotless soul as hell seem'd black,
  That mine through Thee might all be clean.

4 Thou, Lord, for me a sinner made,
  Hast robb'd me of my curse and pain,
Hast died and suffer'd in my stead,
  That I through Thee might live and reign.

5 Now in Thy strength I strive with Thee,
  My Friend and Advocate with God;
Give me the sinless liberty,
  Give me the purchase of Thy blood.

6 Thou art the anchor of my hope,
  The faithful saying I receive;
Surely Thy death shall raise me up,
  For Thou hast died that I may live.

7 Live without sin! If God is true
    I thus shall serve Him all my days,
Shall apprehend whom I pursue,
    And justly triumph in His grace.

8 Satan, with all his arts, no more
    Me from the Gospel's hope can move;
I shall receive the' almighty power,
    And find the pearl of perfect love.

9 Though all the advocates for sin
    Assert their heathenish liberty,
If Jesu's blood can wash me clean
    Sin shall not always dwell in me.

10 Though nature gives my God the lie,
    I all His truth and grace shall know;
I shall, a sinless sinner, I
    Shall perfect holiness below.

11 My flesh, which cries, It cannot be,
    Shall silence keep before the Lord;
And earth, and hell, and sin shall flee
    At Jesu's everlasting word.

THE SAME.

1 O THE cruel power of sin,
    How long shall it endure?
When, O when shall I be clean,
    And pure as God is pure?
From the dead with Jesus rise,
    Be in all His blessing blest,
Gain my calling's glorious prize,
    And enter into rest?

2 O might I this moment cease
  From every work of mine;
Find the perfect holiness,
  The righteousness Divine ;
Righteousness which never ends:
  In himself who feels it wrought,
He no more his God offends
  In deed, or word, or thought.

3 Unto this thrice happy state
  O how shall I attain?
All my time for this I wait,
  And cannot wait in vain;
I shall Thy salvation see,
  I shall do Thy perfect will,
Live in glorious liberty,
  And all Thy fulness feel.

4 O cut short the work, and make
  Me now a creature new;
For Thy truth and mercy's sake,
  The gracious wonder show:
Call me forth Thy witness, Lord;
  Let my life declare Thy power;
Born of God, renew'd, restored,
  O let me sin no more.

5 Fain would I the truth proclaim
  That makes me free indeed,
Glorify my Saviour's name,
  And all its virtues spread:
Jesus all our wants relieves;
  Jesus, mighty to redeem,
Saves, and to the utmost saves,
  All those that come to Him.

6 Jesu, lo! I come to Thee,
   And wait to be sent forth;
If Thy Spirit send forth me.
   A worm shall shake the earth;
I shall Thy great name declare,
   Spread Thy victories abroad,
Be the weapons of Thy war,
   The battle-axe of God.

7 Perfect then Thy mighty power
   In a weak, sinful worm;
All my sins destroy, devour,
   And all my soul transform :
Now apply Thy Spirit's seal;
   O come quickly from above,
Empty me of self, and fill
   With all the life of love.

THE SAME.

1 LORD, I glorify Thy grace,
   Thy truth, and saving power,
Waiting to behold Thy face
   And live in sin no more:
I shall fully be renew'd,
   All Thy promises receive;
Spite of hell, and flesh, and blood,
   I dare at last believe.

2 Can the *Ethiop* change his skin,
   His spots the leopard lose ?
Then may I, inured to sin,
   The path of virtue choose.

Surely in Thy strength I may;
　At Thy word it shall be so,
I shall from my heart obey,
　I shall be white as snow.

3 I have not believed in vain,
　The word of faith is sure:
How should sin in me remain,
　When Jesus saith, " Be pure,
Perfect as your Father is"?
　Father, is there sin in Thee?
Thou art mine, with all Thy bliss,
　When Jesus lives in me.

4 Mine is wisdom, power is mine,
　When Christ is in my heart:
Thou, O Christ, art power Divine,
　Wisdom Divine Thou art!
Soon as Thee my spirit feels,
　Sin no more hath place in me;
Then in me all fulness dwells:
　All fulness dwells in Thee.

DESIRING TO LOVE.

PART I.

1 THEE, Jesu, Thee, the sinner's Friend.
　I follow on to apprehend,
　　Renew the glorious strife;
Divinely confident and bold,
With faith's strong arm on Thee lay hold.
　　Thee, my eternal life.

2 Tell me, O Lord, if Thine I am,
  Tell me Thy new, mysterious name,
    Or Thou shalt never move;
  No, never will I let Thee go,
  Till I Thy name, Thy nature know,
    And feel that God is love.

3 I feel that I have power with God;
  (Thou only hast the power bestow'd.
    And arm'd me for the fight ;)
  A prince, through Thee invincible,
  I pray, and wrestle, and prevail,
    And conquer in Thy might.

4 Thy heart, I know, Thy tender heart
  Doth in my sorrows feel its part.
    And at my tears relent ;
  My powerful sighs Thou canst not bear.
  Nor stand the violence of my prayer,
    My prayer omnipotent.

5 Give me the grace, the love I claim;
  Thy Spirit now demands Thy name,
    Thou know'st the Spirit's will:
  He helps my soul's infirmity,
  And strongly intercedes for me
    With groans unspeakable.

6 Answer, dear Lord, Thy Spirit's groan ;
  O make to me Thy nature known,
    Thy hidden name impart ;
  (Thy title is with Thee the same;)
  Tell me Thy nature, and Thy name,
    And write it on my heart.

7 Prisoner of hope, to Thee I turn,
And, calmly confident, I mourn,
    And pray, and weep for Thee;
Tell me Thy love, Thy secret tell;
Thy mystic name in me reveal,
    Reveal Thyself in me.

8 Descend, pass by me, and proclaim,
O Lord of Hosts, Thy glorious name,—
    The Lord, the gracious Lord,
Long-suffering, merciful, and kind,
The God who always bears in mind
    His everlasting word:

9 Plenteous He is in truth and grace;
He wills that all the fallen race
    Should turn, repent, and live;
His pardoning grace for all is free;
Transgression, sin, iniquity
    He freely doth forgive.

10 Mercy He doth for thousands keep:
He goes and seeks the one lost sheep.
    And brings His wanderer home;
And every soul that sheep might be:
Come then, dear Lord, and gather me.
    My Jesus, quickly come.

11 Take me into Thy people's rest;
O come, and with my sole request,
    My one desire, comply:
Make me partaker of my hope;
Then bid me get me quickly up,
    And on Thy bosom die

PART II.

1 COME, Lord, and help me to rejoice
 In hope that I shall hear Thy voice,
  Shall one day see my God ;
 Shall cease from all my sin and strife,
 Handle and taste the word of life,
  And feel the sprinkled blood.

2 I shall not always make my moan,
 Or worship Thee a God unknown ;
  But I shall live to prove
 Thy people's rest, Thy saints' delight,
 The length, and breadth, and depth, and height
  Of all-redeeming love.

3 I cannot love Thee little, Lord,
 Whenever by Thy grace restored
  I taste how good Thou art :
 Much I shall love, or not at all :
 Forgiven much, I surely shall
  Love Thee with all my heart.

4 O glorious hope of perfect love !
 It lifts me up to things above,
  It bears on eagle's wings ;
 It gives my ravish'd soul a taste,
 And makes me for some moments feast
  With Jesu's priests and kings.

5 Rejoicing now in earnest hope,
 I stand, and from the mountain-top
  See all the land below ;
 Rivers of milk and honey rise,
 And all the fruits of paradise
  In endless plenty grow :

6 A land of corn, and wine, and oil,
  Favour'd with God's peculiar smile,
    With every blessing blest;
  There dwells the Lord our Righteousness.
  And keeps His own in perfect peace
    And everlasting rest.

7 O that I might at once go up,
  No more on this side *Jordan* stop,
    But now the land possess;
  This moment end my legal years,
  Sorrows, and sins, and doubts, and fears.
    An howling wilderness!

8 Now, O my *Joshua*, bring me in,
  Cast out my foes; the inbred sin.
    The carnal mind, remove;
  The purchase of Thy death divide;
  And O, with all the sanctified
    Give me a lot of love.

TITUS II. 14.

*" Who gave Himself for us, that He might redeem us
from* ALL *iniquity."*

1 JESU, Redeemer of mankind,
  How little art Thou known
  By sinners of a carnal mind,
    Who claim Thee for their own;

2 Who blasphemously call Thee Lord,
  With lips and hearts unclean;
  But make Thee, while they slight Thy word.
    The Minister of sin:

3 Who madly plead for sin's remains,
    While, full of slavish fears,
 They *fancy* Thou hast purged their stains,
    And falsely call Thee theirs !

4 O wretched man, who dares divide
    The pardon and the peace !
 In vain for thee the Saviour died,
    Unless He seal thee His.

5 O wretched man, from guilt to dream
    Thy harden'd conscience freed !
 When Jesus doth a soul redeem
    He makes it free indeed.

6 The guilt and power, with all thy art,
    Can never be disjoin'd;
 Nor will God bid the guilt depart,
    And leave the power behind.

7 Faith, when it comes, breaks every chain,
    And makes us truly free;
 But Christ hath died for thee in vain,
    Unless He lives in thee.

8 What is redemption in His blood,
    But liberty within—
 A liberty to serve my God,
    And to eschew my sin?

9 What is our calling's glorious hope,
    But inward holiness?
 For this to Jesus I look up,
    I calmly wait for this.

10 I wait till He shall touch me clean,
    Shall life and power impart,
 Give me a faith that roots out sin
    And purifies my heart.

11 This is the dear redeeming grace,
 For every sinner free;
Surely it shall on me take place,
 The chief of sinners, me.

12 From all iniquity, from all,
 He shall my soul redeem;
In Jesus I believe, and shall
 Believe myself to Him.

13 When Jesus makes my soul His home,
 My sin shall all depart;
And, lo! He saith, " I quickly come.
 To cleanse and fill thy heart!"

14 Be it according to Thy word!
 Redeem me from all sin;
My heart would now receive Thee, Lord;
 Come in, my Lord, come in!

DEUTERONOMY XXXIII. 26, &c.

1 None is like *Jeshurun's* God,
 So great, so strong, so high;
Lo! He spreads His wings abroad.
 He rides upon the sky:
Israel, His first-born son,
 God, the' eternal God, is thine:
See Him in thy help come down,
 The Excellence Divine.

2 Thee the great Jehovah deigns
 To succour and defend;
Thee the' eternal God sustains,
 Thy Maker and thy Friend:

Sinner, what hast thou to dread?
    Safe from all impending harms,
God hath underneath thee spread*
    His everlasting arms.

3 God is thine; disdain to fear
    The enemy within:
God shall in thy flesh appear,
    And make an end of sin:
God the man of sin shall slay,
    Fill thee with triumphant joy;
God shall thrust him out, and say,
    " Destroy them all, destroy!"

4 All the struggle then is o'er,
    And wars and fightings cease:
Israel then shall sin no more,
    But dwell in perfect peace:
All his enemies are gone;
    Sin shall have in him no part;
Israel now shall dwell alone,
    With Jesus in his heart.

5 In a land of corn and wine
    His lot shall be below;
Comforts there and blessings join,
    And milk and honey flow:
Jacob's well is in his soul;
    Gracious dew his heavens distil.
Fill his spirit already full,
    And shall for ever fill.

* The more euphonious reading, " Round thee and beneath
are spread," dates from 1780. The substitution of " *Israel*" for
" Sinner," in line 5, by which the sense is so greatly improved,
has not been traced beyond 1809.

6 Blest, O *Israel*, art thou;
    What people is like thee?
Saved from sin by Jesus now
    Thou art, and still shalt be :
Jesus is thy seven-fold shield.
    Jesus is thy flaming sword;
Earth, and hell, and sin shall yield
    To God's almighty word.

7 God's almighty word shall stand:
    Thine enemies shall fall,
Fade away at His command,
    And sink and perish all:
Liars shall they all be found,
    All who cried, " It cannot be
Sin should ever quit its ground.
    And have no place in thee."

8 Christ shall make thee free indeed
    When He appears within;
Thou on self and pride shalt tread.
    On all the strength of sin;
Thou shalt more than conquer it :
    Thou shalt see it all depart.
See it dead beneath thy feet.
    No longer in thy heart.

9 God, the gracious God and true.
    Hath spoke the faithful word:
He the mighty work shall do:
    Our trust is in the Lord;
He the mountain shall remove.
    He the sinner shall restore.
He shall perfect me in love.
    And I shall sin no more.

MARK XI. 22, 23, 24.

1 JESU, my trust is in Thy word,
    Thy promise I receive;
It ever stands upon record,
    And I in God believe.

2 Thy truth and faithfulness I own,
    Which I shall fully prove;
Thy power shall all in me be shown,
    Thine utmost power of love.

3 Such faith in God through Thee I have,
    I shall be throughly clean;
Thou canst, Thou wilt the sinner save
    From all his inbred sin.

4 Wherefore through Thee to sin I say,
    This mountain in my heart,—
" Be thou removed far hence away,
    For ever hence depart !

5 "No more in me thy being last,
    Have thou no place in me;
In Jesu's name I say, Be cast,
    Be cast into the sea!"

6 It shall be so : I do not doubt,
    The mountain shall depart;
Sin shall be shortly all cast out
    Of my believing heart.

7 Whate'er I ask I shall receive :
    I ask the perfect power
That sin no more in me may live;
    And it shall live no more.

8 I have the things for which I pray
    And fervently desire;
  Jesu, take all my sins away,
    Baptize me with Thy fire.

9 I ask that I may do Thy will
    As angels do above;
  I ask Thee all my soul to fill
    With pure, seraphic love.

10 Whate'er I ask in faith I have,
    As sure as God is true;
  From all my sins Thou soon shalt save.
    And all my soul renew.

11 Things most impossible shall be.
    As sure as God is power;
  And I shall quickly be in Thee,
    And I shall sin no more.

12 Though heaven and earth away shall pass.
    Thy promise cannot move ;
  And I shall taste the perfect grace.
    As sure as God is love !

ROMANS IV. 16, &c.

1 FATHER of Jesus Christ,—my Lord,
    My Saviour, and my Head,—
  I trust in Thee, whose powerful word
    Hath raised Him from the dead.

2 Thou know'st for my offence He died,
    And rose again for me,
  Fully and freely justified
    That I might live to Thee.

3 Eternal life to all mankind
     Thou hast in Jesus given;
  And all who seek in Him shall find
     The happiness of heaven.

4 All nations of the earth are blest
     In Him, who would restore
  And take them all into His rest,
     And bid them sin no more.

5 O God, Thy record I receive,
     In *Abraham's* footsteps tread,
  And wait, expecting to receive
     The Christ, the promised Seed.

6 The word is now gone forth from Thee,
     It must, it must be done;
  My Jesus shall be form'd in me,
     And I shall have a Son.

7 Faith in Thy power Thou seest I have,
     For Thou this faith hast wrought;
  Dead souls Thou callest from their grave,
     And speakest worlds from nought.

8 Things that are not, as though they were,
     Thou callest by their name;
  Present with Thee the future are,
     With Thee the great I AM.

9 In hope, against all human hope,
     Self-desperate, I believe;
  Thy quickening word shall raise me up,
     Thou shalt Thy Spirit give.

10 According to Thy faithful word
     It shall to me be done;
  And I shall soon receive my Lord,
     And I shall have a Son.

11 Regardless now of flesh and blood.
    Of my forlorn estate,
I own my soul is dead to God.
    Yet for the word I wait.

12 I count not now the tedious years
    I have been dead in sin,
But calmly wait till Christ appears,
    Till Jesus lives within.

13 The thing surpasses all my thought:
    But faithful is my Lord,
Through unbelief I stagger not,
    For God hath spoke the word.

14 Faith, mighty faith, the promise sees.
    And looks to that alone,
Laughs at impossibilities,
    And cries, It shall be done.

15 To Thee the glory of Thy power
    And faithfulness I give;
I shall in Christ, at that glad hour.
    And Christ in me shall live.

16 Before Thee I my heart persuade.
    I know that Thou art true.
Fully assured what Thou hast said
    Thou able art to do.

17 Thy truth, and power, and love I plead,
    On this I rest secure;
To all of faithful *Abraham's* seed
    The gracious word is sure.

18 Thy Son Thou hast on all bestow'd.
    That all who Him receive
Might die to sin, and live to God,
    To God alone might live.

19 I, even I, believe in Him,
  Him with my mouth confess;
And faith I know in Thy esteem
  Is counted righteousness.

20 Obedient faith, that waits on Thee,
  Thou never wilt reprove;
But Thou wilt form Thy Son in me,
  And perfect me in love.

FIGHT THE GOOD FIGHT OF FAITH.

[1 *Timothy* vi. 12.]

1 JESU, my King, to Thee I bow;
  Enlisted under Thy command,
Captain of my salvation, Thou
  Shalt lead me to the promised land.

2 Thou hast a great deliverance wrought.
  The staff from off my shoulder broke,
Out of the house of bondage brought,
  And freed me from the' *Egyptian* yoke.

3 Thine outstretch'd arm was bared for me,
  For me by earth and hell pursued;
Thy outstretch'd arm through the Red Sea
  Brought, and baptized me in Thy blood.

4 O'er the vast howling wilderness
  To *Canaan's* bounds Thou hast me led;
Thou bidd'st me now the land possess,
  And on Thy milk and honey feed.

5 I see an open door of hope ;
    (Legions of sins in vain oppose;)
  Bold I with Thee, my Head, march up,
    And triumph o'er a world of foes.

6 Gigantic lusts come forth to fight;
    I mark, disdain, and all subdue,
  I tread them down in Jesu's might,
    Through Jesus I can all things do.

7 Lo ! the tall sons of *Anak* rise ;
    Who can the sons of *Anak* meet ?
  Captain, to Thee I lift mine eyes;
    And lo ! they fall beneath my feet.

8 Passion, and appetite, and pride
    (Pride, my old, dreadful, tyrant foe)
  I see cast down on every side,
    And conquering I to conquer go.

9 My Lord in my behalf appears :—
    Captain, Thy strength-inspiring eye
  Scatters my doubts, dispels my fears,
    And makes the hosts of aliens fly.

10 Who can before my Captain stand ?
    Who is so great a King as mine ?
  High over all is Thy right hand,
    And might and majesty are Thine.

11 Jesu, my soul takes hold on Thee,
    I arm me with Thy Spirit's might ;
  Humbly assured of victory,
    I underneath Thy banner fight.

12 Thy Spirit lifts the standard up,
    When as a flood the foe pours in :
  I see the cross, hold fast my hope,
    Believe, and more than conquer sin.

13 With holy indignation fill'd,
    When by the prince of hell withstood,
Firm I resist ; I grasp my shield,
    And quench his fiery darts with blood.

14 Single, a thousand foes I chase,
    I turn and blast them with my eyes :
Trembles the world before my face,
    Their prince with all his legions flies.

15 Having done all, by faith I stand,
    And give the praise, O Lord, to Thee ;
Thine holy arm, Thine own right hand
    Hath got Thyself the victory.

16 Wherefore to Thee my soul I raise,
    My soul in Thee securely boasts,
Exults, and glories in Thy praise,
    And triumphs in the Lord of Hosts.

17 Wisdom, and power, and strength, and might
    Thou, Lord, art worthy to receive ;
Honour and riches are Thy right,
    And blessings more than earth can give.

18 Help us to praise our glorious King,
    Ye church of the first-born above :
Let angels and archangels sing
    The triumphs of all-conquering love.

19 Let earth and all her fulness still
    Rejoice His greatness to proclaim,
And everlasting praises fill
    The heaven of heavens with Jesu's name.

I AM DETERMINED TO KNOW NOTHING SAVE JESUS CHRIST, AND HIM CRUCIFIED.

[1 *Corinthians ii. 2.*]

1 VAIN, delusive world, adieu,
With all of creature good !
Only Jesus I pursue,
Who bought me with His blood :
All thy pleasures I forego,
I trample on thy wealth and pride :
Only Jesus will I know,
And Jesus crucified.

2 Other knowledge I disdain.
'Tis all but vanity ;
Christ, the Lamb of God, was slain,
He tasted death for me ;
Me to save from endless woe
The all-atoning Victim died ;
Only Jesus, &c.

3 Turning to my rest again,
The Saviour I adore ;
He relieves my grief and pain,
And bids me weep no more ;
Rivers of salvation flow
From out His head, His hands, His side ;
Only Jesus, &c.

4 Here will I set up my rest ;
My fluctuating heart
From the haven of Thy breast
Shall never more depart :

Whither should a sinner go?
His wounds for me stand open wide ;
  Only Jesus, &c.

5   What though all I am is sin?
      Sin cannot break my peace,
Here is blood to wash me clean
      From all unrighteousness ;
This shall make me white as snow.
On this for all things I confide ;
  Only Jesus, &c.

6   What though earth and hell engage
      To shake my soul with fear,
Calmly I defy the rage
      Of persecution near ;
Suffering faith shall brighter glow,
As gold when in the furnace tried ;
  Only Jesus, &c.

7   Him to know is life and peace
      And pleasure without end ;
This is all my happiness,
      On Jesus to depend,
Daily in His grace to grow,
And ever in His faith abide ;
  Only Jesus, &c.

8   O that I could all invite
      This saving truth to prove !
Show the length, and breadth, and height.
      And depth of Jesu's love !
Fain I would to sinners show
The blood which all may feel applied ;
  Only Jesus, &c.

9   Him in all my works I seek,
      Who hung upon the tree;
    Only of His love I speak
      Who freely died for me :
    While I sojourn here below,
  Of nothing will I think beside ;
    Only Jesus will I know,
      And Jesus crucified.

THE SAME.

1   Let the world their virtue boast,
      Their works of righteousness :
    I, a wretch undone and lost,
      Am freely saved by grace :
    Other title I disclaim,
  This, only this, is all my plea ;
    I the chief of sinners am,
      But Jesus died for me !

2   Let the stronger sons of God
      Their liberty assert,
    Justly glory in the blood
      That made them pure in heart :
    I am full of guilt and shame,
  My heart as black as hell I see ;
    I the chief, &c.

3   Happy they whose joys abound
      Like *Jordan's* swelling stream,
    Who their heaven in Christ have found.
      And give the praise to Him ;
    Let them triumph in His name,
  Enjoy their full felicity :
    I the chief, &c.

4 Blest are they, entirely blest,
  Who can in Him rejoice,
 Lean on His belovèd breast,
  And hear the Bridegroom's voice :
 Meanest follower of the Lamb.
His steps I at a distance see ;
 I the chief, &c.

5 Outward comforts have I none,
  Or sensible delight ;
 Joy is to my soul unknown,
  My day is turn'd to night :
 But my God is still the same,
No shade of change in Him can be ;
 I the chief, &c.

6 I, like *Gideon's* fleece, am found
  Unwater'd still and dry,
 While the dew on all around
  Falls plenteous from the sky :
 Yet my Lord I cannot blame,
The Saviour's grace for all is free ;
 I the chief, &c.

7 Still I see His unfelt grace
  Descending from above,
 But can neither pray nor praise.
  Nor fear my God, nor love :
 Yet He suffer'd to redeem
My soul from all iniquity ;
 I the chief, &c.

8 Surely He will lift me up,
  For I of Him have need ;
 I cannot give up my hope,
  Though I am cold and dead ;

To bring fire on earth He came ;
O that it now might kindled be !
I the chief, &c.

9   Jesu, Thou for me hast died,
And Thou in me wilt live ;
I shall feel Thy death applied,
I shall Thy life receive :
Yet, when melted in the flame
Of love, this shall be all my plea,
I the chief of sinners am,
But Jesus died for me !

PLEADING THE PROMISE OF SANCTI-
FICATION.

Ezekiel xxxvi. 23, *&c.*

1 God of all power, and truth, and grace,
Which shall from age to age endure,
Whose word, when heaven and earth shall pass,
Remains, and stands for ever sure :
2 Calmly to Thee my soul looks up,
And waits Thy promises to prove,
The object of my steadfast hope,
The seal of Thine eternal love.
3 That I Thy mercy may proclaim,
That all mankind Thy truth may see,
Hallow Thy great and glorious name,
And perfect holiness in me.
4 Chose from the world if now I stand
Adorn'd in righteousness Divine,
If brought into the promised land
I justly call the Saviour mine,--

5 Perform the work Thou hast begun,
  My inmost soul to Thee convert,
Love me, for ever love Thine own,
  And sprinkle with Thy blood my heart.

6 Thy sanctifying Spirit pour,
  To quench my thirst and wash me clean ;
Now, Father, let the gracious shower
  Descend, and make me pure from sin.

7 Purge me from every sinful blot,
  My idols all be cast aside ;
Cleanse me from every evil thought,
  From all the filth of self and pride.

8 Give me a new a perfect heart,
  From doubt, and fear, and sorrow free ;
The mind which was in Christ impart,
  And let my spirit cleave to Thee.

9 O take this heart of stone away,
  (Thy sway it doth not, cannot own,)
In me no longer let it stay ;
  O take away this heart of stone.

10 The hatred of the carnal mind
  Out of my flesh at once remove ;
Give me a tender heart, resign'd,
  And pure, and full of faith and love.

11 Within me Thy good Spirit place,
  Spirit of health, and love, and power ;
Plant in me Thy victorious grace,
  And sin shall never enter more.

12 Cause me to walk in Christ my Way;
  And I Thy statutes shall fulfil,
In every point Thy law obey,
  And perfectly perform Thy will.

13 Hast Thou not said, who canst not lie,
  That I Thy law shall keep and do ?
 Lord, I believe, though men deny ;
  They all are false, but Thou art true.

14 O that I now, from sin released,
  Thy word might to the utmost prove :
 Enter into the promised rest,
  The *Canaan* of Thy perfect love.

15 There let me ever, ever dwell ;
  Be Thou my God, and I will be
 Thy servant : O set to Thy seal ;
  Give me eternal life in Thee.

16 From all remaining filth within
  Let me in Thee salvation have ;
 From actual and from inbred sin
  My ransom'd soul persist to save.

17 Wash out my deep original stain—
  Tell me no more it cannot be,
 Demons or men ! The Lamb was slain,
  His blood was all pour'd out for me.

18 Sprinkle it, Jesu, on my heart !
  One drop of Thine all-cleansing blood
 Shall make my sinfulness depart,
  And fill me with the life of God.

19 Father, supply my every need ;
  Sustain the life Thyself hast given :
 Call for the never-failing Bread,
  The manna that comes down from heaven.

20 The gracious fruits of righteousness.
        Thy blessings' unexhausted store,
    In me abundantly increase,
        Nor let me ever hunger more.

21 Let me no more, in deep complaint.
        My leanness, O my leanness ! cry :
    Alone consumed with pining want,
        Of all my Father's children, I !

22 The painful thirst, the fond desire,
        Thy joyous presence shall remove.
    While my full soul doth still require
        Thy whole eternity of love.

23 Holy, and true, and righteous Lord,
        I wait to prove Thy perfect will :
    Be mindful of Thy gracious word,
        And stamp me with Thy Spirit's seal.

24 Thy faithful mercies let me find,
        In which Thou causest me to trust :
    Give me the meek and lowly mind.
        And lay my spirit in the dust.

25 Show me how foul my heart hath been.
        When all renew'd by grace I am ;
    When Thou hast emptied me of sin.
        Show me the fulness of my shame.

26 Open my faith's interior eye ;
        Display Thy glory from above.
    And all I am shall sink and die,
        Lost in astonishment and love.

27 Confound, o'erpower me with Thy grace :
  I would be by myself abhorr'd.
  (All might, all majesty, all praise,
  All glory be to Christ my Lord !)

28 Now let me gain perfection's height :
  Now let me into nothing fall,
  Be less than nothing in Thy sight,
  And feel that Christ is all in all.

BEHOLD THE MAN !

1   ARISE, my soul. arise ;
      Shake off thy guilty fears :
    The bleeding Sacrifice
      In my behalf appears ;
    Before the throne my Surety stands.
    My name is written on His hands.

2   He ever lives above
      For me to intercede.
    His all-redeeming love.
      His precious blood, to plead :
    His blood atoned for all our race,
    And sprinkles now the throne of grace.

3   Five bleeding wounds He bears.
      Received on *Calvary ;*
    They pour effectual prayers.
      They strongly speak for me :
    Forgive him, O forgive ! they cry,
    Nor let that ransom'd sinner die !

4   The Father hears Him pray,
     His dear Anointed One,
   He cannot turn away
     The presence of His Son ;
His Spirit answers to the blood,
And tells me I am born of God.

5   My God is reconciled,
     His pardoning voice I hear,
   He owns me for His child ;
     I can no longer fear,
With confidence I now draw nigh,
And Father, Abba, Father, cry !

TITUS II. 11, &c.

1 We magnify the gift of God,
   The common Saviour praise ;
A talent is on all bestow'd,
   A seed of saving grace.

2 To every soul it comes unsought,
   To raise him from his fall ;
To all it hath appear'd, and brought
   Salvation unto all.

3 From all ungodliness and sin
   It teaches us to fly,
Forbids to touch the thing unclean,
   Or but in thought comply.

4 From every earthly low desire,
   From every creature-love,
It calls, and bids our hearts aspire
   And seek the things above.

5 It teaches us, and not in vain,
    All evil to eschew ;
  From every sin we now refrain,
    And every good pursue.

6 Sober, and just, and godly here,
    Whoe'er the grace receive,
  With sin and Satan ever near,
    A sinless life we live.

7 Our soul is changed, our heart is clear.,
    Our inward strife is o'er ;
  Here in this present world of sin
    We live, and sin no more.

8 The power of godliness we show,
    To carnal minds unknown,
  And perfect holiness below,
    And live to God alone.

9 Worthy, we walk with Him in white,
    Holy and perfect here,
  Till Christ with all His saints in light
    Shall gloriously appear.

10 We look for that thrice blessed hope,
    When time and death shall end,
  And Christ, the Judge, to take us up,
    Shall with a shout descend.

11 Jesus, the great tremendous God
    Our Saviour, shall come down ;
  To all who conquer'd through His blood
    He gives the starry crown :

12 That blood which He for all did shed,
    To make us throughly clean,
  To save, and make us free indeed
    From every spot of sin.

13 For this He hung upon the tree,
      For this His life He gave;
  Our souls from all iniquity,
      Our ransom'd souls, to save.

14 A royal priesthood to ordain,
      An holy, chosen seed;
  And bring them to a perfect man,
      And make them like their Head.

15 He died, that we to sin might die,
      And live to God alone;
  He died, our hearts to purify,
      And make them all His own.

16 This is the dear, peculiar race,
      The people doubly bought,
  The' elect of God, who sought His face,
      And found the God they sought.

17 Zealous of all good works they live,
      And all good tempers show;
  And still to God the glory give,
      And live His life below.

18 This is the fellowship of saints:
      I see it, Lord; I see
  The grace which answers all our wants,
      The grace which is for me.

19 The glorious prize I now pursue,
      For full redemption wait;
  And soon I shall attain unto
      My primitive estate.

20 Heaven I shall have within my breast,
       Nor envy those above,
   When taken into Jesu's rest
       And perfected in love.

IT IS TIME FOR THEE, LORD, TO LAY TO
   THINE HAND: FOR THEY HAVE DES-
   TROYED THY LAW.

[*Psalm cxix.* 126.   P. B. V.]

1   Jesu, the Truth, the Way,
          The Life, in us appear;
      Thy glorious arm display,
          And bring salvation near,—
      The great salvation Thou hast wrought,
      Above the reach of human thought.

2   Flesh, earth, and hell deny
          The freedom of Thy sons:
      And scornfully they cry,
          "Where are the perfect ones?"
      They dare Thee all Thy power to show,
      "Thou canst not make us saints below."

3   Answer their challenge, Lord;
          Thy witnesses call forth,
      Send out the quickening word,
          Renew the face of earth;
      Now the new heavens and earth create,
      Restore us to our first estate.

4   Lay to Thy mighty hand,
        The work is worthy Thee :
    A world of foes withstand,
        And say, It cannot be,
We cannot full redemption have,
Thou canst not to the utmost save.

5   Arise, O jealous God,
        Come quickly from above ;
    Thy law they have destroy'd,
        The holy law of love,
The perfect law of liberty,
The law of life which is in Thee.

6   With Thee the potsherds strive,
        They give their God the lie ;
    They teach, " We cannot live
        And not with sin comply ;"
Thy word of none effect they make :
Come, for Thy truth and mercy's sake.

7   Eternal God, come down
        With Thy victorious cross,
    Thy genuine gospel own,
        Maintain Thy righteous cause.
No longer let Thy foes blaspheme ;
Come, Jesu, mighty to redeem !

8   Thy controversy, Lord,
        Do Thou Thyself decide ;
    And let Thy faithful word
        Be to the utmost tried :
To Thee we make our bold appeal,
Declare the counsel of Thy will !

9   Is it Thy will to save
          Our souls from every sin ?
      Say, Jesu, wouldst Thou have
          Thy righteousness brought in ?
      Us wouldst Thou wholly sanctify ?
      Or have we, Lord, believed a lie ?

10   No, no, the witness cries !
          " Ye shall as God be pure,
      Whoe'er on Christ relies
          To him the word is sure :"
      And I, even I shall perfect be,
      And Christ shall live His life in me.

11   Sin shall not always live,
          Or in our flesh *remain;*
      We did not, Lord, receive
          The word of truth in vain :
      The word of truth shall make us free,
      The Spirit's cry is " Liberty !"

12   The acceptable year
          Of Jesus is at hand;
      Prisoners of hope, appear.
          Go forth at His command,
      And show yourselves from sin set free :
      The Spirit's cry is " Liberty !"

13   We surely shall obtain
          (When Jesus enters in)
      A liberty from pain,
          A liberty from sin ;
      We then shall more than conquerors be.
      The Spirit's cry is " Liberty !"

14   His call we now obey,
            Our full consent we yield ;
        Man shall not tear away
            Our anchor or our shield.
        Us from the gospel hope cast down,
        Subvert our faith or take our crown.

15   The sin-atoning blood
            Its full effect shall have;
        Whom it hath brought to God
            It inwardly shall save.
        From all iniquity release,
        And 'stablish us in perfect peace.

16   The Holy One shall live,
            And in our hearts abide;
        To us a portion give
            Among the sanctified ;
        We all shall say, "The work is done,
        We all are perfected in One."

HE THAT BELIEVETH SHALL NOT MAKE HASTE.

[*Isaiah xxviii.* 16.]

PART I.

1 WITNESS Divine, the Just and True,
    Jesu, to us this promise seal,
  Our haste of unbelief subdue,
    And bid our fluttering hearts be still !
2 That power which stopp'd the mid-day sun,
    Turn'd back the tide, and chain'd the sea,
  Be in our rapid spirits shown,
    And make us truly wait on Thee.

3 Arrest our nature's headlong course,
    (We would be poor, despised, forlorn,)
  Baffle our skill, unnerve our force,
    Our carnal confidence o'erturn.

4 Great Helper of the friendless Thou,
    Thou Strengthener of the feeble knees,
  O let our souls before Thee bow,
    And sink into a sweet distress.

5 We cannot see without Thy light,
    Without Thy light we *would* not see ;
  We have no wisdom, help, or might,
    But Lord, our eyes are unto Thee.

6 O let us not presume to take
    The matter out of Thy great hand :
  Who can the Rock of Ages shake?
    The sure Foundation still shall stand.

7 Let others rush with trembling haste,
    With eager wrath Thy cause defend;
  Our soul is on Thy promise cast,
    And lo ! we calmly wait the end.

8 Though we our hands do not lift up,
    The tottering ark shall never fall :
  It never shall to *Dagon* stoop :
    Thy kingdom ruleth over all.

9 Steadfast our anchor is and sure,
    It enters now within the veil ;
  Thy church, immovably secure,
    Defies the powers of earth and hell.

PART II.

1 COME, O Thou greater than our heart,
      And make Thy faithful mercies known ;
  The mind which was in Thee impart,
      Thy constant mind in us be shown.

2 From anger set our spirits free,
      It worketh not Thy righteousness;
  In patience let us wait on Thee,
      And quietly our souls possess.

3 Jesu, to whose supreme command
      All things in heaven, earth, hell, submit.
  Upon us lay Thy mighty hand,
      And self shall sink beneath Thy feet.

4 O let us by Thy cross abide,
      Thee, only Thee, resolve to know,
  The Lamb for sinners crucified,
      A world to save from endless woe.

5 Take us into Thy people's rest,
      And we from our own works shall cease ;
  With Thy meek Spirit arm our breast,
      And keep our minds in perfect peace.

6 Lift up, and fix our steadfast eye
      On Thee the Father's favourite Son,
  Thee our Great Head, gone up on high,
      Firm on Thine everlasting throne.

7 Though earth and hell Thy rule oppose,
      The Lord is king, Messiah reigns ;
  Till Satan, sin, and all Thy foes,
      And death, the last of all, be slain.

8 Jesu, for this we calmly wait ;
 O let our eyes behold Thee near,
Hasten to make our heaven complete,
 Appear, our glorious God, appear !

PART III.

1 UNCHANGEABLE Almighty Lord,
 Our souls upon Thy truth we stay ;
Accomplish now Thy faithful word,
 And give, O give us all one way.

2 O let us all join hand in hand
 Who seek redemption in Thy blood,
Fast in one mind and spirit stand,
 And build the temple of our God.

3 Thou only canst our wills control,
 Our wild unruly passions bind,
Tame the old *Adam* in our soul,
 And make us of one heart and mind.

4 Speak but the reconciling word,
 The winds shall cease, the waves subside :
We all shall praise our common Lord,
 Our Jesus, and Him crucified.

5 Giver of peace and unity,
 Send down Thy mild pacific Dove ;
We all shall then in one agree,
 And breathe the Spirit of Thy love.

6 We all shall think and speak the same
 Delightful lesson of Thy grace,
One undivided Christ proclaim,
 And jointly glory in Thy praise.

7 O let us take a softer mould ;
  Blended and gather'd into Thee,
To us Thy Father's name declare,
Under one Shepherd make one fold,
  Where all is love and harmony.

8 Regard Thine own eternal prayer,
  And send a peaceful answer down ;
To us Thy Father's name declare,
  Unite and perfect us in one.

9 So shall the world believe and know
  That God hath sent Thee from above.
When Thou art seen in us below,
  And every soul displays Thy love.

PART IV.

1 THE Lord is king, and earth submits.
  Howe'er impatient, to His sway ;
Between the cherubim He sits,
  And makes His restless foes obey.

2 All power is to our Jesus given ;
  O'er earth's rebellious sons He reigns.
He mildly rules the hosts of heaven,
  And holds the powers of hell in chains.

3 In vain doth Satan rage his hour,
  Beyond his chain he cannot go ;
Our Jesus shall stir up His power,
  And soon avenge us of our foe.

4 Jesus shall His great arm reveal,
  Jesus, the woman's conquering Seed.
(Though now the serpent bruise His heel.)
  Jesus shall bruise the serpent's head.

5 The enemy his tares hath sown:
   But Christ shall shortly root them up,
Shall cast the dire accuser down,
   And disappoint his children's hope :

6 Shall still the proud *Philistine's* noise,
   Baffle the sons of unbelief,
Nor long permit them to rejoice,
   But turn their triumph into grief.

7 Come, glorious Lord, the rebels spurn ;
   Scatter Thy foes, victorious King !
And *Gath* and *Askelon* shall mourn,
   And all the sons of God shall sing.

8 Shall magnify the sovereign grace
   Of Him that sits upon the throne,
And earth and heaven conspire to praise
   Jehovah, and His conquering Son.

THE LORD'S PRAYER PARAPHRASED.

1 FATHER of all, whose powerful voice
   Call'd forth this universal frame,
Whose mercies over all rejoice,
   Through endless ages still the same :
Thou by Thy word upholdest all,
   Thy bounteous love to all is show'd.
Thou hear'st Thy every creature's call,
   And fillest every mouth with good.

2 In heaven Thou reign'st, enthroned in light,
   Nature's expanse beneath Thee spread ;
Earth, air, and sea before Thy sight,
   And hell's deep gloom, are open laid.

Wisdom, and might, and love are Thine;
　Prostrate before Thy face we fall,
Confess thine attributes Divine,
　And hail the Sovereign Lord of all.

3 Thee, Sovereign Lord, let all confess,
　That moves in earth, or air, or sky,
Revere Thy power, Thy goodness bless,
　Tremble before Thy piercing eye.
All ye who owe to Him your birth,
　In praise your every hour employ;
Jehovah reigns! Be glad, O earth,
　And shout ye morning stars for joy.

4 Son of Thy Sire's eternal love,
　Take to Thyself Thy mighty power;
Let all earth's sons Thy mercy prove,
　Let all Thy bleeding grace adore.
The triumphs of Thy love display;
　In every heart reign Thou alone,
Till all Thy foes confess Thy sway,
　And glory ends what grace begun.

5 Spirit of grace, and health, and power,
　Fountain of light and love below,
Abroad Thine healing influence shower,
　O'er all the nations let it flow.
Inflame our hearts with perfect love,
　In us the work of faith fulfil:
So not heaven's hosts shall swifter move
　Than we on earth to do Thy will.

6 Father, 'tis Thine each day to yield
　Thy children's wants a fresh supply;
Thou cloth'st the lilies of the field,
　And hearest the young ravens cry:

On Thee we cast our care ; we live
  Through Thee, who know'st our every need :
O feed us with Thy grace, and give
  Our souls this day the living Bread.

7 Eternal, spotless Lamb of God,
  Before the world's foundation slain,
Sprinkle us ever with Thy blood ;
  O cleanse, and keep us ever clean.
To every soul (all praise to Thee)
  Our bowels of compassion move,
And all mankind by this may see
  God is in us, for God is love.

8 Giver and Lord of life, whose power
  And guardian care for all are free,
To Thee in fierce temptation's hour
  From sin and Satan let us flee.
Thine, Lord, we are, and ours Thou art ;
  In us be all Thy goodness show'd ;
Renew, enlarge, and fill our heart
  With peace, and joy, and heaven, and God.

9 Blessing and honour, praise and love,
  Co-equal, co-eternal Three,
In earth below and heaven above,
  By all Thy works, be paid to Thee.
Thrice Holy, Thine the kingdom is,
  The power omnipotent is Thine ;
And when created nature dies
  Thy never-ceasing glories shine.

REVELATION I.

VERSES 4, 5, 6.

1 O THAT the life-infusing grace,
    The pure and perfect peace of God,
  Might now descend on *Israel's* race,
    The church He purchased with His blood!

2 The souls peculiarly His own,
    On them the choicest gifts descend
  From Him that sitteth on the throne,
    Ancient of Days which never end.

3 He was from all eternity,
    Pure essence, life, and light, and power;
  He is when time no more shall be,
    He is and shall be evermore.

4 From God to all His church below,
    From the seven spirits before His throne,
  From Jesus, let the blessing flow;
    Jesus is God's co-equal Son.

5 The true and faithful Witness He,
    The First-begotten of the dead,
  Prince of the kings of earth—to Thee
    Be everlasting homage paid.

6 Amazing height of love Divine!
    We praise with all Thy hosts above
  The' unutterably great design,
    The mystery of redeeming love.

7 From actual and from inbred sin
    Us thou hast wash'd in Thine own blood;
  Thy blood hath more than made us clean,
    Hath made us kings and priests to God.

8 Wherefore to Thee all honour, praise,
   Dominion, power, and thanks we give,
 While to the glory of Thy grace
   Through all eternity we live.

VERSE 7.

1 BEHOLD, He comes ! and every eye
   Shall see Him in the clouds draw near ;
 The Judge, to those who made Him die
   In vain, shall terribly appear :

 Who pierced Him by their sins beneath,
   Exposed afresh, and crucified,
 Renounced their interest in His death,
   And, bought by Him, their Lord denied.

3 Rebellious worms, they would not take
   The grace He waited long to give,
 But cast His words behind their back.
   And *would* not come to Him and live.

4 Him shall they see with wrath return
   'Gainst those who made His offers vain.
 And all the tribes of earth shall mourn.
   Adjudged to everlasting pain.

5 The unbelieving world shall wail,
   And gnaw their tongues, and gnash their
       teeth ;
 But we, who let His grace prevail,
   Shall never taste that second death.

6 We with our Lord shall always live.
   The God of our salvation praise,
 To Him alone rejoice to give
   The glory of His sovereign grace.

7 Come, gracious Lord, we wait Thy day,
    We languish to be taken home;
No longer let Thy chariot stay;
    Come, gracious Lord, to judgment come.

VERSES 10, 11, &c.

1 SAY, which of you would see the Lord?
    Ye all may now obtain the grace,
Behold Him in the written word,
    Where *John* unveils the Saviour's face.

2 Clear as the trumpet's voice He speaks
    To every soul that turns his ear;
Amidst the golden candlesticks
    He walks: and lo! He now is here!

3 Present to all believing souls,
    They see Him with an eagle's eye;
Down to His feet a garment rolls,
    Stain'd with a glorious crimson dye.

4 A golden girdle binds His breast.
    (Whence streams of consolation flow,
Milk for His new-born babes, who rest
    In Him nor other comforts know.)

5 His form is as the Son of Man;
    His eyes are as a flame of fire,
They dart a sin-consuming pain,
    And life and joy Divine inspire.

6 His spotless purity of soul
    We by a lovely emblem know;
His head and hairs are white as wool,
    White are they as the driven snow.

7 Glitter His feet like polish'd brass,
　　That long hath in the furnace shone ;
　Brighter than lightning is His face,
　　Brighter than the meridian sun.

8 As many waters sounds His word,
　　Seven stars he holds in His right hand.
　Out of His mouth a two-edged sword
　　Goes forth : before it who can stand ?

9 Lord, at Thy feet we fall as dead ;
　　Lay Thy right hand upon our soul,
　Scatter our fears, Thy Spirit shed,
　　And all our unbelief control.

10 Tell us, " I am the First and Last,
　　Who lived and died for all am I !
　And lo ! My bitter death is past,
　　And lo ! I live no more to die.

11 " I have the keys of death and hell."
　　Amen ! Thy record we receive ;
　And wait till Thou our spirits seal.
　　And all in all for ever live.

A PRAYER FOR THE BISHOPS.

1 Draw near, O Son of God, draw near,
　　Us with Thy flaming eyes behold,
　Still in Thy falling church appear,
　　And let our candlestick be gold.

2 Still hold the stars in Thy right hand.
　　And let them in Thy lustre glow,
　The lights of a benighted land,
　　The angels of Thy church below.

3 Make good their apostolic boast,
    Their high commission let them prove,
Be temples of the Holy Ghost,
    And fill'd with faith, and hope, and love.

4 The worthy successors of those
    Who first adorn'd the sacred line,
Bold let them stand before their foes,
    And dare assert their right Divine.

5 Their hearts from things of earth remove;
    Sprinkle them, Lord, from sin and fear!
Fix their affections all above,
    And lay up all their treasure there.

6 Give them an ear to hear the word
    Thou speakest to Thy churches now;
And let all tongues confess their Lord,
    And let all knees to Jesus bow.

A PRAYER FOR LABOURERS.

1   Lord of the harvest, hear
      Thy needy servants cry;
Answer our faith's effectual prayer,
      And all our wants supply.

2   On Thee we humbly wait,
      Our wants are in Thy view:
The harvest truly, Lord, is great,
      The labourers are few.

3   Convert, and send forth more
      Into Thy church abroad,
And let them speak Thy word of power,
      As workers with their God.

4   Give the pure gospel word,
        The word of general grace:
    Thee let them preach, the common Lord,
        Saviour of human race.

      O let them spread Thy name,
        Their mission fully prove,
    Thy universal grace proclaim,
        Thy all-redeeming love.

6   On all mankind forgiven
        Empower them still to call,
    And tell each creature under heaven
        That Thou hast died for all.

ANOTHER.

1 JESU, Thy wandering sheep behold !
        See, Lord, with yearning bowels see
    Poor souls that cannot find the fold,
        Till sought and gather'd in by Thee.

2 Lost are they now, and scatter'd wide,
        In pain, and weariness, and want :
    With no kind shepherd near to guide
        The sick, and spiritless, and faint.

3 Thou, only Thou, the kind and good
        And sheep-redeeming Shepherd art :
    Collect Thy flock, and give them food,
        And pastors after Thine own heart.

4 Give the pure word of general grace ;
        And great shall be the preachers' crowd,
    Preachers, who all the sinful race
        Point to the all-atoning blood.

5 Open their mouth, and utterance give;
    Give them a trumpet-voice to call
A world, who all may turn and live
    Through faith in Him that died for all.

6 In every messenger reveal
    The grace they preach, divinely free,
That each may by Thy Spirit tell,
    " He died for all, who died for me."

7 A double portion, from above,
    Of that all-quickening Spirit impart;
Shed forth Thine universal love
    In every faithful pastor's heart.

8 Thy only glory let them seek ;
    O let their hearts with love o'erflow ;
Let them believe, and therefore speak,
    And spread Thy mercy's praise below.

9 Mercy for all be all their song,
    Mercy which every soul may claim,
Mercy which doth to all belong,
    Mercy for all in Jesu's name.

10 To Thee, for all men lifted up,
    O let them still their witness bear,
And, shouting from the mountain-top,
    The Saviour of the world declare.—

11 " He willeth not the sinner's death,
    He died for all, He none pass'd by ;
Since we would now resign our breath,
    For every soul of man would die."

UNTO THE ANGEL OF THE CHURCH OF EPHESUS, WRITE. &c.

Revelation ii. 1, *&c.*

1 O Thou that dost the churches bear,
    The stars in Thy right hand uphold,
Who walkest now with jealous care
    Amidst the candlesticks of gold ;

2 Poor, guilty, abject worms, to Thee
    In our declining state we call ;
See, Thy degenerate people see,
    Nor let our tottering *Sion* fall.

3 Our works of faith Thou once didst know,
    Our patient hope and labouring love ;
We would not bear Thy Romish foe,
    We dared that Antichrist reprove.

4 We tried him by the written word,
    Through all his snares and fetters broke,
As *Satan's successor* abhorr'd,
    And cast away his iron yoke.

5 Him and his god, and sin and death,
    We more than conquer'd through Thy name ;
The witnesses resign'd their breath,
    And clapped their hands amidst the flame.

6 For their dear suffering Saviour's sake,
    Immovable the champions stood,
Nor fainted at the rack, or stake,
    But water'd all the church with blood.

7 Yet O ! how quickly, Lord, hast Thou
    Whereof Thy people to reprove !
Fallen, alas ! Thou see'st us now,
    We now have left our former love.

8 Our wine with water mixt, our gold
    Is dim, our shipwreck'd faith is dead,
No more our tokens we behold,
    Our martyrs all to heaven are fled.

9 O could we call to mind the grace,
    The glorious grace from which we fell,
Live o'er again the ancient days,
    And do the works Thou lov'st so well !

10 O that we might through Thee repent,
    And timely turn to Thee, and live !
So should Thy grace our doom prevent,
    Thou wouldst abundantly forgive.

11 Before Thou dost in vengeance come,
    Our candlestick far off remove,
And fix the' unalterable doom,
    O let us weep, believe, and love.

12 Call on us, by thy Spirit call,
    Yet once again our church restore.
Show us Thy grace is over all,
    And lift us up to fall no more.

VERSE 7.

1 HEAR, all that will, the Spirit hear,
    What He to all the churches saith:
" Fight the good fight till Christ appear,
    And give the prize to conquering faith.

2 " The tree of immortality,
    Which in the midst of *Eden* stands,
The conqueror's due reward shall be,
    Though guarded by cherubic bands.

3 " I will remove the sword of flame;
    (It first shall the old *Adam* slay;)
  The tree of life Myself I am,
    And open to Myself the way."

4 To him that overcomes at last
    Surely I will My fulness give,
  He of the tree of life shall taste,
    And free from sin for ever live.

UNTO THE ANGEL OF THE CHURCH IN SMYRNA.

VERSES 8, 9, &c.

1 HEAR, Jesu; hear, the First and Last,
    The Alpha and Omega Thou,
  Who once for every man didst taste
    Of death, and ever livest now.

2 Still let Thy gracious Spirit strive,
    And conquer a rebellious race;
  In us Thine ancient work revive,
    Thy sanctifying work of grace.

3 O that to Thee our deeds were known,
    Acknowledged and approved by Thee.
  Such as Thou didst in *Smyrna* own,
    Such as in us Thou once didst see!

4 The patient, meek, and lowly mind,
    True poverty of spirit, bestow,
  And rich in faith we'll cast behind
    Whate'er of good appears below.

5 We then the power of faith shall prove,
    Nor shrink from persecution near,
But more than conquer in Thy love,
    Thy perfect love which casts out fear.

6 Though earth and hell at once engage,
    And fiends and formal saints conspire,
The synagogue of Satan rage,
    And threaten us with racks and fire ;

7 Bold shall we stand in Thy great might,
    For Jesu's sake count all things loss,
With beasts, and men, and devils fight
    Beneath the banner of Thy cross.

8 Shall Satan into prison cast ?
    To prison we with Christ will go,
And gladly bear, till all are past,
    These light afflictions here below.

9 But make us faithful unto death;
    But arm us in that fiery hour,
And we shall all obtain the wreath,
    And die for God, to die no more.

TO THE ANGEL OF THE CHURCH IN PERGAMOS.

VERSES 12, 13, &c.

1 O Thou that hast the two-edged sword,
    Let us Thy warning voice receive ;
Give us an ear to hear Thy word,
    Give us to tremble and believe.

2 We dwell where Satan keeps his seat ;
    Our fathers would not Thee disclaim,
  They would not to Thy foes submit,
    But kept the faith, and held Thy name.

3 They held it fast in evil days ;
    Faithful to Thee the martyrs stood,
  And turn'd against the storm their face,
    And strove, resisting unto blood.

4 But we, alas ! deserve Thy blame
    For tamely bearing with Thy foes,
  Who dare deny the Saviour's name,
    And all Thy gospel truths oppose.

5 The devil's factors still we hear,
    The sinful advocates for sin,
  Who cause the little ones to err,
    And teach they never can be clean.

6 We suffer them for sin to plead;
    Still they promote the devil's cause,
  Deny that Thou for all hast bled,
    And stain the glory of Thy cross.

7 Before Thy people's face they cast
    The stumbling-block of creature-love;
  " The power of sin must always last,
    The power thou never canst remove."

 8 They speak ; and we, to ill inclined.
    Have gladly drank the poison in,
  And gratified the carnal mind,
    The idol of indwelling sin.

9 But let us plead for sin no more,
   But let the stumbling-block depart,
Our vile idolatries be o'er,
   Thine, only Thine, be all our heart.

10 Lord, we renounce whoe'er oppose
   And fight against Thy saving power ;
Consume not us among Thy foes,
   Nor let Thy two-edged sword devour.

11 O let us of Thy strength take hold,
   Thine utmost promises embrace,
The Finisher of faith behold,
   The God of all-victorious grace.

12 To him that conquers in Thy might
   Thou wilt the hidden manna give ;
Thou hast obtain'd it as Thy right,
   And he shall Thy deserts receive.

13 Thou, Lord, wilt give him a white stone,
   A new mysterious name impart,
To none but the receiver known,
   Christ in a pure and sinless heart.

UNTO THE ANGEL OF THE CHURCH IN
THYATIRA.

Verses 18, 19, &c.

1 O Son of God, whose flaming eyes
   A sin-consuming virtue dart,
To scatter all Thy foes arise,
   And search, and purify our heart.

2 Lift up Thy feet of burnish'd brass,
 Satan, the world, and sin tread down;
Pity a froward, faithless race,
 And call us yet again Thine own.

3 The service which our fathers paid,
 The faith Thou didst in them approve.
Of this we now have shipwreck made,
 And lost our hope and left our love.

4 The prophets of smooth things we hear,
 Who all Thy promises deny,
Entrap Thy servants in their snare,
 And catch them with a soothing lie.

5 They teach them things unclean to eat,
 To fold their arms and take their ease.
Spiritual whoredom to commit,
 Mammon and God at once to please.

6 Darkness they make with light agree,
 And heaven with hell, and Christ with sin ;
They say the God of purity
 Dwells in a cage of birds unclean.

7 Great Searcher of the heart and reins,
 Whose eyes our inmost substance see,
Who dost, to all, rewards and pains
 According to their works decree ;

8 Avert from us the heavy doom
 Of such deniers of their Lord;
(Whose wrath shall to the utmost come
 On all that dare corrupt His word;)

9 On us no other burden lay,
    On us, and all who have not known
What Satan and his preachers say,
    But still for full redemption groan.

10 Our knees confirm, our hands lift up,
    Our hearts from things of earth remove,
And guide into a patient hope
    And looking for Thy perfect love.

11 Let us hold fast the pledge of good,
    The grace Thou hast already given,
Till all our hearts are Thine abode,
    And find in Thee their present heaven.

12 O let us conquer all our foes,
    And active to the end endure,
Maintain Thy works, whoe'er oppose;
    To working faith the word is sure.

13 Power over hell, and earth, and sin,
    The lawful conqueror shall receive ;
An everlasting power brought in,
    Power without fear or sin to live.

14 Power to o'erturn, subdue, control
    The nations with an iron rod ;
(Implanted in the new-born soul
    The wisdom, and the power of God ;)

15 Power over sins, to hew, and slay
    Them all with a continued stroke,
And scatter as the potter's clay,
    As vessels into shivers broke.

16 Power to maintain his victory,
   The perfect life of faith to live;
 Power, as the Father gave to Thee,
   Thou to the conquering soul wilt give.

17 Wilt give him the bright Morning Star:
   The Morning Star, O Christ, Thou art:
 And lo! we see Thee gleam from far,
   And wait Thy rising in our heart!

UNTO THE ANGEL OF THE CHURCH IN SARDIS.

Chapter iii. 1, 2, &c.

1 O THOU whose eyes run to and fro
   Through earth, and every creature see,
 What is it which Thou dost not know?
   All things are manifest to Thee.

2 Thou hast the spirits, seven and one,
   Thou hast the stars in Thy right hand,
 And all our works to Thee are known:
   How shall we in Thy judgment stand?

3 Thou know'st we take in vain Thy name,
   While dead in trespasses we live;
 Thee for our Lord we falsely claim,
   While to the world our hearts we give.

4 A powerless form, a lifeless sound,
   Our works as vanity are light;
 Wanting, alas! they all are found,
   And worse than nothing in Thy sight.

5 O that we now might turn again,
   And cherish the last spark of grace,
Strengthen the things that yet remain,
   And call to mind the ancient days.

6 Surely we did Thy faith receive,
   We heard with joy the gospel word :
O let us now repent and live,
   And watch to apprehend our Lord ;

7 Stir ourselves up, renounce our ease,
   Before Thy sudden judgments come ;
And watch, and pray, and never cease,
   Till Thou repeal our threatening doom.

8 A few Thou still hast left, who stand
   And depecrate the' impending blow,
Protectors of a guilty land,
   And guardian angels here below.

9 They, by Thy mercy reconciled,
   For our unhappy *Sardis* plead ;
Harmless, and pure, and undefiled,
   They ever in Thy footsteps tread.

10 Before they see the realms of light,
   Deserving here through Thy desert.
Worthy they walk with Thee in white.
   In spotless purity of heart.

11 Partakers of the life Divine,
   Who in the fight of faith o'ercome,
They all shall in Thine image shine,
   Made ready for their heavenly home.

12 They *here* shall be redeem'd from sin,
    Shall *here* put on their glorious dress,
  Fine linen, pure, and white, and clean,
    The saints' inherent righteousness.

13 Love, perfect love, expels all doubt,
    Love makes them to the end endure ;
  Their names Thou never wilt blot out ;
    Their life is hid, their heart is pure.

14 Their names Thou wilt vouchsafe to own
    Before Thy Father's Majesty,
  Pronounce them good, and say " Well done,
    Enter, and ever reign with Me."

TO THE ANGEL OF THE CHURCH IN PHILADELPHIA.

VERSE 7. &c.

1 HOLY and True, who hast the key
    Of *David*, full of grace and power,
  None opens what is shut by Thee,
    And none can shut Thine open door.

2 O help Thy little church below,
    Noted for their fraternal love ;
  Accept us in Thyself, and know
    Our souls, and all our works approve.

3 Open a door to preach Thy word,
    Which neither earth or hell can close ;
  Let all proclaim the common Lord,
    Who died to save a world of foes.

4 A little strength Thou see'st we have,
    We trust that Thou art still the same ;
  Save, Jesu, to the utmost save
    Thy people who confess Thy name.

5 We dare not give our God the lie;
    Saviour from sin, we Thee receive ;
  Though Satan's synagogue deny,
    We *here* a sinless life shall live.

6 Who falsely call themselves Thine own
    Shall then indignantly submit;
  Thy mighty hand shall cast them down,
    And make them bow before our feet.

7 Then all the advocates for sin,
    The carnal *self-elect*, shall know
  Thy blood hath made us throughly clean,
    And wash'd from all our sins below.

8 Thy cleansing blood, by faith applied,
    Gave us a love that cast out fear :
  And lo! with all the sanctified
    We plead for a perfection here.

9 But let us to the end endure,
    Nor ever let Thy promise go,
  Till all our hearts and lives are pure,
    And every soul is white as snow.

10 Let us Thy word of patience keep,
    Nor from the gospel hope remove ;
  But sow in confidence, to reap
    The harvest of Thy perfect love.

11 So shall Thy grace our souls preserve
    From sore temptation's fiery hour,
  When all who plead for sin shall swerve,
    And fall, perhaps to rise no more.

12 We know Thou wilt not long delay ;
    Let no seducer cast us down,
  Or tear our confidence away.
    Or spoil us of the promised crown.

13 That crown the conqueror *here* receives.
    Who the good fight of faith hath won :
  While without fear or sin he lives,
    He lives to God, and God alone.

14 Establish'd by Almighty hands,
    He shows forth all Thy grace and power.
  In God's eternal temple stands
    A pillar, and goes out no more.

15 The name and city of Thy God
    Thou didst to him on earth impart.
  And shedd'st Thy perfect love abroad.
    And wrote Thy nature on his heart.

16 Thy Father *here* Thou didst reveal,
    To him Thou here Thyself hast given,
  And mark'd him with the Spirit's seal,
    A citizen and heir of heaven.

17 This is our glorious calling's prize;
    Saviour, at this our wishes aim :
  Restore us to our paradise,
    Inscribe us. Lord, with Thy new name.

18 To all whom Thou hast given an ear
    The perfect grace make haste to give.
  And sanctify us *wholly* here,
    And to Thy heaven of heavens receive.

UNTO THE ANGEL OF THE CHURCH OF THE LAODICEANS.

VERSE 14. &c

PART I.

1 AMEN to all that God hath said,
    Witness Divine, the Just and True,
Who wast before the worlds were made.
    Whose being no beginning knew.

2 With guilty self-condemning fear,
    With humble self-abasing shame,
Thy Spirit's dreadful charge we hear,
    Nor dare throw off the' imputed blame.

3 God of unspotted purity,
    Us and our works canst Thou behold?
Justly we are abhorr'd by Thee,
    For we are neither hot nor cold.

4 We call Thee Lord, Thy faith profess,
    But do not from our hearts obey ;
In soft *Laodicean* ease
    We sleep our useless lives away.

5 We live in pleasures, and are dead ;
    In search of fame and wealth we live ;
Commanded in Thy steps to tread,
    We seek sometimes. but never strive.

6 A lifeless form we still retain,
    Of this we make our empty boast,
Nor know the Name we take in vain :
    The power of godliness is lost.

7 The power we daringly deny,
    A fancied good, a madman's dream;
The truth itself we deem a lie,
    The promised Holy Ghost blaspheme.

8 How long, great God, have we appear'd
    Abominable in Thy sight?
Better that we had never heard
    Thy word, or seen the gospel light.

9 Better that we had never known
    The way to heaven through saving grace,
Than basely in our lives disown
    And slight and mock Thee to Thy face.

10 Thou rather wouldst that we were cold,
    Than seem to serve Thee without zeal;
Less guilty if, with those of old,
    We worshipp'd *Thor* and *Woden* still.

11 Less grievous will the judgment-day
    To *Sodom* and *Gomorrah* prove,
Than us, who cast our faith away
    And trample on Thy richer love.

PART II.

1 YET still we glory in Thy name,
    O Christ, as though we knew Thy grace;
Thee with unhallow'd lips we claim,
    A lukewarm, worse than heathen, race.

2 We say that we with goods abound,
    Are rich, and full, and need no more;
Nor know that we are wretched found
    With Thee, and bare, and blind, and poor.

3 O let us our own works forsake,
  Ourselves and all we have deny,
Thy condescending counsel take,
  And come to Thee, pure gold to buy.

4 Gold that can bear the fiery test,
  And make the buyer rich indeed:
Adorn us in the milk-white vest,
  And over us Thy mantle spread.

5 When this unspotted robe we wear,
  Our sins are cover'd all by Thee;
No longer doth our shame appear,
  Salvation in Thy light we see.

6 Touch'd by an unction from above,
  Our eyes are open'd to perceive
The mystery of redeeming love,
  The death by which alone we live.

7 Beholding as with open face
  The glory of the Lord, we go
From strength to strength, from grace to grace.
  And perfect holiness below.

8 O might we through Thy grace attain
  The faith Thou never wilt reprove,
The faith that purges every stain,
  The faith that always works by love.

9 O might we see in this our day
  The things belonging to our peace,
And timely meet Thee in Thy way
  Of judgments, and our sins confess;

10 Thy fatherly chastisements own,
     With filial awe revere the rod,
   And turn with zealous haste, and run
     Into the outstretch'd arms of God.

11 Behold, Thou standest at the door,
     Thou knockest long at every heart,
   Ready the sinner to restore,
     And lift the fallen up, Thou art.

12 Thou callest all men to repent;
     And all men may obey Thy call,
   They may, the stoniest *may*, relent;
     Thy death hath bought the grace for all.

13 What Thou hast lent we all may use,
     We all our talents may improve;
   We need not, Lord, Thy grace refuse,
     Or stop our ears against Thy love.

14 Thou hast obtain'd for us a power
     Thy proffer'd mercy to embrace;
   And all may know their gracious hour,
     And all may close with saving grace.

PART III.

1 SAVIOUR of all, to Thee we bow,
     And own Thee faithful to Thy word;
   We hear Thy voice, and open now
     Our hearts to entertain our Lord.

2 Come in, come in, Thou heavenly Guest;
     Delight in what Thyself hast given,
   On Thy own gifts and graces feast,
     And make the contrite heart Thy heaven.

3 Smell the sweet odour of our prayers,
  Our sacrifice of praise approve,
And treasure up our gracious tears,
  And rest in Thy redeeming love.

4 Beneath Thy shadow let us sit,
  Call us Thy friend, and love, and bride,
And bid us freely drink and eat
  Thy dainties, and be satisfied.

5 O let us on Thy fulness feed,
  And eat Thy flesh, and drink Thy blood !
Jesu, Thy blood is drink indeed,
  Jesu, Thy flesh is angels' food.

6 The heavenly manna faith imparts;
  Faith makes Thy fulness all our own,
We feed upon Thee in our hearts,
  And find that heaven and Thou art one.

7 An heaven begun on earth we feel,
  Who conquer in the glorious strife,
And pass o'er sin, and earth, and hell,
  Triumphant, to eternal life.

8 The fulness of eternal bliss
  We shall from Thee receive above;
This the reward of conquests, this
  The crown of all-victorious love.

9 Conqueror of sin, and hell, and death,
  As Thou the dreadful fight hast won,
And wearest now the' immortal wreath,
  And sittest on Thy Father's throne;

10 So shalt Thou grant to all that fight
    And conquer in Thy mighty name,
  To claim the kingdom as their right,
    Their sufferings and their crown the same.

11 Who bore Thy cross shall wear Thy crown,
    Shall triumph in Thy victory,
  And in Thy glorious throne sit down,
    And reign in endless bliss with Thee.

THE SPIRIT AND THE BRIDE SAY, COME!

[*Revelation xxii. 17.*]

1 LORD, I believe Thy work of grace
    Is perfect in the soul;
  His heart is pure who sees Thy face,
    His spirit is made whole,

2 From every sickness. by Thy word,
    From every sore disease,
  Saved, and to perfect health restored.
    To perfect holiness.

3 He walks in glorious liberty,
    To sin entirely dead;
  The Truth, the Son hath made him free,
    And he is free indeed.

4 He lives. when Thou hast fully wrought
    The work of faith with power,
  Upright in deed, and word, and thought
    He lives, and sins no more.

5 Throughout his soul Thy glories shine,
    His soul is all renew'd,
And deck'd in righteousness Divine,
    And cloth'd and fill'd with God.

6 In spirit join'd, and one with Thee,
    And purged from all his stains,
No wrinkle of infirmity,*
    No spot of sin remains.

7 He knows Thee now as he is known,
    Thy fulness he receives;
Flesh of Thy flesh, bone of Thy bone,
    In Thee he ever lives.

8 This is the rest, the life, the peace
    Which all Thy people prove;
Love is the bond of perfectness,
    And all their soul is love.

9 Thy people are all sanctified;
    And Thou shalt say to me,
" Thou art all fair, My love, My bride,
    There is no spot in thee."

10 O joyful sound of gospel grace !
    Christ shall in me appear:
I, even I, shall see His face,
    I shall be holy here.

11 I shall from every sin be free;
    (The word of God is sure;)
Walk before Him, and perfect be,
    And pure as God is pure.

* *I. e.,* Such infirmities as David speaks of, Psalm ciii. 3.

12 This heart shall be His constant home;
    I hear His Spirit's cry,
  " Surely," He saith, " I quickly come,"
    He saith, and cannot lie.

13 The God of truth Himself hath sworn;
    On Him my soul relies;
  My soul, on wings of eagles borne,
    Shall fly, and take the prize.

14 The glorious crown of righteousness
    To me reach'd out I view;
  Conqueror through Him, I soon shall seize
    And wear it as my due.

15 The promised land from *Pisgah's* top
    I now exult to see;
  My hope is full (O blessed hope !)
    Of immortality.

16 My fluttering spirit fatigues my breast,
    And swells and spreads abroad,
  And pants for everlasting rest,
    And struggles into God.

17 I feel and know Him now in part;
    His love my heart constrains,
  Its near approach expands my heart,
    And fills with pleasing pains.

18 He visits now the house of clay,
    He shakes His future home :
  O wouldst Thou, Lord, on this glad day
    Into Thy temple come !

19 With me I know, I feel. Thou art;
      But this cannot suffice,
   Unless Thou plantest in my heart
      A constant paradise.

20 My earth Thou water'st from on high;
      But make it all a pool;
   Spring up, O well! I ever cry,
      Spring up within my soul!

21 Come, O my God, Thyself reveal;
      Fill all this mighty void,
   Thou only canst my spirit fill:
      Come, O my God, my God!

22 Fulfil, fulfil my large desires,
      Large as infinity;
   Give, give me all my soul requires,
      All, all that is in Thee!